MY ISLAND SECRET

MY ISLAND SECRET

A Novel By

2FeetPro.com

This is a work of fiction. Names, characters, businesses, places, events, locales, and incidents are either the product of the author's imagination or used in a fictitious manner. Any similarity to actual persons, living or dead, or actual events is purely coincidental.

ISBN 979-8-218-07121-9

The author can be contacted via Facebook: Bernard Semiopenminded Harris

Cover Art: 2FeetPro.com
Font for MY ISLAND SECRET | "Love Coffee" | sourced from dafont.com/khurasan.d5849
Font for BERNARD HARRIS | "Master of Break" | sourced from dafont.com StereoType Clément Nicolle
Font for SEMIOPENMINDED | "The Bold Font" | http://www.newboldtimes.com

Cover Model: Lakisha LelaMone Greene. @houseoflelamone. Owner and CEO at Le'lamone' Beauty. Co-founder of Fashion Night Out RVA. Fashion Designer/Stylist at House of Le'laMone. Talk Show Host of Style Live.

I was once considered a problem child. To me, I was just busy.
Just active. Yes, yes, I got into things just like most young boys
but the village that I grew up in kept me on the straight and narrow path.

One family member that was always like a second mom and a queen in
our village was my cousin, Josephine Moody. She was loved by many
and a pillar in the community. She inspired me to be better
even when some family members thought I would never amount to anything.

Hurtful as it may seem, she pushed me. Disciplined me.
And loved me as if I was one of her own. These are things that
I will treasure 'til the end of my days.

For all you have done and what I'm to become –
this book belongs to you, with all my love.
May you rest in peace 'til we meet again.

Love You!

Acknowledgements

Each and every person is inspired by someone and, in a lot of cases, these people are behind-the-scenes until someone makes light of who they are. Family and friends make up the DNA of the man you see today. I couldn't be myself without the support of some very near and dear people.

There should be no surprise who I love with all my heart – my mom – Mary L. Harris. This woman is my rock, my foundation. Her struggles and accomplishments inspired me to be the best in all that I do. I still, today, run everything by her as I did as a child. Her opinion matters to me as the cement to the bricks of our family bond. No one will ever stand between the love we share. Thank you, Mom!

Gloria Moody, now Gloria Smith AKA First Lady Smith AKA G'Money my love. This woman has secrets of my life that we will take to the grave. She's one I'd give my life to save hers.

Robert Moody AKA Bobby, my right-hand man. Another one who has secrets that we will not only treasure but we will take into the next world. Thanks, cuz, for all the late-night talks and continued support.

Michael Moody, my muscle, my big dude. He has been nothing but genuine throughout our entire lives. This teddy bear of a man is the one that will turn grizzly if you push him. Thanks, cuz, for all the love and support. Your kind words got me through when I needed it the most.

Latrice Moody, one of my youngest but very knowledgeable cousins. Words can't express the love I have for her and her support. She encouraged me and told me I would be great in whatever I do. Thanks, Trice.

Michael and Sindy Greene, childhood friends, true friends for many years - along with my two beautiful God Children Aja and Avery. Their love and support have been part of my foundation for years and I sincerely thank them for being there when I needed them most.

Leslie Simon and Anita Jones, my two island women, who not only gave me insight on island women and culture, they also provided me with continuous support in creating this novel. Thanks, Ladies.

Karen Harris, my sister. The protector. She's also the interrogator of any new females that may come into the family circle. She doesn't have a problem letting you or anyone know how much she loves her baby brother. Thanks, K, for the continued support and protection.

Honorable mention for Renee Johnson who cast very knowledgeable insight on being open and free with my writing style. Thanks Renee.

And last, Ms. Neena Love, my Editor and Publisher. Thanks for pushing me beyond the limits I could ever think to imagine. Thanks for believing in me and seeing my vision and taking me to new heights. I will cherish it for the rest of my life. Thanks for making my dream come to fruition.

1

BEEP. BEEP. BEEP.

It is 5 a.m., and Brian and Stacey awaken to the subtle sound of their alarm clock. Not ready to get out of bed yet, Brian reaches over and lightly taps the snooze button.

BEEP. BEEP. BEEP.

It is 5:15 a.m., and the alarm is going off again. Stacey reaches over the bed, retrieves her back scratcher, positions it to the cord of the alarm clock, and snatches it from the wall.

"Another hour. I just need one more hour," says Stacey as she reaches for the covers and pulls them over her head.

Brian lifts the covers and admires the beauty of his wife. *Mmm.* Brian thinks, *my wife is simply lying beside me and my man is rock hard. Morning sex is just what I need to get my day started.* He lies in awe and the only thing he can think about is how his wife Stacey keeps her body nice, tight, and right, and all he wants to do is be in her secret garden.

Brian gets up to close the bedroom door and asks Alexa to play songs by Maxwell, Stacey's favorite music artist. Now, he must select the right tune because he knows the perfect song will set the tone. Brian pulls the covers back and again is in awe, with pure admiration for Stacey's body, which looks like a honey-glazed donut. The only thing Brian is thinking about is how much he wants to lick it, kiss it, suck it and nibble on it.

For this to go down the way he wants it to, Brian has to play his cards correctly because Stacey is all about romance. There would be no just-sticking-it-in. Brian needs to mentally fuck her first by using his words to relax her mind, body, and soul, so he was pulling out all his cards. One sure way of getting that honey bun was to give Stacey a massage. He sensually rubs her shoulders, then her waist, and down to her thighs, in and out. He reaches for her fruit basket and feels it warm and creamy. Brian thinks he is home free, so he pulls his man out. Brian is so hard. His dick is aching. He slowly inches up to Stacey and attempts to slide in from the back. Stacey turns to him and asks, "What are you doing?"

Brian's facial expression, along with his man, drops like a ton of bricks. He becomes enraged but quickly realizes that if he wants this to go down, he must be sensitive to the situation.

Brian and Stacey have been together for eighteen years and have two lovely children, Ashley and Malcolm. Prior to having children, Brian and Stacey were inseparable. When you saw one, you saw the other. They did everything together. They even enjoyed sports, such as basketball and football. Hell, as much as Stacey screamed at the television, one would think she was more of the coach than the fan. Their sex life was off the chain, literally. Every day and wherever, it didn't matter, they got it on. But just imagine driving in the Indy 500 and going from 240mph to 10mph. Their sex life went from every day and wherever to now almost a mission impossible. Lately, Stacey has shown less interest in sex and the relationship, which makes Brian wonder. But he isn't about to call it quits because he wants it to work. He loves his family. He is willing to do whatever it takes to hold on.

"What's wrong?" Brian asks Stacey.

"I'm just not in the mood," Stacey replies.

"Are you sick?"

"No. I'm just not in the fucking mood," Stacey repeats angrily.

Brian is pissed. *This is some bullshit*, he thinks to himself as he snatches the sheets off the bed and heads for the shower. "Fuck! Fuck!" Brian shouts.

Now, I'ma have to get myself off to relieve this sexual frustration. Brian is so mentally fucked up. No matter what he does, he can't concentrate enough to nut. He walks out of the bathroom and slams the door with an earth-shattering sound. Brian's eyes are red like a four-alarm blaze. If looks could kill, everything in sight would be on fire. He walked through the house, slamming doors and cabinets. At this point, he does not care who he wakes. Everyone is going to get up. Do you think a woman scorned is bad? Try a sexually frustrated, angry man. Hell, hath no fury!

As Brian leaves for work, thoughts are racing through his mind. *I give this woman everything, and all I request is a little head or some sex from time to time. Most women dream of having a man like me. I wash clothes every week. I do the grocery shopping and make repairs on the house and cars, take her on two trips a year, give her money randomly, and make time for her whenever she needs or asks for it. I spend an enormous amount of time with the kids, yet I can't get a piece of ass when I want it. I love my wife, but sometimes I wonder if I'm being used. A man has needs and feelings too, and right now, I need to get laid in the worst way. Something has got to give! And quick!*

Brian storms out, not speaking or saying goodbye to anyone. As he drives to work, he has all kinds of thoughts, and none are good. Brian drives aggressively, speeding and weaving in and out of traffic. Out of nowhere, he sees blue lights in his rearview mirror.

Damn, this is all I need, Brian thinks as he reduces his speed and pulls over, hoping it isn't him the officer is pursuing. However, to his dismay, the officer speeds up and rides his bumper to let him know to pull over.

The trooper steps to the window and says, "License and registration."

The trooper sees that Brian is in uniform and recognizes that he is either a city cop or a correctional officer.

The trooper asks, "What's the rush, Mr. Phillips?"

"My apologies, sir. I woke up late and I'm just trying to make it to work before roll call," Brian replies.

"I know what you mean. Do you need an escort?" the trooper asks.

Feeling relieved, Brian responds, "Yes."

"What exit are you headed to?"

"Exit 98," Brian answers.

"Tell you what, I can cover you to 96."

They both nod in agreement, and the trooper returns to his vehicle.

While waiting for the trooper to pull back onto the road, Brian thinks to himself that *being blue has its advantages*. As they race down the interstate, Brian's mind is still on the incident that happened earlier that morning between him and his wife. He is still sexually frustrated, but he realizes that he needs to calm down and think about it from a woman's perspective. Make no mistake, he loves his wife and his family, but he is having thoughts of cheating, and he knows he has to figure out a better way to handle the situation. Several thoughts come to mind. However, he is locked in on one idea, in particular, that he was pretty sure would get his wife's attention. He decides to send her two dozen yellow roses, along with an apology, to her job in hopes that it will soften her up.

So many thoughts are running through his mind, both good and bad. Brian and Stacey were good not too long ago. They used to have sex practically every day. Then it went to five times a week, then down to three times a week, then down to once a week, to twice a month. There was no warning, no notice, and no explanation for the complete shutdown. For the life of Brian, he rattled his brain trying to figure out why. Stacey started as the most loving, notable wife. She was very attentive, caring, and family oriented. Their life was incredible. They did everything together. But then, without a moment's notice, Stacey became very distant. It seemed like she withdrew from the relationship for reasons uncertain. Throughout their relationship, Brian has remained the same lovable husband that most women dream of having. Communication was essential to him. However, it was not on the to-do list anymore. The more Brian fought for it, the more Stacey pulled away. He knew he was feeling this way because of her actions, which spoke of not wanting to be in the relationship anymore. Living in a relationship of confusion was troublesome and heartfelt. The uncertainty of not knowing was killing Brian inside and destroying the very fiber of what had tied them together in the first place.

Brian arrives at work. He checks in and then steps away to the break room to call the florist by Stacey's job. *Maybe, just maybe, this will be the thing to soften her up,* he thinks to himself after placing the order for the delivery. Brian feels that he is not only a good man but a man most women would dream of having. He will do whatever it takes to get in Stacey's good graces. Lord knows he needs it, especially with how he feels right now.

After ordering the flowers, Brian returns to the floor to begin his day with roll call. He still isn't in a good head space because of his sexual frustration, so anyone who gets on his mother fucking nerves is going to feel it. Surprisingly, those assholes must have been able to read his mind and see his facial expression. They knew he was not up to dealing with any bullshit because they didn't bother him at all. He appreciates them for leaving him alone.

Brian's lunch break is approaching, and he expects to hear from Stacey because he knows that she is well aware of his lunchtime. Cell phones aren't allowed on his job, but he'd taken a chance and snuck it in, hoping he would hear from her. He sits in the cafeteria, anticipating a phone call or text showing her appreciation for the delivery she should have already received at work. He keeps looking at his phone, waiting for it to vibrate, but nothing, not even a voice mail. Lunch had come and gone, and he didn't get any calls, no texts, or voice mails. Brian's anger is unimaginable. It is so prevalent that even his colleagues started noticing and were asking him if everything was okay. Brian responds yes, but who was he fooling? Surely not himself, or anyone else, for that matter. What he did know was that he needed to get it together. He is sexually frustrated, but all everyone can see is an angry black man.

As the day continues, Brian feels the need to recheck his phone on his last break, and again, nothing. No text, missed call, or voice mail. Now Brian is tunnel vision angry, so everyone that he'd come in contact with was going to feel it. Who would think all this anger could come from not getting some ass? Brian wondered if this was how it felt from an addict's perspective because he was definitely feenin'.

It was quitting time, and everyone on the job had been spared. As Brian walked to his car, he thought he had done everything right in the player's handbook, but the results had him feeling otherwise. He glanced at his phone again, and still, nothing. The more he looks at it, the more it angers him.

Brian gets in his car and races through the parking lot, tires squealing. He is expressing road rage in its rarest form and makes it to the interstate reaching 90mph. Three minutes into his speeding frenzy, he sees blue lights again. *Shit, here we go again,* Brian thinks to himself, hoping it isn't the same trooper from earlier that morning.

The trooper summons Brian to turn the engine off and drop the keys out the window. Brian complies. The trooper approaches his vehicle and asks for his identification. Brian complies. The trooper asks, "What's the rush?" Brian had a quick response earlier that morning when he was stopped the first time, so he had to come up with something quickly this time as well.

Brian looks at the trooper and says, "I apologize, sir, but my wife and son were in a car accident and have been rushed to the ER. I was trying to get to them and wasn't paying attention to my speed."

The trooper observes Brian's uniform and badge and asks, "What exit are you heading to?"

"Exit 36," Brian responds.

"Allow me to provide you an escort," says the officer, then gives Brian his license, registration, and keys back and walks to his car.

I'm going to hell, Brian thinks to himself. He convinces himself that the damage has already been done, and if he is going to be sexually frustrated, he has nothing to lose. But then, he started to feel bad because now, in his mind, he may be directing his family's path into unforeseen danger because of the lie he'd just told. Brian is in disbelief that good pussy would have him acting this way. However, here he was, and he couldn't wait until he arrived home. His focus is now on Stacey and how he may strangle her when he sees her.

When the trooper and Brian arrive at Exit 36, the trooper turns off his blue lights. Brian flashes his headlights twice to thank the officer for the escort. Brian proceeds to his house. As he approaches the house, he notices that Stacey's car isn't in the driveway. Usually, Stacey would be home before his arrival, which causes Brian to wonder even more.

Brian enters the house and is greeted by his daughter with overwhelming love as she hugs and kisses him. Ashley is a daddy's girl who loves everything about her father. In her eyes, the sun rises and sets on her dad, and there is nothing anyone can say to make her feel differently about him.

"Hey, baby girl," Brian says, returning his affection by hugging and kissing Ashley on her cheek. "How was your day?"

"Good. I missed you, Daddy," Ashley responds.

"I missed you too, baby girl. Where's your brother?"

"He's in his room."

"Hmm, okay. Where's your mother?"

"I'm not sure," Ashley states.

"Did she call?" Brian asks, trying not to show his anger.

"No," Ashley answers.

Although Brian has several other questions, he does not feel the need to interrogate Ashley about her mother's whereabouts. Brian observes the clock, and it is as if every tick and tock is a jab to his side. In his mind, Stacey needs to have a good got damn reason for being late. At this point, being dead is about the best excuse he could think of.

Brian needs to ease his mind. He needs a distraction from his thoughts about what he may do to Stacey, so he walks to his son's room with Ashley on his heels. Ashley is Brian's oldest child, at twelve years old, and Malcolm is the youngest, at eight. More like eight going on eighty. Malcolm is incredibly witty for his age and has a very carefree attitude, which is the opposite of his sister.

"Little man, take a break from that game and come speak to your dad," Brian says as he walks into Malcolm's room.

"Oh, hey, Dad," Malcolm responds with a nonchalant attitude.

"Hey, Son. I hope you know your lesson as well as you know that game. Is this the only thing you've been doing since you came home from school?"

"Awww, Dad, chill."

"Chill? I think you've forgotten who you are talking to. Let me remind you that you are not talking to one of your friends," Brian says sternly.

By the sound of Brian's tone, Malcolm knew he had crossed the line. Ashley even shook her head in disbelief at Malcolm's response. Brian is huge on discipline and respect, so it was a no-brainer for Malcolm to snap back into reality. Malcolm knew that whatever he said next would need to be on the level of respect that Brian demanded from both he and Ashley. Otherwise, there would be a punishment coming, and soon!

"Okay, okay, Dad. I get it," Malcolm says, trying to smooth things out with his father.

"Alright, Son. Keep what I said in mind. There's more to life than video games. I need you to remember that."

"Yes, sir. I understand, Dad."

While Brian is tough, he also remembered what it was like being a kid. Tough love is what he knows, so he exhibits it. Malcolm and Brian high-five each other and displayed their signature handshake.

2

It is now three hours past Stacey's expected time of arriving home. Brian didn't dare call her because they had this thing about trusting one another and allowing each other space. But, her lateness was wearing thin on him, not to mention the tension between his legs ached like a migraine. Thirty more minutes was all Brian had agreed to with his conscience before he would initiate a call. As soon as the thought crosses his mind, he glances at the surveillance camera and sees headlights slowly lighting up the driveway. Shortly after, the image of Stacey's car appears as clear as day.

Brian swiftly makes a bee-line to the shower. He wants to allow Stacey time to settle before he drills her ass. The shower is hot, just like Brian's temperament. The room is foggy, just as the thoughts rapidly cross his mind. Every moment of being in that shower, Brian thinks of ways he is going to cross-examine Stacey's ass.

Stacey is clever and witty, slick with the tongue and always on point, so Brian knows he has to be on top of his game. He will have to pull a 'Johnny Cochran' to handle the argument he is about to have with his wife. Brian vigorously washes his body over and over, so much that he begins to prune. Just as he is about to exit the shower, he hears the click of the bathroom door open.

"Is there any room in there for me?" Stacey asks softly. Her soft-spoken voice sounds as if she was the radio host of the midnight slow jams, seducing Brian's ears. At that moment, all the rehearsed, profound words that Brian had thought to use had gone out the got damn window. He was dick dumb when he laid eyes on Stacey, who was standing just outside the shower door.

Brian imagines every article of clothing Stacey had on slowly being removed – her six-inch heels, black mini-skirt, and sheer white blouse, with lace bra and panty set. He imagines all the things she exhibited to him when they first met. Her every move is magnified in Brian's imagination. The steam in the room helps to set the tone of a romantic love scene and the anticipation of Stacey getting in the shower with him had his dick throbbing. Reality sets in. She is three hours late. Brian is mentally torn between keeping an erection or becoming America's Top Detective. Stacey has some real explaining to do.

The shower door clicks and everything Brian had thought to ask is forgotten. Stacey slowly enters the shower. The warm water runs down her angelic, pecan-toned body. She soaps up her washcloth ever so slowly. She covers every inch of her body with soap. Brian watches. It seems to move in slow motion as if it is a peep show on 42nd Street in the city.

The smell of the shea butter Dove soap heightens Brian's senses, and his dick is now as solid as a kitchen pipe. Stacey slowly backs up on Brian, and instantly his dick knows where home is. His penis is like a programmed iRobot that knows where to find the center of heaven.

Brian slowly caresses Stacey's left breast while using his right hand to explore her secret garden. Stacey firmly places her hands on the shower wall and moans in ecstasy. Brian gently grabs Stacey's throat as he slides his rock-hard pipe into her warm pussy and proceeds to pound it with authority, fast then slow. Slow then fast.

"Yes, Daddy," Stacey responds between moans.

Brian leans back, and with one last thrust, he explodes inside her.

"Damn girl, I needed that," Brian mildly expresses in a baritone voice.

Brian leans back against the shower wall. Stacey turns to him and hugs him passionately while softly kissing his neck, causing Brian's eyes to roll behind his eyelids in sexual pressure. This feeling of desire is what he longed to feel from his wife, and his man stood at attention again. Brian is dick dumb for sure. The lack of intimacy has made him contemplate the unimaginative. But now, the very thought of Stacey being late, not calling or texting, was null and void, all due to that quick session of intimacy. Stacey turns to Brian, hugs him close, and expresses her thanks for the beautiful flowers.

"You're welcome, baby. I'm glad you like them," Brian responds. With all that tension and anger, it is almost incomprehensible to think that Brian wanted to cause harm to his wife of eighteen years. *I must be crazy,* Brian thought to himself. All day, he had been thinking the craziest of thoughts. Then, in a matter of moments, his anger and frustration had vanished with a nut. And to think, it never had to come to this if Stacey would just give up the goods like she used to.

Stacey tries to exit the shower. Brian grabs her wrist and asks, "Where you think you going?"

Stacey smiles. "Hmm, my big daddy ain't done yet?"

KNOCK. KNOCK.

At that moment, they both regretted for a second that they had children. "Mommy, are you in there?" Ashley asks.

"Yes, baby. Just a minute. I'll be right out."

Brian turns the water pressure in the shower up to muffle the sound. "We're not done yet," Brian whispers in Stacey's ear. She raises her leg on the side of the tub, and Brian slides his pipe between her legs. As he slowly enters Stacey's paradise of pleasure, he watches her cream all over his magic stick. Stacey moans and tries to refrain from being too loud because she knows Ashley was just outside the bathroom door.

"Ohhh yes, Daddy. It's yours. This is your pussy!" Stacey says solemnly.

"Whose pussy is it?"

"Yours, Daddy," Stacey moaned in that sexy whisper she always does when she is turned on.

KNOCK. KNOCK.

"Mommy," Ashley interrupts them again.

Stacey answers, attempting to sound calm and composed, "Yes, baby girl."

"I need your help."

Stacey turns to Brian and says, "Daddy, we're gonna have to finish this later." Brian shakes his head.

Stacey backs away slowly while grabbing Brian's chin with her index and thumb fingers, and with a sexy squint in her eye, she whispers, "Don't worry, Daddy. I got another surprise for you. Save some of that energy." Brian smiles like a kid who has just received a new bike.

"Okay. Okay. Now, we're talking." Brian turns the shower off, and they both exit the bathroom. When they walk into the bedroom, Brian asks, "What are we eating?"

"I'm not really hungry," Stacey responds.

Brian is taken aback by her response and thinks, *let me file that.*

Stacey continues, "I'm a go ahead and make something quick, like spaghetti."

After dinner, Brian and Stacey send the kids to bed with kisses and goodnight wishes. They cuddle up to watch a movie. A particular scene in the movie triggers Brian and he can't help the thoughts crossing his mind. The fact that it had been a couple of weeks since they'd had sex, her not being hungry this evening, and her coming in late with no excuse like it was okay didn't sit well with him. He wants to address his concerns, but not at the risk of pissing Stacey off, so he decides to play it cool and give her a massage in hopes that it will get her in the mood for a discussion. When he finishes the massage and feels it is safe to go to the next step, Brian slips his shorts off and pokes Stacey on the side of her leg with his rock-hard man. Stacey turns and slightly rolls her eyes with attitude.

"What's wrong?" Brian asks.

Stacey frowns and spats, "What now? You didn't get enough earlier?"

"Really? I'm confused. Wasn't it you who said save some energy because you had a surprise for me later? Now it's a problem? Are you no longer attracted to me? I don't turn you on anymore? What?" Brian pleads for understanding.

Stacey stammers, "No, that's not it—"

"Then, what is it?" Brian asks, cutting her off. At that moment, Brian wanted to rip her clothes off and fuck the shit out of her! She had him contemplating taking it!

"Is that all you think about?" Stacey asks.

"All I think about?" Brian asked with a slightly elevated voice, then threw his hands up in frustration. "What's the problem?" he asks again, somewhat subdued and contemplative.

Stacey replies, "I don't know. I just don't feel like it lately."

Brian held his head. "I understand if you're physically sick, on your cycle, or have had a bad day at work. I get it. But you just not being in the mood is killing me. I'm trying to understand, but you're not giving me much to work with."

"You wouldn't!" Stacey storms off.

Brian is beyond upset at this point. He grabs his shorts, shirt, and shoes and heads out the room, then the front door. He gets in his car, revs the motor, and burns out of the driveway. Brian is driving with no regard, exceeding speeds of 120mph. His adrenaline is pumping, and his mind is racing. He thinks to himself, *what am I missing?* He begins to calm down, slows the car down, and thinks, *what am I doing wrong?*

He pulls the car to the side of the road and looks to God for answers. He prays silently, “Please, Lord, show me another way. I can’t see what I’ve done or where I’ve gone wrong. Please provide me with a light to follow.”

RING. RING.

Brian picks up his cell phone and sees his sister, Karen, is calling. He hesitates but decides to answer.

“Hey, Sis. What’s up?”

“Hey, little brother. What’s up with you?” Karen responds.

“Nothing much, just the usual,” states Brian.

“What? That woman getting on your nerves again?”

Brian laughs in silence, trying to figure out how she knew what was happening in his house. “Yeah, a little. How’d you know?”

“I can hear it in your voice, little brother. I’ve known you all your life, so I know when something is wrong. What is it this time? She overspent on a card? She missed a bill? Or she ain’t giving you no sex?”

Brian thinks, *damn, she’s good or is it just the norm?* “Well, Dr. Phil-letta,” Brian says with a smile, “It’s kinda the sex thing. I’m seriously sexually frustrated. I haven’t cheated, but I’m contemplating it.”

“Oh, wait a minute,” Karen says, “Not the pope of the relationship world. Hold the phone. Am I hearing this right?”

“Yes! You heard me right!” Brian fires back.

“Oh, okay. So, what’s really going on?” Karen asks with a concerned voice.

“She hit me off with a little appetizer earlier today, then when we were done, she told me to save my energy, and we would finish later.”

“Why?” Karen asked curiously.

“Because Ash interrupted us while we were in the shower. Before today, it had been weeks since we’d been together. She tries to make it seem like all I do is ask for sex. I mean, who else should I expect sex from other than my wife?” Brian states, frustrated.

Karen sneers, “Hmmm, I’m not gonna say it.”

“Say what?” Brian asks.

“Me and Mommy tried to tell you she’s an opportunist. She saw you for your worth, baby brother. You’re a good guy, don’t ever think you’re not. Me and Mommy raised you right.”

“You and Mommy?”

They both laugh.

"I know I'm a good dude, so how do I fix this? Give me some of that woman's intuition."

"Well, what changes have you noticed in her behavior besides no sex? Has her eating habits changed? Does she come home late? Has her appearance changed? Is she wearing new perfume? Does she walk different? Does she appear happy, even when she isn't engaging or interacting with you?" Karen asks, giving Brian something to think about.

Damn, Brian thought to himself, *she's hitting on all the cylinders.* Karen had just run the perfect profile on Stacey.

"Well, Sis, I can say that just about everything you've said is happening."

"I don't mean to make an already bad situation any worse, baby brother, but my intuition says it's a man. Either she's trying to get him, or she has him, and she's fucking him," Karen says carefully.

"What!" Brian screams into the phone.

"Calm down."

"What do you mean calm down? You just said she's fucking another man, and I should be calm? Fuck no!" Brian shouts.

"You see? All you men are just alike. Y'all get all bent outta shape when you think someone else is fucking your woman. Have you ever thought you could be boring her? Or you're just not exciting anymore? Maybe it's your routine."

"My routine?" Brian repeats, confused.

"Yes, doing the same thing every time you two are together."

"That's no excuse to fuck someone else," Brian states.

"One would think that, but to be very honest, sometimes what you feel really isn't. It just so happens to be just what it is. You're right. That's no excuse to be with someone else. However, nowadays, the silliest things can turn out to be the component. People don't honor or respect marriage anymore. Most times, it's all about the show and the material things that usually comes with it. Most men can't accept or see it. Y'all take a woman for granted. You wanna pound the pussy and beat it up, but never massage it or make love to it. Don't get me wrong. There's nothing wrong with y'all beating it, but not all the time. Be gentle," Karen schools Brian.

"Not me. That's not my style," Brian retorts.

"You have to be spontaneous," Karen insists.

Brian immediately thinks about some of the things he'd done to impress his wife. The roses he'd just sent were a perfect example.

"I try to be spontaneous, but there's always an excuse," he replies.

"Well, it's something. Listen to her, ask her close-ended questions, watch a movie with her, ask her questions during the movie, watch her reactions and listen to her responses."

"Okay, okay, Phil-letta. I get it. Your words of wisdom humble me."

Karen laughs and says, "What's a big sister for?"

"Yeah, yeah. I'll talk to you later," Brian says and ends the call.

As he drives home, Brian continuously plays the information he'd just received from Karen back and forth in his mind when a song by Heatwave, called Mind Blowing Decisions, plays on the radio. Old songs like this one always remind Brian of the bible because it reflects the past, the present, a repeat of history, and what's to come. However it may have been, or however it seemed, Brian needs to fix his situation, but he isn't sure how to do it.

3

Brian walks into the house feeling calm. Everything is dark and still. It is so quiet that you could hear a feather hit the floor. To Brian's surprise, Stacey is still awake, and her face brightens when he walks into the room. Brian is shocked by the softness of her facial expression. The scent of vanilla fills his nose, and the slightly tinted lightbulb casts a glow on Stacey's face. Her red satin gown was nice and tight in all the right places. Brian couldn't help himself. Just looking at his wife turns him on.

Stacey noticed him looking at her and asked, "Are you okay?"

Before Brian can answer, she continues, "I'm sorry, baby, I don't know what's going on with me or why I'm feeling this way. I'm sorry."

Stacey rises from the bed, reaches out to Brian, and hugs and kisses him repeatedly while she apologizes. She reaches for his man, lowers her head, and begins to massage it with her mouth. It felt so good to Brian and so wrong, all at the same time. His mind said to stop her, but his body said, *let's get it*.

He hated to do it, but he stopped her.

"No, stop. I don't want it this way. I want you to desire me. I don't want you to pretend just to silence me. Do you understand me?"

"Yes."

"This feels like you're only doing it because I got angry and left. I don't want you to feel guilty," Brian says. He wraps his arms around her as tightly as possible, then kisses her and tells her he loves her. He wants to make love to her mentally. He needs to get her mind off his anger and make her feel safe and loved so she would give him all her mind, body, and soul like they used to be.

"I love you," Brian whispers while holding Stacey ever so close. Brian asked Alexa to shuffle songs by Maxwell as they fell asleep.

The following day, Brian is the first to rise. Shortly after, Ashley was up, then Malcolm.

"Good morning, guys," Brian greeted his kids.

In harmony, Ashley and Malcolm both respond, "Morning Dad."

Ashley rushes to Brian's side for her morning hug while Malcolm reaches up to give Brian a high five.

"Hey, I have an idea," Brian said.

"Yes, Dad," Ashley responds as Malcolm looks on with anticipation.

"Why don't we surprise Mommy with breakfast in bed?"

"Sure," Ashley says while Malcolm nods.

"Let's cook pancakes, eggs, and sausage. I would like to make some grits too, but they don't come out right. Can you teach me?" Ashley asks Brian.

"Sure, baby girl," Brian confirms.

"Malcolm, get the silverware and plates. Ashley, get that pot and fill it halfway with water. I'll start on the pancakes and sausage." Brian has his kids working like they are in a well-trained military camp.

"Okay, baby girl, we need to boil some water on high, then lower it once we get it to the right temperature. Then, we wanna slowly add the grits and stir. The key to cooking grits is to keep stirring them until they get to the texture of your desire," Brian explains.

"I got it, Dad. Move over, sir. Let me do it," Ashley says anxiously.

"Okay, it's all yours," Brian says, passing the spoon to Ashley.

"Malcolm, rinse those plates and silverware and dry them."

"Yes, sir. Dad, can I ask you a question?"

"Sure, little man. What's up?"

"Why do I have to rinse off dishes that are supposed to be clean?"

"Well, Son, although the dishes may be clean, they can still accumulate dust and floating debris, so just to be on the safe side and not to take any of it into our mouths, we do a quick rinse," Brian answers Malcolm.

"I get it now. That makes sense," Malcolm responded.

"Okay, good."

"Ashley, how are those grits coming?" Brian asks as he finishes the pancakes.

"Good. I think the grits are done," Ashley says, proud of her creamy pot of grits.

"Okay, turn the burner on low and start your eggs," Brian instructs.

"On low?" Ashley repeats.

"Yes, keep it on low so that it will stay warm," Brian confirms, then turns his attention back to Malcolm.

"Okay, Malcolm, get the sausage out."

Brian slices the sausage in half and lightly fries it to a crisp. "Okay, guys, I think we did it. Everything looks good," Brian announces.

The kitchen is heavy with the scent of a delightfully balanced meal that would convince anyone who wasn't hungry that they actually were. They all took part in preparing the breakfast meal, but Malcolm took the initiative to prepare Stacey's plate.

As Malcolm approached the bedroom door, they all took the time to observe Stacey's beautiful smile. It made Brian hopeful that this could be the turning point that would change their relationship and get Stacey back to loving him like old times. He began thinking of the many things Stacey liked to do, then had a great idea.

What woman would refuse a day of pampering? he thought to himself. He steps away and looks up the number to her favorite nail salon. Once he makes the appointment, he thinks, *why not include a full body massage to top it off for her?* So, he calls and sets that appointment as well. He loves his wife and wants to show her how much she means, so he pulls out all the stops just for her. Once he locks in the appointments, he returns to the bedroom with his family. Stacey is still smiling as she eats her breakfast. She seems to appreciate the gesture her family has made for her.

"Aww, thanks, guys. This was a nice surprise," Stacey says to Brian and the kids.

"Mommy, I made the grits and eggs," Ashley announces with a fulfilling smile.

"You did? They are delicious, baby. Thank you."

"You're welcome," Ashley replies, smiling from ear to ear.

"Mom, I made your plate," Malcolm says, feeling insufficient.

"And you did a wonderful job. Everything looks nice and tastes good," said Stacey.

Brian is glad that Stacey approves of her breakfast. He is ready to let her know that breakfast is only the beginning, so he moves closer to her and says, "Okay, so when you're done, I have something planned for you. Take your time and enjoy your food and when you're finished eating, get dressed and meet me downstairs." Stacey smiles.

Brian leaves the room and enters the bathroom. He removes all the linen and cleans the bathroom to meet his OCD specifications. He finishes by placing a fresh, new washcloth and towel out for Stacey. As she entered the bathroom, she noticed that it had been cleaned and the linen had been replaced. The shine of the chrome on the faucets and the scent of bleach let her know the bathroom had been cleaned with precision. Brian enters the bathroom.

"Is there anything else you need?" he asks.

"No. Thanks," Stacey responds.

"Okay, wear something comfortable."

"Comfortable?" Stacey asks.

"Yes. I need you to be comfortable, so there is no need to overdo it. Jeans or sweats will do."

"Why don't you pick something out for me?"

"Oh, no problem. Your wish is my command."

Brian certainly had just the outfit in mind. He pulls out a pair of black leggings, a white top, and a pair of sandals. He sorts through her lingerie drawer and pulls out a black laced bra and thong set he loves. He returns to the bathroom doorway with a light smile and says, "All set."

Brian sits on the edge of the bed as Stacey exits the bathroom wearing a plum plush rob with her body slightly damp and glistening. Stacey is Brian's fantasy that has come true. She is beautiful, intelligent, and graceful. Through all his admirations, he cannot help but get slightly aroused. The very sight of Stacey turns him on. She makes him feel like a teenager. All her wrongs were right, and when he thought she was wrong, he couldn't help but to forgive her. His love for her is unimaginable, and he will do just about anything to make her happy, even though he feels neglected because she isn't as affectionate as he desires.

"You're amazing!" Brian announces to Stacey.

"Hmm?" Stacey stops in her tracks and looks at Brian.

"You're amazing!" Brian repeats. "I don't regret, for one day, ever wanting you to be my wife."

"Aww, babe. That was sweet."

"I mean it. You make me crazy."

Blushing, Stacey says, "Thank you, babe," and reaches for Brian's chin.

Brian smiles. As Stacey walked over to the bed, she observed the clothes Brian had laid out for her to wear.

"Interesting choice," she says.

"Yeah, it's sufficient for today."

"Okay, can you at least tell me where we're going?"

"No, babe," Brian says with a sinister grin.

"Just get your clothes on before we have to make other plans."

Stacey lotions herself and gets dressed. She looks at Brian and smiles at him with her chestnut brown eyes and deep dimples. At that moment, Brian decides to exit the room because the temptation is too great.

"Babe, I'ma be downstairs," Brian says, getting up to leave before he did something that would surely make Stacey late for her appointment.

"Okay, I'll be down in a few," Stacey replies.

When Brian makes it downstairs, he goes into the family room and reaches for his cell phone. He finds his sister's name in his contacts and sends her a text message.

"Be here in an hour," the text message to Karen reads.

"Okay," Karen replies.

Brian takes the time to entertain Ashley and Malcolm while waiting on Stacey to finish getting dressed. Shortly after that, Stacey walks downstairs looking super sexy in her leggings. The scent of her Versace perfume fills the room. Brian is in the middle of a conversation with the kids, but he is immediately distracted and stares at Stacey's hourglass figure. He is captivated by her presence.

RING. RING.

"I got it!" Malcolm announces as he gets up to answer the door.

"Hey, Auntie Karen!" Malcolm shouts.

"Good morning, handsome," she replied to Malcolm, giving him a big hug.

Karen walks into the house with an abundance of energy. She hugs Brian and Stacey, then walks over to Ashley to admire how much her beautiful niece is growing up. Karen receives the warmest greeting from everyone, especially Malcolm and Ashley. She is their only aunt and the favorite by far. She is also like a mother to them, and they share everything with her.

"Guys, I have a surprise," Karen says with a sarcastic grin.

Yes, Auntie. What is it?" Malcolm and Ashley both ask anxiously.

"Who wants to go to Big Bob's Playland?"

"Me! Me!" Malcolm says, jumping up and down.

"Ummm, I'm a little too grown for that, but I'll ride out with y'all," Ashley says, slightly rolling her eyes.

"Aw, Ashley, you know we'll find something girly to do before the day is over," Karen says to Ashley, assuring her that she will have a good time too. Stacey and Brian smile.

"Aw, Karen, you didn't have to," Brian says, giving Karen a half hug.

"What did you think we were going to do? Sit around the house while y'all go out and have a good time?"

"Umm, ahh, no," Brian mutters.

"Okay, good. So, guys, let's go," Karen says, and without wasting another moment, Brian and Stacey walk out the front door.

Brian holds the door for Stacey as she climbs into his black M3. He slides into the driver's seat and lowers the convertible.

"I love you," Brian says silently.

"I love you too," Stacey replies.

BZZZ. BZZZ. BZZZ.

Stacey's phone started vibrating. She reaches in her pocketbook and, without pulling the phone out or looking at it, hits the side button to stop it from vibrating. Brian lays eyes on her for a moment but does not respond.

BZZZ. BZZZ. BZZZ.

Stacey's phone vibrates over and over. This time, she does not respond. Instead, she tries to ignore the texts. Brian cannot ignore it, so he asks, "Is everything alright?"

"Oh yeah, everything is fine. I keep getting those junk advertisement notices," Stacey responds, trying to keep her cool.

Brian raises his eyebrows and says, "Oh, okay." And with that, he turned the music on his satellite radio station, put his shades back on, and cruised on the interstate until they reached their destination.

Brian and Stacey continued their day as he had planned. They arrived at the nail salon and enjoyed the VIP treatment, which included a private room and their choice of wine. They enjoyed listening to the smooth sounds of Sade's Cherish the Day and sipping on Chardonnay as the attendant gently massaged their feet. Everything was perfect. From the music to all the surprises Brian had pre-planned, Stacey is overwhelmingly pleased. But Brian isn't quite finished yet. He still has three more surprises for his beautiful wife. First, a hot oil massage at the spa, dinner, and finally, a nightcap at the Marriott. He is excited about what is to come, but before he and Stacey continue his plans, Brian initiates a call to Karen.

RING. RING.

Karen answers, "Hello."

"Hey, Sis," Brian greets.

"Hey, what's up?"

"Can you do your baby brother a huge favor?"

"Sure, what is it?" Karen asks.

"Can you watch your niece and nephew for a night?" Brian asks with his fingers crossed.

"Hmm, a whole night?" Karen asks.

"Yes. You said to be spontaneous," Brian reminds Karen.

"Yeah, I did. Go for it, little brother. I got you," Karen assures Brian.

"Thanks, Sis! I really appreciate it. Love you."

"Love you too."

"Kiss the kids for me," Brian says.

"I will," Karen said and ended the call.

During the hot oil massage session, Brian breaks the news to Stacey. Dinner is next on the schedule, and he takes Stacey to her favorite restaurant, Olive Garden. Stacey is pleasantly surprised. Stacey's masseur is tall, muscular, and extremely handsome. While Brian's masseuse is striking, dazzling, and downright breathtaking. Her hands feel muscular, while her physique suggests she is soft and sexy. Brian and Stacey envision a discreet metacognition that they'd held a personal fantasy about their respected professionals. Unlike Stacey, Brian is unable to contain himself. Unfortunately, he becomes aroused, causing his masseuse to pause with a sparkle in her eye and a glowing face. She suggests that Brian roll over to avoid bringing any attention to himself from Stacey and her masseur, who were about five feet away. Brian takes the advice from his masseuse, rolls over with his towel, and quietly exits the room.

"Babe, I'ma go to the bathroom," Brian says quietly.

"Okay, babe," Stacey replies, too relaxed to open her eyes.

"I have one more surprise for you," Brian informs her.

BZZZ. BZZZ. BZZZ.

Stacey's phone starts vibrating again. Thinking that Brian had exited the room this time, she picked up the phone and viewed the text. Brian stops at the door before leaving the room and observes her action of dismissing the text after viewing it. Stacey wraps up her session and exits the room to the waiting arms of Brian. Brian gives the attendants a nice tip and thanks them for their superb and professional pampering, then walks out of the spa, arm in arm with Stacey.

"Babe, what's next?" Stacey asks.

"Well, we're on the way to have dinner at your favorite restaurant, and I made arrangements for Karen to watch the kids while we spend some alone time together," Brian replies with a genuine look of love on his face.

Stacey's pleasant smile quickly changed to the look of a deer caught in headlights.

"Hmm, oh really?" Stacey replies.

"Is that a problem?" Brian asked with a concerned look.

"No, no. I was just asking, babe."

"Okay. Well, I hope you like my surprise," Brian says, feeling some kind of way.

Stacey turns her head side to side, almost in disbelief, and replies, "Okay."

"Is that okay?" Brian asks.

"Oh yeah. That's fine, babe."

During dinner, Stacey expresses to Brian how much she appreciates the pampering. Brian had gone out of his way to continue being the charming man most women dream about.

"The night is young, babe, and I still have one more surprise for you."

"Really? What is it?"

"Be patient."

Brian and Stacey drive through the city streets as Stacey sings along with the classic, old-school music playing through the speakers. Brian gazes at Stacey occasionally, and she appears to be pleased. Seeing her smile made him smile.

They slowly pull up to the Marriott. "What are we doing here?" Stacey asks.

"This is the last part of my surprise," Brian states, studying Stacey's facial expression. The smile he witnessed on her face just a few moments ago has disappeared.

"Surprise? Hmm, what about the kids?"

"Relax, babe. I took care of that already. They're in good hands with Karen for the night."

"Hmm. Okay," Stacey replies, reluctantly.

Once they enter the hotel, Brian approaches the courtesy counter and provides his ID and credit card. The attendant returns his credentials and issues a room card for room# 321. Brian turns to Stacey, flashes the card, then grabs Stacey's hand and leads her to the elevator. Once they are off the elevator and in the room, Brian slowly undresses Stacey and leads her into the bathroom. He runs a bath and massages Stacey's body from head to toe.

BZZZ. BZZZ. BZZZ.

Stacey's ring tone on her phone begins playing. Brian exits the bathroom, turns to Stacey, and asks, "Did you want me to get that?"

"No," Stacey replies.

Brian tries to keep an open mind. He does not want to think the worst about the texts Stacey has ignored all day. He returns from the mini-bar with a small bottle of wine, then climbs into the jacuzzi with Stacey. They talk and laugh as soft music plays in the background. After about 45 minutes of relaxing with each other, Brian and Stacey exit the bathroom. They decide to watch a movie in bed.

"This is still your day, so you pick what movie we will watch," Brian says to Stacey as he passes her the remote.

"Hmmm, let's see what's playing on Netflix," Stacey says as she changes the channel to the streaming network and begins to search for an exciting movie to watch.

BZZZ. BZZZ. BZZZ.

Stacey's phone starts vibrating. She reaches for the phone, glances at it, then dismisses it. "I don't know why I keep getting these robo calls," she says, trying to downplay an argument she feels is brewing.

Robo calls? But those were texts, Brian thinks to himself. He wonders why Stacey feels the need to lie to him. "Hmm, I don't know, babe."

"I think I may need to change my number."

Change your number? I think that may be a little extreme," Brian states.

"Yeah, maybe."

Determined to keep his cool, Brian dismissively asks, "Did you find a movie for us to watch?"

"Hmmm, I'm still searching. Do you want to watch an action movie? Or a love story?" Stacey asks.

"Babe, whatever you want, is what I want," Brian responds, and Stacey smiles.

Brian gets out of bed to put his phone on the charger in the bathroom. He had his phone on vibrate, but he wanted to turn the ringer on because Karen had the kids, just in case something happened with them. As he approaches the bathroom, he looks back and sees Stacey reaching for her phone, assumingly checking her messages. As Brian continues to the bathroom, he can't help but wonder what is going on in his wife's world and why she is being so distrustful. He is contemplating the idea of ruining their fantastic day and confronting her about what is going on. He knew that sooner or later, he would have to face it. He wanted answers, but was now the time to demand those answers? Brian finishes plugging up his phone and returns to the bedroom to see Stacey trying to tuck her phone under her pillow. Brian raises his eyebrow skeptically and asks, "Is everything okay?"

"Yes, babe. Why?"

Brian sighs before responding. "Your demeanor. You're acting different."

Stacey tries to smile convincingly. "No, I'm fine. Really, I'm okay, babe."

Many thoughts are circulating through Brian's mind regarding Stacey's movements as of late. The situation is similar to the conversation he'd had with Karen. Brian decides to let it go for now and enjoy the rest of the evening with his wife. The night is winding down, and Brian and Stacey barely speak to one another. Brian falls asleep during the movie, leaving Stacey awake to do whatever she was doing behind his back.

The following day, Brian and Stacey get up and prepare to head home. There is still obvious tension in the air, and the conversation is limited to simple and dry good morning pleasantries. Stacey appears overly eager for an unknown reason, and Brian is standoffish. Still confused, Brian is left to assume what is happening with his wife and her phone. Her movements aren't making sense, and he needs answers. After they go downstairs and have the continental breakfast at the hotel, they ride home in ominous silence. Stacey tries to make small talk, but Brian is more interested in getting answers about what is going on with her. The entire idea is to show Stacey how much he loves her, but Brian feels it is all a waste. Once they arrive home, they are greeted with open arms by Malcolm and Ashley. This small moment warms Brian's heart despite his thoughts about his wife.

"Hey, guys. Did y'all miss us?" Brian asks the kids.

"Yeah!" Both Ashley and Malcolm eagerly answer.

"What did y'all do?" Ashley asks.

Before Brian or Stacey could answer Ashley's question, Malcolm steps up with a big smile and asks, "Did you bring us something back?"

"Not this time," Brian replies as he rubs Malcolm on the head.

Ashley shoves Malcolm and mutters, "It's not always about you."

"I didn't say it was!" Malcolm shouts at Ashley. The two begin to shove one another as siblings do.

"Okay, okay! Enough you two!" Brian says with authority.

"That's right," Karen says. "We didn't have a problem before, and we aren't about to have one now. Understood?"

"Yes, ma'am," they both respond.

"I was about to tell you guys all that we did and how much fun we had, but that just went out the window because you all are acting like you have no sense," Stacey says as she looks at Malcolm and Ashley with a displeased face.

"I'm going to lay down," Brian says.

"Sis, thank you so much for watching the kids. I'ma talk to you later."

"Oh, okay. Is everything okay?" Karen asks with concern.

"I'm just a little tired. I'm alright," Brian says, trying to sound as convincing as he can.

"Okay then," Karen says, not convinced. Karen hugs her brother, then has a little one-on-one girl talk with Stacey about the latest social media drama, calls the kids down to hug them, and then leaves. Stacey settles Malcolm and Ashley for the evening, then joins Brian in bed.

4

BEEP. BEEP. BEEP.

5 a.m.

Brian hit the snooze button

BEEP. BEEP. BEEP.

It's 5:15 a.m. Monday morning, back to the grind. Brian reaches and accidentally knocks the alarm over, then turns it off. Brian's heart is beating rapidly. It doesn't hurt, so it doesn't trigger a genuine concern.

"Hey, babe," Brian says to Stacey.

"Yes," she responds.

"Feel this," Brian says, then takes Stacey's hand and places it on his chest.

"What is it?" Stacey asks.

"Do you feel how fast my heart is beating?"

"Oh, yes, I do. Does it hurt?" Stacey asks.

"No."

"It could be something you ate. Did you sneak and eat something late last night?"

"No, I didn't," Brian says.

"Go take an aspirin," Stacey instructs.

Brian goes downstairs to the kitchen, pulls the aspirin bottle out of the medicine cabinet, gets a bottle of water out of the refrigerator, then swallows the aspirin and gulps down the entire bottle of water. Brian feels like something isn't right, but he goes on with his morning, hoping that whatever is possibly wrong will correct itself. He returns to his room, finishes dressing, kisses Stacey and the kids, and heads out.

When Brian arrives at work, he checks in and proceeds to roll call as usual. During roll call, a colleague addresses him.

"Phillips," a female colleague named Teresa shouts.

"Yes," Brian answers.

"Are you feeling okay?"

"Yes. Why do you ask?"

"You don't seem like yourself."

Brian pulls Teresa to the side and confidently expresses his concern about his situation to her.

"Well, I think you should play it safe. Why don't you go down to the infirmary and have them check you out," Teresa says to Brian with a look of concern on her face.

"No, I'll be fine. If it gets worse, I'll go," Brian assures her.

"Okay, don't play. I'ma check-up on you," Teresa says sternly.

"Okay," Brian says with an appreciation for her concern.

When lunchtime arrives, Brian is at his post. Sergeant Thomas approaches him. "Officer Phillips."

"Yes, sir."

"How are we doing, sir?" the Sergeant asks Brian.

"Fine, sir."

The Sergeant looks at Brian and barks, "On the contrary. I've heard differently."

"Infirmary! Now!" Sergeant Thomas instructs Brian with a firm voice.

Brian looks at the Sergeant in confusion and responds, "Excuse me, sir?"

"You heard me! Infirmary! Now!" repeats the Sergeant, almost screaming.

When Brian arrives in the infirmary, several inmates are waiting to be seen. It is cold, and there is a thick silence in the room that he'd never experienced before. The room has an odor similar to the doctor's office, which gives Brian a sick feeling in his stomach. Brian looks over the room and notices an empty bed, medical tools, and supplies.

The next moment, the nurse enters the room and announces, "Mr. Phillips."

Brian stands up and confirms, "Yes, that's me."

"You can follow me," the nurse states.

Brian walks through the door and follows the nurse to an unmanned area. Once she verifies Brian's identity and takes his vitals, she explains to him that she will take two vials of blood from him and run tests to determine what is going on. Once the nurse finishes, she asks Brian if he has any questions for her. When Brian answers that he doesn't have any questions, she instructs him that the doctor will be in soon and walks out of the room.

The doctor enters the room shortly after announcing, "Good afternoon, Officer Phillips. I'm Dr. Patel. Can you tell me what's going on?"

"I'm not really sure. I woke up this morning and noticed my heart was beating abnormally," Brian responds.

"Are you in any pain?" the doctor asks.

Brian shakes his head and says, "No, sir."

The doctor looks at Brian with discernment and says, "You wouldn't lie to me, Officer Phillips, would you?"

Brian repeats, "No. No, sir. No pain."

"Well, it appears that something is going on in there, so I'm recommending that you contact your primary physician. Who might that be?"

"Ummm, Dr. Bernstein, sir."

"Okay. Would you like to call him? Or shall I?"

"I'll call him, sir."

"Okay, I want you to call before leaving our office, so I'm going to release you to the front office to do so now."

"Okay. Thank you, sir," Brian states, becoming even more nervous about what is going on with him.

Brian walks out of the examination room to the front office and asks the young lady at the desk if he can use the phone to make a call.

"Yes, sir. You can follow me to this room for privacy and make your phone call here," the front desk person says as she escorts Brian to a small room. Once the front desk person walks out of the room and closes the door, Brian calls Dr. Bernstein and explains what is happening.

"Mr. Phillips, what tests have you taken?" Dr. Bernstein asks Brian.

"My blood was drawn, and an EKG was performed."

Dr. Bernstein then requests to speak with Dr. Patel to get further information on Brian's condition. A few moments later, Dr. Patel walks into the room with Brian and takes over the phone call with Dr. Bernstein. Brian cannot hear the entire conversation between the two doctors but has heard enough to know something is wrong. *Lord, don't let this be it for me. I have a wife and two wonderful children that I have to be here for. I'm not ready to go yet,* Brian thinks as he waits for Dr. Bernstein to end the call with Dr. Patel and give him the verdict.

"Okay, thank you for the information, Dr. Patel. We will proceed with this plan of action," Dr. Bernstein says to Dr. Patel. Dr. Bernstein instructs Brian to report to the ER at once, and he will meet him there. Brian falls back in his seat with thoughts of disbelief. *Did he just say go to the ER? What is happening to me? Why am I going to the ER?* It hit him that something serious is happening to him. But how serious is it? And why isn't anyone telling him anything more than to go to the ER? He wanted to ask so many questions, but he had become numb.

"I know you must have many questions, Officer Phillips, but at this point, we want to get you to the ER and checked in. Then, we will fill you in on everything that's happening and what we plan to do." Brian looks at Dr. Patel, feeling like he is in the twilight zone. He is unsure what to think or how to feel and simply says, "Okay."

Sergeant Thomas enters the room and escorts Brian to the car. When they leave for the ER, Sergeant Thomas turns the vehicle siren and lights on, as a courtesy, to expedite the transport. The hospital staff greets Brian and Sergeant Thomas upon their arrival.

"Mr. Phillips, we have been expecting you." Brian turns to meet the voice that is speaking to him.

"Mr. Phillips, I am Dr. Weinstein. I will be taking care of you until Dr. Bernstein arrives."

Brian nods and replies, "Okay, Dr."

Still confused and in disbelief, Brian asks, "What's the urgency?"

Dr. Weinstein replies, "Well, can you tell me how you are feeling now?"

"I woke up this morning and noticed that I kinda had a rapid heartbeat. I wasn't too concerned because I wasn't in any pain. It was just a rapid beat, and I dismissed it because I felt no pain. I honestly didn't think it was much to be concerned about," Brian explains.

Before Dr. Weinstein could comment, Stacey walks into the room. Brian feels instant relief at the sight of her face. She is just as confused as Brian is. She had gotten a call from Sergeant Thomas telling her that Brian was transported to the ER and that she needed to meet him there. When she attempted to ask what happened, she was advised to get to the ER as soon as possible, and her questions would be answered. Now that she has arrived, she asks the million-dollar question again, "What's going on?"

"Mrs. Phillips, I presume?" Dr. Weinstein turns to Stacey and asks.

"Yes, Dr. What seems to be the issue? What's going on with my husband?" Stacey asks impatiently.

Brian immediately feels happy that she had bossed up to get answers that he hadn't been able to obtain.

"Well, we are trying to sum some things up with his condition. Have you noticed anything different with your husband? What was his last meal, if you can recall?"

Stacey looks confused and responds, "No, sir. Things have been pretty normal. We had spaghetti last night, which is a very normal meal for us."

Dr. Weinstein further probed. "Does he take any supplements, enhancements, or Viagra?"

"No. None," Stacey answers.

"Well, it appears we have a serious issue then."

Brian's facial expression went into panic mode upon hearing those words from Dr. Weinstein. He'd become overwhelmed his heart rate began to increase even more. Dr. Weinstein notices the monitor levels increase and immediately starts to console Brian.

"Mr. Phillips, I need you to remain calm. You're in good hands."

"Yes, babe. Please stay calm. I won't let anything happen to you," Stacey chimes.

Brian turns to Stacey with tears in his eyes.

"Mr. and Mrs. Phillips, in order for us to get ahead of this thing, we must move quickly," Dr. Weinstein states.

Brian turns to Dr. Weinstein and asks, "What do we need to do?"

"Mr. Phillips, you have a condition called Arrhythmias. In other words, irregular heartbeat. This can lead to a stroke, heart attack, or even sudden cardiac arrest if untreated. So, we need to do an Electrical Cardioversion, or in layman's terms, shock your heart, reset it and cause it to beat at a normal rhythm again."

Upon hearing this news, Brian immediately becomes excited again and responds, "Wait! Wait! Wait! Hold on!"

Brian was scared to death. At that moment, he had never been so scared in his life. He could see what people meant when they said they could see their life flash before their eyes. As nervous as he was, he felt that if the fear alone didn't kill him, then knowing that he needed to have his heart shocked would certainly do it.

Brian turned to Stacey and said, "I love you. Call my mom and the kids and let them know what's going on before they take me back, just in case things go, you know."

Stacey looks at Brian and replies, "Babe, you're gonna have to listen to the doctor. All that other stuff can wait."

"Stacey! Do what I say! Damn! Do what I say! I need this!" Brian shouts at Stacey.

Understanding that Brian is serious, Stacey immediately pulls her phone out of her pocketbook and calls Ashley's cell phone.

RING. RING.

Ashley sees it's her mother calling and answers, "Hey, Mom. Wassup?"

"Ashley, where is your brother?" Stacey responds.

Ashley recognizes the urgency in Stacey's voice and responds, "He's in his room. What's wrong, Mom?"

"Ashley, get your brother, now!"

"Okay, okay. Hold on, Mom."

Ashley puts her hand over the speaker of the phone and yells, "Malcolm, come down here! Mom is on the phone and has something important to tell us now!"

Malcolm is downstairs and standing in front of Ashley in less than a minute. Ashley put the phone on speaker and said, "Mom, he's here."

Stacey then walks back into the room and says, "The kids are on the phone."

Brian lies there trying to figure out how to explain to his kids what was happening to him. He is overwhelmed and starts crying. Stacey's heart melts. "Kids, hold on for a second," she says to Ashley and Malcolm. She mutes the phone and gets some tissue from the bathroom for Brian to wipe his face. "Are you sure you can do this?" she asks Brian out of concern.

"Yes, I need to talk to them," he says. Brian takes a moment to pull himself together, then grabs the phone from Stacey. "Kids, Dad isn't doing well. I'm not sure as to what's really going on, but I wanted to tell you guys that I love you very much. I needed to hear your voices before the doctor tries to fix whatever is going on."

"Doctor tries to fix what's going on? Dad, what are you talking about? What happened? Where are you?" Ashley's voice quivers as she tries to understand what Brian is saying.

Brian pauses for a moment, trying to fight back his tears. "Baby girl, I wasn't feeling my best when I left for work this morning, so I saw the doctor, and now I'm at the ER. But I don't want you to worry. I am in good hands, and I will be just fine."

"Dad, do you promise you're gonna be alright? Dad, I need you. Please, please tell me you're gonna be alright. Please, Dad."

Malcolm, in shock, adds, "Yes, Dad, tell us you're gonna be okay."

"Son, I love you and your sister very much, and I'm gonna do whatever I must to get better."

"Okay, Dad. I love you," Malcolm says.

"I love you, Dad," Ashley says and ends the call.

The phone rings, but there is no answer. Stacey tried several times, then called her cell phone. Stacey, emotionless, leaves the room and calls Brian's mom.

RING. RING.

I wonder what Stacey wants with me? She doesn't call me, Barbara thinks as she picks up her phone. "Hello, Stacey. Is everything okay?" she says, answering her phone.

"Mrs. Phillips, we are at the hospital, and your son wants to talk to you."

Barbara's heart stops. Stacey hands Brian the phone. Brian says, "Mom, I don't have much time because I'm on the way back to have a procedure done. If all doesn't go well, I just needed to hear your voice and tell you that I love you."

"Wait? What?" Barbara shouts.

"Mom, I have to go," Brian says.

Stacey takes the phone and says, "It's his heart."

Barbara shouts, "Where are you guys? Where are you?"

"St. James Hospital."

Barbara hangs up and rushes to the hospital.

5

Barbara is like the daily journal; all news gets to the family through her. So, you can imagine what happens next. She calls the entire family and advises them that Brian is in the hospital and it is serious. Yep, you guessed it. After Barbara arrives at the hospital, the family starts coming by the dozens. Barbara rushes to the nurse's station and asks the nurse where she can find her son, Brian Phillips. Stacey overhears the commotion and addresses Barbara from the rear.

"Mrs. Phillips, I'm here."

Barbara turns to Stacey and asks, "Where is my son?"

Stacey looks with disbelief because of the way Barbara addresses her. Barbara repeats herself with more hostility. Stacey responds, "Mrs. Phillips, you may be better off asking the Doctor."

"Maybe I should," Barbara responds with a side-eye. Moments later, Brian's cousin, Sara, walks up with his sister.

"Mom, calm down," says Karen.

The rest of the family, unaware of the history of Barbara and Stacey, watches ever so closely. You see, both Barbara and Karen have always been overprotective of Brian. When he brought Stacey home to meet them, it was an instant "no" for both of them. Karen always tried to explain to Brian that he was caught up on the pretty face, beautiful skin, and big ass, but as women, she and Barbara could see what he couldn't see. Barbara always warned Brian that Stacey was a no-good opportunist, but he always brushed it off, thinking that his mom and sister would learn to accept Stacey. However, it never happened. The entire time that Brian and Stacey had been together, Stacey's relationship with Barbara and Karen had been rocky.

While all the mayhem was happening in the lobby, the doctor walked in and said, "Mrs. Phillips."

Both Barbara and Stacey answer, "Yes."

The doctor says, "I need to speak with the wife of Mr. Phillips."

Barbara jumps up and says, "Well, I'm his mother."

Dr. Weinstein addresses Barbara and says, "No disrespect, Mrs. Phillips, but I really need to speak to his wife."

Barbara angrily responded, "Well, I'm not going anywhere."

Stacey turns to Dr. Weinstein and says, "It's okay."

Dr. Weinstein explains, "Mr. Phillips is going to be okay. He's not completely out of the woods, but there has been a change for the better."

Barbara asks, "What seems to be the problem?"

Dr. Weinstein states, "Of course, you know it's his heart."

Barbara gasps. "His heart? How serious is it?"

Dr. Weinstein answers, "It appears to be Atrial Fibrillation, also known as A-Fib. Now, before everyone gets excited, please understand that many people live with this, and it can be controlled with a good diet and exercise."

Everyone nods their heads with shock. They are somewhat relieved that Brian still has his life. "Can we see him?" Barbara asks.

"For now, I'd like to keep the visits to a minimum and with minimal excitement," Dr. Weinstein says.

"Ok, whatever is best for Brian," Stacey responds.

Barbara rolls her eyes with disgust.

"Ladies, out of concern for my patient, I'm going to need you two to leave the attitude at the door. Is that understood?" states Dr. Weinstein.

Both Barbara and Stacey remain silent.

"Ladies, is that understood?" Dr. Weinstein asks again. "If not, I will suggest to my staff that he have no visitors until I deem it ok."

Barbara responds, "I understand, Doctor. I will do it for my son." Stacey nods in agreement.

"Ok then, he's in room 227."

Barbara turns to Karen and says, "There will be minimal visitors at this time. I will let your brother know you're here. Let the others know, and I'll tell Brian his family is here for him."

"Ok, Mom," Karen responds with tears in her eyes. Barbara and Karen hug each other.

Stacey goes to the room, feeling the heat of not being received well by some of his family. And for good reason because of her past behavior. By the time they both reach the room, Brian is knocked out and sleeping peacefully. Stacey kisses Brian goodnight as Barbara looks on with a bitter expression.

"I'ma stay with my son," Barbara utters silently.

"Ok, that's fine. I'll go home and see about the kids," Stacey responds dryly, then walks out of the room.

Barbara walks out to address the family. They ask a series of questions, but she has little to share. However, she did leave everyone with the words. He's *in God's hands*. Night falls, and the morning comes quickly. Barbara had stayed up all night to see her son wake up. When Brian finally opened his eyes, his mom was always there by his side. "Good morning, Mother."

"Good morning, Son. How are you feeling?"

"Well, I really don't feel any different. I'm not in any pain, just feel a little tired. Did you stay all night?"

"Do you even have to ask?" Barbara responds.

"No, I guess not. Where's Stacey?"

"Home, I presume, with your kids. Boyyyyyy…"

"Mother don't. Not today," Brian says, stopping Barbara in her tracks.

"I don't understand why," Barbara starts shaking her head out of worry and concern, "that girl, or should I say your wife, is nothing but trouble. I don't know how you're gonna deal with that for the rest of your life."

"Mother."

"Don't mother me," Barbara says.

"Now isn't the time," Brian replies.

RING. RING. *Saved by the bell*, Brian thinks.

"Hey, baby brother."

"Hey, Sis, what's up?" Brian asks.

"You. How are we doing?" Karen asks with concern for her brother.

"I just woke up. I haven't talked to the doctor yet, but for now, it looks like I'ma make it," states Brian.

"Well, that's good to hear. Where's Mom?"

"Right here. Where else?" Brian answers, smiling at his mom.

Karen chuckles. "I bet she's bleeding your ears about your wife."

"Yes," exclaims Brian.

Karen chuckles again.

"Listen, I'm headed into work. I just wanted to check in on you and see how you were doing."

"I appreciate that," Brian responds.

"Hey, girl." Brian overhears a voice in the background.

"Hey, you boo loving already?" the unfamiliar voice asks. Both parties laughed

"No, silly, this is my brother," says Karen.

"Brother?"

"Yeah, my brother," Karen repeats.

"All this time I've known you, you've never mentioned a brother."

"That's because I don't tell you everything, Thotianna."

Brian laughs.

"Oh damn, I almost forgot you were there, baby brother. Take care of yourself, and I'll hit you up later."

"Ok, Sis. Love you," Brian says.

"Love you too," replies Karen and ends the call.

"Well, Son, I'm glad to see you and your sister are close. It gives me hope that if something should ever happen to me, I can rest knowing your sister is right there for you," Barbara explains.

"Yes, Mother, as I am for her," Brian assures Barbara.

"Son, I'ma check with the nurse and head out to get cleaned up, but I'll be back."

"Yes, Mother, I know you will."

Barbara walks up to Brian lying in bed and puts her hand on his forehead as if she were checking to see if he has a fever, but she is silently thanking God for taking her son through the medical procedure and bringing him through it. Knowing that his mother is praying for him, Brian closes his eyes and silently receives the prayer that she is praying over him. After about two minutes, Barbara finally breaks the silence and says, "Ok, Son, you take care of yourself. If you need anything before I get back, you call me."

"Ok, Mom, I will," Brian answers, appreciating his mom's genuine love and concern for him.

Barbara gives Brian a forehead kiss and leaves the room.

RING. RING. As the door is closing, Brian's phone rings. He picks his phone up and sees that it is Stacey. *Wow, right on cue, as if she knew my mom just left*, Brian thinks to himself.

"Hey," Brian answers.

"Hey, is your mom still there?"

"No, she's not. Why?"

"Brian, I can't do your mother. She just won't leave things alone."

"And for good reason, Stacey. You haven't been the model wife."

"I know I've made mistakes, and I live with them every day."

"I'm sure," Brian says.

"What do you mean by that?"

"Nothing, Stacey. Just forget it," Brian tries to dismiss it.

"No, if you have something to say, Brian, get it out," Stacey pushes.

"Stacey, I'm not about to sit here and argue with you about your relationship with my mother. You two need to work on that. As for your other discretions and past antics, I choose to forget about them, so let it go."

"No, I will not," Stacey responds.

"Stacey, for the last time, knock it off," Brian suggests, becoming aggravated.

Stacey, refusing to take the hint and let it go, starts screaming into the phone. Brian, unable to return the energy she was giving him, ends the call. When he hangs up the phone, he wonders how Stacey could call him and start an argument knowing that he was laid up in the hospital having issues with his heart. Could the stress of his marriage be why he is having heart issues? He truly loved his wife, but was holding on to his marriage really worth it if it was beginning to affect his health? He has so much to think about and consider, but at this moment, he just can't bring himself to it, so he turns over in his bed and goes to sleep.

Later, during Karen's lunchtime, she calls to check on Brian. "Hey, baby brother."

"Hey, Sis," Brian said, with anguish in his voice. He had taken a nap earlier, hoping to calm down and rest his mind from his conversation with Stacey. But when he woke up, it was the first thing he thought about, and he was still aggravated.

"What's wrong?" Karen asks, immediately becoming concerned.

"Nothing. I'm good," Brian lies because he didn't want to get into it.

"Now, come on, baby brother. I told you I always know when something is wrong with you."

"Yes, I know. I don't want to talk about it, but I know you're not gonna let it go until I do."

"Hmmm, you know me so well. So, save us both the trouble and tell me what's going on," Karen says to Brian.

"If it's not your mom, it's Stacey," he says with disappointment.

"I know. I heard. You know your mother. She's still your mother and will always be 'til the day she leaves this earth."

Before Brian could respond, he heard another voice speaking to his sister.

"Hey, girl."

"Hey Allison," Karen responds to the voice.

"I guess you're on the phone with your brother again."

"As a matter of fact, Ms. Nosey, I am."

"Well, I just wanted to know what we are doing for lunch."

"Baby brother," Karen says to Brian before responding to Allison.

"Yeah, I know the drill," Brian responds to Karen.

"I'll hit you later," Karen promises.

"Sure thing," Brian says.

Karen hangs up with Brian and directs her attention to Allison. "Girl, you can be so rude sometimes," Allison said to Karen.

"Rude?" Karen asks. "That's family. I'm not being anything."

Allison's phone rings, and she goes from a calm, cheerful person to an angry, Tasmanian devil. "Batty hole, Batty hole! Girl, if I didn't have these two kids, I woulda left his ass a long time ago," says Allison. (Translation, asshole in her native tongue).

"Why? What's wrong?" Karen asks.

"You know this MF has a password on his phone all of a sudden, and he thinks his ass is slick. He's been talking to some bitch."

"Really?" Karen asks.

"Yes, really!" Allison responds with frustration.

"Do you think he's cheating on you?"

"No telling, girl. He hasn't been saying anything like that over text. Otherwise, I would have done a Lorena Bobbitt on his ass!"

Karen laughs.

"What's funny?" Allison asks Karen.

"Nothing, girl. I'm just laughing at your crazy ass. I know what you're going through. That's why I'm single. I've seen it with my brother and how it's damn near torn him apart," Karen says, shaking her head.

"Really?" Allison asks, looking confused.

"Yes, really," Karen confirms.

"So, what did he do?"

"Ironically, he keeps giving her the benefit of the doubt by using the excuse that everyone messes up, and he stayed."

"Yeah, we do, but fucking someone else is far more than a fuck up," Allison responds.

"You love your brother."

"Yes. He's like my best friend," states Karen.

"I see that," Allison says. "That's good. It tells me y'all had a good upbringing. You know, I'm close to one of my brothers, too. We share every…" Allison stops talking about her brother and quickly changes the subject. "So, Karen, you have any pictures of this mystery man brother of yours?"

"Of course, I do," Karen responds, matter of factly.

"Bitch! Well, let me see them!" They both laugh.

Karen pulls out her phone. Allison glances at the photo and says, "Hold up. Damn girl, your brother is fine as hell."

"Hold on, tramp," Karen fires back.

"You're married, and he is too!"

"I know, but damn, I got eyes, and from what I can see, your damn brother is fine as hell! And it looks like he's packing that meat!"

"Girl, bye!" Karen dismisses Allison.

"I'm serious! In my Country, he's called a hot boy," Allison says.

"Girl, I don't care what y'all call them. That's still my brother! Anyway, what's going on with you and Winston?"

"If I had to say, that damn bumboclat is up to some fuckery with some other rasshole."

"Hold on, girl. You know when you get mad, I can't understand a word you're saying. English, please. English."

"In short, I'm saying that MF is fucking some other bitch and me. I just need proof," Allison explains.

"Ok, so what you plan on doing?" Karen asks.

"I'ma get my proof, best believe that! Then he can suck yuh madda!"

"Oh, I see," Karen says as she looks on with an instinctive expression.

"So, when can I meet this hot boy?" Allison asks playfully.

"Put some water on that cat. My brother is married too, and he loves his wife. Almost too much," Karen says, shaking her head.

"Karen, I just need someone to talk to and make me laugh other than you. That male attention that another woman can't give me."

"I hear you, girl," Karen says. "Calm down. I'll see what I can do." Karen thinks to herself, *my brother could use a friend*. But she also feels that the thought of it could make him angry, so she would have to test the waters, per se, and see if he would be interested.

After work, Karen calls Brian. "Hey, little brother. How are things? Is your mother there?" she asks.

"No, she isn't," Brian replies.

"How about Stacey?"

"She's not here either," Brian responds.

"Damn, little brother. So, you're all alone?" Karen asks with concern.

"Mommy will be here shortly, and I haven't spoken to Stacey," states Brian.

"What's up with that?" Karen asks Brian curiously.

"She's probably mad at me from our conversation earlier," Brian says.

"Mad or not, she doesn't have the decency to call and check on your wellbeing? I'm confused and hurt at the same time. Your life is on the line right now, and I can't help but feel like she let an argument supersede her love for you. But, enough of that because I'm getting angry," Karen says, changing the subject. "Anyway, do you remember that voice you heard in the background when I was on the phone with you the other day?"

"Yes. What about it?" asks Brian.

"Well, I think my co-worker has a crush on you."

"A what?" Brian asks, confused.

"You heard me. A crush," Karen repeats.

"Now, how on earth is that humanly possible when she doesn't even know me?" questions Brian.

"I kinda showed her the picture of you at Malcolm's party. You know, the one with you in the t-shirt?" Karen asks.

"Yeah," Brian responds.

"Well, she saw the picture, and it was a love at first sight kinda thing. Now, before you get bent outta shape, let me explain."

"Explain what? When can I meet her?" Brian asks.

"Hmm," Karen looks at the phone in disbelief, "What did you say?"

"I'd love to meet her," states Brian.

"She sounds interesting. Where is she from? I believe I heard an accent," he says.

"She's a Jamaican girl, and her name is Allison."

"Ok," replies Brian.

"She's married with two kids. Sound familiar?"

"Yeah, it does."

"Well, the sooner I get freed from this medical prison, the sooner we can hook up," says Brian.

"Ok, sounds like a plan," Karen responds.

"Cool beans." They both laugh.

"Ok, baby brother. Take care of yourself, and we'll talk soon," Karen says and ends the call.

6

Karen feels a sense of regret for having called Brian about Allison. She knows her brother loves his wife and that he could be making an impulsive decision based on the anger he feels toward his wife. She also knows that Brian and Allison have much to lose if they get caught. She looks at her phone, wondering if she should go through with setting them up. *Why am I feeling guilty? Brian is a grown man. He has been through a lot with Stacey, and meeting Allison could be refreshing in his life right now. Besides, there's nothing wrong with having a friend,* Karen tries to convince herself through her thoughts. She dials Allison's number and gives her the news.

"Girl, guess what?"

"Whaaaat!" Allison asks curiously.

"I just got off the phone with my brother, and you're not gonna believe what he had to say."

"Whaaaat? Bitch, stop with this guess who, what, and when shit!"

"Girl, he said when he gets out, y'all can hook up!"

"Oh," Allison says with a secret smile.

"Bitch, ummm, hello. You think I don't know you?" Karen asks.

"What?" questioned Allison.

"I know you. I can see your Jamaican ass smiling from ear to ear.

So, before we go any further, I need you to remember that you are a married woman, and my brother is a married man. So, that means y'all are just friends," demands Karen.

"Friends? I guess you forgot we grown." They both laugh.

"Girl, I'm not looking for anything. I just want some male company, someone to make me laugh and make me feel like a woman again. I miss feeling sexy and wanted, you know?" states Allison.

"I hear you, girl. Just be careful," Karen requests.

"I will," Allison replies.

"Friends," Karen says.

"Yes, friends," Allison assures. "Ooooh, girl. Hold on, my girl, Anita is calling." Allison clicks over to answer the incoming call. "Hey girl, what's going on?"

"Girl, do I have some tea for you," Anita responds.

"Hold on," Allison says and clicks back over to Karen. "Hey, K."

"Yeah, yeah. I know the drill. You gonna cheat on me with the next bitch," says Karen, and they both laugh.

"Girl, do your thing and tell Anita I said hey," said Karen.

"Ok, I will," Allison responds and ends the call.

"Nita," Allison says, rejoining the call with her friend.

"Yeah, girl," answers Anita.

"I just hung up with Karen, and you're not gonna believe this!" Allison says, bubbling with excitement.

Now extremely curious about what Allison is about to reveal, Anita says, "Believe what? Girl, what is it?"

"Her brother is a hot boy!"

"Bumba!" (Translation, holy crap).

"Really? Do tell," says Anita.

"Girl, I looked at his picture on her phone and was like, Blurtneet!" (Translation, Oh my God!).

Anita smiles and says, "So, what does all this mean?

"Well…"

"Well, what, bitch?" Anita demands. "You up to no good!"

"Girl, I feel like a little payback," says Allison.

"Payback?" Anita asks.

"Yeah, I found some text messages on Winston's phone. He was planning to meet this bitch for lunch, and lord knows what. He's been coming in late or staying in the city at his brother's house, so he says, so he can be close to work and not have to drive home and turn around a couple of hours later to be back," Allison explains. "I can smell the fuckery."

(Translation, bull shit).

"Intuition."

"Yes, girl, I'ma play it by ear. I'll keep Karen's brother around for safe keeping," Allison exclaims.

"Safekeeping, hmm."

"Yes, girl."

"Well, do what you have to do. I'ma support you with whatever decision you make because I wanna see you happy. You're a good girl, but a sneaky bitch, too," Anita says, and they both laugh.

"So, what's the mystery man's name?" asks Anita.

"Brian," Allison answers.

"Brian. Hmm, I can't wait to see who's getting my girl's panties wet and what he looks like." They both laugh hysterically.

"Well, I'ma keep you posted in detail," Allison says.

"Yes, do that," Anita replies.

"Ok, girl, get back to me."

"Ok," Anita said and ended the call.

Brian receives some favorable news. Dr. Weinstein informed him that his pressure looked good, his heart rate was normal, and he might be able to leave the hospital in a day or two. *That is excellent news*, he thinks. However, with all that good news, he can't help but think that Stacey had only come to the hospital once. Not to mention that she hadn't brought the kids. With that on his mind, he calls home.

RING. RING.

"Hello," Ashley answers.

"Hey."

"Hey, Daddy. I miss you."

"I miss you too, baby girl."

"Daddy, when are you coming home?"

"Soon, baby girl. Soon," Brian says.

"Why haven't you guys come to see me?"

"Mommy said you weren't able to have visitors," Ashley replies.

"What?" Brian could feel his blood pressure hit the roof.

"Where's your mother?"

"She's not here, Dad. She hasn't come in yet. She's been working late, so I've been the lady of the house," Ashley explains.

"Aw, and I know you've been good at it too, baby girl. Where's your brother?"

"Where else?"

"Playing that game," Brian says as he shakes his head.

"Well, baby girl, when your mother comes in, tell her I want y'all to come and see me."

"Ok, Dad."

"Ok, baby girl. Love you," Brian says.

Before Ashley can respond, Brian's mother, Barbara, walks into his room.

"Love you, too. Bye, Daddy," Ashley says and ends the call.

Barbara catches the tail end of Brian's call but cannot discern who he was talking to before hanging up. She still decides to jump all over it.

"Was that your dear, loving wife? She asks sarcastically.

"No," Brian says. "It was your granddaughter."

"Oh, how's my little princess doing?" Barbara asks, easing up a bit.

"She's ok. They should be coming up later," Brian replies.

In disbelief, Barbara says, "I can't wait to see them."

"Yeah, me too," Brian responds.

"So, what is the doctor saying?"

"Well, good news. He says everything appears to be almost normal, and I should be getting outta here in the next day or so."

"That's great news! I know you can't wait. However, home isn't where you should be just yet," Brian's mom says.

Brian knows where his mother is going with this. As much as he doesn't want to go there with her, he knows he can't ignore her. He takes a deep breath and asks, "And what's that supposed to mean, Mother?"

"You know that got damn wife of yours."

"Mother, enough. I may not have the perfect model wife, but she's still my wife, and you're gonna have to respect that."

"I don't have to respect…you know what? Never mind!"

"Mother, please," Brian pleads.

"Ok, let's drop it," she replies.

The nurse walks into the room, and Brian thinks, *Saved! There is a God!*

"Mr. Phillips? I'm nurse Betty, and I'm gonna take your vitals." The nurse pulls the blood pressure machine to Brian's bed, wraps the cuff around his arm, and taps the button on the device for it to begin taking his blood pressure. She puts a thermometer under his tongue to record his temperature. Once the thermometer beeps, she pulls it out of Brian's mouth. 98.6 normal temp. Shortly after, the blood pressure machine goes off, letting the nurse know it is complete. She looks at the final recording of Brian's blood pressure and says, "Oh my, Mr. Phillips. Is everything ok?"

"Yes, why? Brian asks, looking at the nurse in confusion.

"Your pressure is through the roof. I'ma have to issue you some Vasotec."

"What's that?" he asks.

"Meds that should help to get your pressure back to normal levels," the nurse explains. "I'm going to step out and get your medicine. Do you need anything else right now?"

"No, I'm fine. Thank you," Brian says, starting to feel nervous again because he wants to go home but knows that would not be possible if he has a setback.

"Ok, I'll be right back," says the nurse, then walks out of the room.

Brian turns and looks at his mother, and she looks away. A few moments later, the nurse returns with two pills in a small white cup and some water. Brian swallows both pills and finishes the water. The nurse tells him to take it easy and get some rest. She informs him to push the nurse call button if he needs anything. Brian agrees, and she exits the room.

Moments after the nurse leaves Brian's room, the phone rings endlessly, and visitors start coming in after work. It was like Grand Central Station in Brian's room. The medication had made him a little drowsy, but every time he closed his eyes and dozed off, the phone rang, and his room door was opening by another visitor. Finally, after about three hours, the phone stopped ringing, and the visitors left. During that entire time, no Stacey and no kids. Not even a phone call. Brian tried to contain his feelings, but it was tearing him apart.

He calls Stacey's cell phone but no answer.

There is no way this bitch could still be working, Brian thinks. He calls home.

RING. RING.

Ashley answers after the third ring.

"Hey, Dad."

"Hey, princess. Where's your mom?"

"I don't know, Dad. She hasn't called."

Brian is beyond pissed. He tries to keep his cool because his mother is sitting in the recliner beside his bed with her antennas all the way up. She can hear everything and is eating it up. But while she is seemingly taking pleasure in Brian's disappointment with his wife, his blood pressure begins to spike again. It is so bad that he starts feeling faint. When Barbara notices the change in Brian's behavior and sees that he is starting to fade, she immediately summons the nurse. She takes the phone out of Brian's hand and says, "Ashley, Ashley baby, Daddy is gonna have to call you back. Brian! Brian!" she yells out.

7

Brian is unconscious. Barbara screams out, "Nurse! Help! Help! My son!"

A nurse runs into the room. She instructs Barbara to leave and calls, "Code blue! Code blue! Stat!" The medical team rushes in and administers oxygen and a sedative. The nurse finds Barbara outside the room and asks her what events caused Brian to pass out.

Barbara lies and says she isn't sure. She goes into a daze and is furious! If Stacey is thinking about coming to the hospital, she needs to think twice. It is best for her to stay far away at this time because Barbara has the look of murder in her eyes. Once Barbara emerges from her daze, she hears the nurse say, "Well if he had hopes of going home today, that's not gonna happen now."

Once the sedative kicked in, Brian relaxed and fell asleep. Barbara, on the other hand, was on a war path. She steps out of the room and attempts to call Stacey, but just as she'd thought, there is no answer. That may have been good, for Stacey and Barbara's sake, because had Stacey answered her phone, nothing nice would have come out of Barbara's mouth. Barbara paces back and forth in the hall with her mind going one hundred miles per minute. She needs to vent because if not, she feels like she will explode. She pulls out her phone and calls Karen.

"Karen."

"Yes, Mom."

"You know this damn girl hasn't come up or called your brother? You know she got me heated!"

"Yes, Mother, but I think you should just stay out of it," Karen says.

"Stay out of it? Brian called Stacey to ask her why she hadn't been up here with the kids to see him, but of course, she didn't answer her phone. So, he called the house, and Ashley told him Stacey hadn't been home or called them. It upset him so bad that his blood pressure spiked, and the nurses had to rush in and give him medicine to try and stabilize it again! So, how am I supposed to stay out of it? That's my child, and it's hard to see him going through all of this when I know he deserves so much more."

"What? His blood pressure spiked again? Is he ok? I'm on the way up there now!" Karen shouts, almost in a panic.

"No, you don't have to leave work to come up here. He is asleep now. His nurse said he needs rest, so he will be fine," Barbara assures Karen.

For a moment, there is silence on the phone as Karen tries to digest all the information. She breaks the silence and says, "Well, Mother, I'm glad they were able to stabilize his pressure. I understand your concern about Brian and Stacy, but it's Brian's marriage. He is a grown man, and you have to let him handle it. I agree with you that he deserves more, but we just have to trust that in due time, God will provide him what he's deserving of."

"I guess you're right. I just needed to vent," Barbara says.

"I know, Mother. Get some rest and make sure my brother is good. Tell him I love him, and I'll talk to you tomorrow."

"Ok. Love you."

"Love you too," Karen says and ends the call.

Dr. Weinstein greets Brian the following day, "Good morning, Mr. Phillips. How are you feeling this morning?"

"I'm feeling good, Dr.," Brian replies, trying to sit up some in the bed.

"You wanna tell me what happened yesterday?"

"I'm not sure what you mean, doctor," Brian answers hesitantly. Brian knows exactly what Dr. Weinstein is referring to. He wants to be transparent with the doctor but is hesitant to speak openly with his mother in the room.

"Why did your blood pressure spike all of a sudden?"

"Well, umm…" Brian knew that Barbara would be upset if he asked her to leave the room, but this was about his health, so he decided to take the risk. He slowly turns to her and says, "Mother, do you think we could have a minute?" As Brian already knew, Barbara immediately is upset that he was asking her to leave the room.

She does not want to risk his blood pressure spiking again, so she simply says, "Sure, Son."

As soon as Barbara leaves the room, Brian begins, "Doctor, I'm having some personal issues."

"Personal? Anything you want to talk about?" Dr. Weinstein asks Brian curiously.

"Well, I'm not sure how to say this," Brian states cautiously.

"The easiest way to say it is by just saying it," the doctor confirms.

"I kinda feel like my wife is seeing someone else."

"Have you confronted her on this assumption?" the doctor asks.

"No, I haven't. It's just a strong gut feeling," admits Brian.

"Ok, well, gut feelings aren't proof or fact. Listen, I don't want to scare you or make you nervous, but I have to be candid with you. Your health is on the line here, so if you don't have solid proof that your wife is being unfaithful to you, I would suggest you let it go. Likewise, if your gut feeling is so strong that you can't let it go, I would suggest you let it go." At that moment, Dr. Weinstein gave Brian a look that said, *you know what I'm saying.*

Brian looks down and instantly catches on. The doctor does not want to advise him to leave Stacey, but he wants Brian to know the seriousness of the situation if he continues to hold on to anything causing his health to fail, including his wife. Brian looks up at the doctor and asks, "You mean my wife?"

"I mean, whatever it is, including your wife, your job, whatever, because if you continue at this rate, you could have a massive heart attack, and there will be little that any of us will be able to do for you if that happens. Is that what you want?" the doctor asks Brian sternly.

"No," Brian answers humbly.

"Then, I advise you to get to the bottom of whatever it is that's bothering you and put an end to it. Mr. Phillips, I know it's a hard decision, especially when you love someone. However, you can't force something that isn't meant to be. And with that, I'ma leave you to think about it."

Brian's head falls into his chest. "Ok, doc. I appreciate the talk, and I will make some changes, I promise," Brian assures Dr. Weinstein.

"Good, 'cause I'ma need you to be healthy to pay this bill." They both laugh as Dr. Weinstein exits the room. "Good day, Mr. Phillips."

"Oh, Dr. Weinstein," Brian calls to the doctor. "How much longer do you think I'll be here?"

"Keep your pressure down, and you could be out in a day or so," Dr. Weinstein answers and exits the room.

As Barbara returned to Brian's room, the phone rang. It's Stacey.

"Hey."

"Hey, Stacey."

Barbara can hardly contain herself and starts to say something until Brian gestures for her to be silent, so she leaves the room again.

"Is that your mother?" Stacey asks.

"Yes."

"Well, you know I haven't been up there 'cause I wanted to avoid that drama."

"Drama?" Brian asks, needing more of an explanation from Stacey.

"Yes, drama. You know your mother isn't trying to give me any slack."

"I get it, but at the same time, Stacey, I'm your husband, and here is where you should be, not running and hiding from my mother. Listen, we are gonna have to work on some things, or we're gonna have to do away with some things."

"Meaning what?" Stacey asks.

"Us."

"Us what, Brian? What the hell are you saying?"

"Listen, we aren't gonna argue about this. We are gonna discuss this civilly," Brian says, trying to remain calm.

"Yes, starting with your mom."

"Stacey, enough. The two of you are never gonna get anything resolved if one of you can't be the bigger person."

"Why does it have to be me?" Stacey asks.

"Why can't it be you, Stacey? Why can't you be the one to take the initiative to settle the score with my mom? You know I need the both of you in my life, and I need you both on good terms. You don't love me enough to make that happen?"

Stacey is silent. She loves her husband and knows that he has a valid point, but she just doesn't have it in her to approach his mother civilly because she has never been civil with her.

"On another note," Brian interrupts her thoughts, "the doctor said I could be outta here in about a day or so, as long as I keep my pressure down."

"Ok, sounds good. I was calling because I was gonna bring the kids up."

"Bring 'em," Brian confirms.

"Umm…," Stacey starts, but Brian cut her off.

"Umm, nothing. Bring my kids. I'll deal with my mother."

"Ok."

"See you in a few," Brian says.

"Yes, I'll be there," Stacey replies and ends the call.

Barbara returned to the room, on cue, as if she had been standing at the door listening to the conversation between Brian and Stacey.

"So, why?" she asks Brian, demanding an answer.

"Mother, stop! She's on her way, and I need you to chill out!" Barbara rolls her eyes with disbelief. "Mother, I'ma tell you the same thing I just finished saying to Stacey. The two of you need to find a way to fix the drama between you. I need both of you in my life, but I will not continue to be in the middle of what's going on between you. I love you, Mother, but I need you to play nice when my family gets here, or I'ma ask you to leave," Brian says sternly.

Barbara looked at Brian and couldn't believe what she was hearing. "What?"

"Yes, Mother."

"Well, I guess I'ma just go home because after all that broad has been putting you through since you've been here, I know when I see her, I'm gonna want to curse her out," Barbara says as she starts picking up her things to leave.

"Mother, I understand and appreciate your concern for me, but I am a grown man, and I have to make my own decisions when it comes to my marriage. I need you to be here for me, so that means I need for you to stay out of it and just be my mom," Brian replies.

Barbara glares at her son and sees the pleading in his eyes. She wants to be there for Brian, but it is hard for her because she can see the train wreck that is about to happen if he stays with Stacey. Her heart can't take seeing her son in devastation. She puts her pocketbook and jacket down, walks to Brian's bed, looks in his eyes, touches his hand, and says, "Son, I understand what you're saying, and I understand what you're asking of me, but I see what's up the road for you if you stay with that woman, and my heart will not allow me to be a part of it. But I will be waiting on you when the bottom falls out, so call me when she disappoints you."

And with that, Barbara turns around, picks up her things, and walks swiftly toward the door.

"Mother," Brian calls out.

"Goodnight!" Barbara says without turning around and leaves the room.

Fifteen minutes later, Stacey and the kids arrive. Ashley springs through the door with the biggest smile and shouts, "Daddy!" and walks up to the side of the bed to give Brian the tightest hug.

"Hey Princess," Brian says with a big smile.

Malcolm approaches Brian's bedside and gives him a high five. At this moment, Brian knows that this is what he has been missing. "What's up, Dad."

"Nothing much, Son. You holding it down?"

"Yeah, Dad. You know it," Malcolm says proudly.

"That's good. I have missed you guys," Brian says to both of his kids.

"We missed you too, Dad," they both respond to Brian in harmony.

"So, Dad, when are you coming home?" Ashley asks Brian.

"Hopefully, in a day or so," Brian responds.

"Great! And when you get home, I can cook for you," Ashley says excitedly.

"Yes, Princess. Yes, you can."

Brian and the kids spend time talking and enjoying each other's company as Stacey sits in the chair and acts standoffish. After about twenty minutes, Stacey stands up and says, "Ok guys, we are about to go. Say bye to Daddy so he can get some rest."

"Aw, Mom, we just got here. We're not ready to leave Dad yet," Malcolm says with great disappointment. Brian is disappointed too, but he does not want to participate in making his kids feel any worse, so he takes them both by their hands and says, "Don't worry guys, I'll be home in a day or so, and we can spend all the time we want together. Besides, it's getting late, and you have school tomorrow. Call me when you get home so I can say good night before you go to bed, ok?"

"Ok, Dad. Please hurry up and get better so you can come home," Ashley says, laying her head on Brian's chest.

"I will, baby girl. I love you both, and I'll see you real soon," Brian says, fighting back the tears. "Now, y'all go with your mom and be good."

"Bye Dad," they both said in harmony. Malcolm reaches over and gives Brian a high five. As they exit the room, Brian notices that Stacey does not kiss him. She did not get close to him throughout their ten-minute visit. His mind wonders where their relationship is going. While Brian is still in deep thought, there is a knock on the door, and a nurse walks into the room. "Mr. Phillips. It's time for me to take your vitals."

The nurse stands at the computer in silence, recording the information into Brian's chart. He is on edge, praying that his numbers are back to normal. He breaks the silence, "Ok, lay it on me."

The nurse turns to Brian and surprises him, "Everything looks good. Who knows, someone may be going home tomorrow."

"What? Really?" Brian says excitedly.

"Yes. It appears you will go home tomorrow, providing there are no setbacks."

"That's great! Oh wow!" Brian is pleased and excited to hear this good news.

"Well, Mr. Phillips, keep up the good work, and if everything goes well, don't hesitate to come back and see me sometime," the nurse says with a flirty smile.

Brian's eyes light up with surprise as he watches the nurse walk towards the door. When she gets to the door, she turns around and says, "Oh, by the way, it's Cheryl."

"Hmm?" Brian asks for clarity.

"My name is Cheryl," she repeats.

"Oh, okay," Brian says. *Hmmm...there is nothing sexy about me lying in this hospital bed with a half gown on, but I'm still pullin' the chicks!* Brian thinks to himself with a devilish smile on his face. *If Stacey knows what I know, she better get her shit together! And quick!* He continues with his thoughts, feeling his ego growing larger by the second. He snaps himself out of his 'I'm the man' moment and picks up his phone to call his mom and let her in on the good news.

"Thank you, Jesus! I knew you would come through for my boy!" Barbara shouts on the phone after Brian tells her what the nurse said. He hangs up with his mom and calls Karen to fill her in. She cries tears of joy in her excitement about the news.

8

Brian wakes up feeling good physically, the best he has felt since he arrived at the hospital. He is confident that he will hear the words from the doctor that he wants to hear. He sits up a little and stretches. He feels cooped up and wants to get out of the hospital, smell the outside air, feel the breeze on his face, and soak up some Vitamin D! He wants to be with his kids again. And unfortunately, he needed to get out of there to figure out what was going on with his marriage. He has some decisions to make. *I don't want to think about it right now. I'll cross that bridge when I get to it; Brian* thinks to himself as he walks over to the window and peers through the blinds.

He gazes out the window for a few minutes, admiring the beautiful sun that is shining, the birds that are flying, and the people that he could see walking in and out of the hospital. Just as he walks to the bed, there is a knock on the door, and the doctor walks in. "Good morning, Mr. Phillips," Dr. Weinstein greets as he enters the room. "Everything looks good, sir."

"Great! That's great," Brian says with excitement.

"So, I'm going to sign your discharge papers."

Brian smiles because his discharge is an answer to his prayers. It means he is doing much better. It means he can now go home to be with his family. It means he has to find out what is going on with his wife. The smile begins to fade from his face. Now, he has to face the reality of what has been on his mind and what could have possibly landed him in the hospital in the first place. Still not ready to deal with it, his thoughts go to Karen's co-worker, and a smile slowly reappears on his face. The idea that someone is interested in him is fascinating, and it pumps his ego. It makes him feel alive and full of confidence, a feeling he hasn't felt in a long time. He hates to admit it, but he is anxious to meet this mysterious young lady.

"Mr. Phillips, take great care of yourself and remember what we spoke about yesterday. From now on, consider your health first. Let go of everything that is not good for you, ok?"

"Yes, sir, Dr. Weinstein. I understand," Brian says.

"Alright, sir, I don't want to see you here again, but I'm here if you need me," Dr. Weinstein says, walking towards the door.

The discharge papers arrive, indicating that Brian can leave after 2 p.m. He calls Stacey to pick him up, but no answer. He leaves a message on her voice mail to call him back ASAP. He takes a shower, gets dressed, and packs his things. When Brian looks at the clock, it is 1:30 p.m., and he still has not received a return phone call from Stacey. The last person he wants to call is his mom because he knows where that call will go, so he calls his sister.

RING. RING.

"Hey, Sis. I was wondering if you could do me a favor. Can you come get me?"

"Get you? What happened to…"

Brian cuts her off. "Don't ask and don't tell your mother," he informs.

"Ok. What time are you getting discharged?" Karen asks.

"2 p.m."

"2 p.m.? It's already 1:51. Never mind. I'll make up an excuse and see you soon," Karen assures.

Karen makes it to the hospital to pick Brian up. As he gets into her car, his phone rings. It's Stacey. It is now 3:10 p.m.

"Hello."

"Yes, I received your message to call," responds Stacey.

"Never mind," Brian says.

"What do you mean?" Stacey asks.

"I mean, never mind," Brian repeats. "I took care of what I needed."

"Ok then," Stacey says and ends the call.

Brian arrives home around the same time the kids come from

school. Ashley notices Karen's car and runs to it.

"Auntie Karen!"

"Hey, sweetie."

Malcolm walks up to Karen's car shortly after. "Hey, Auntie," Malcolm says and kisses Karen. "What's up? Mom and dad aren't here."

"On the contrary," Karen says. "Your dad is…"

Before Karen can complete her sentence, Ashley says, "Really? No way! Is he in the house?" Ashley rushes to the door, and shortly after, Malcolm follows and takes off for the door to see his dad.

"Dad!" Ashley yells out.

"Yes, Princess."

"You're home!"

"Yes, baby. Daddy's home." Ashley reaches up and kisses Brian, then gives him the tightest hug. "Aw, thank you, baby. I needed that," Brian says, still holding on to his daughter. Malcolm walks in with a smile from ear to ear, then gives Brian a high five.

"What's up, little man," Brian says, looking his son up and down.

"Nothing much," Malcolm says.

"We're glad you're home, Dad," Ashley says.

"Yeah," Malcolm chimes in.

"I'm glad to be home. I have missed you both so much," Brian says, still looking his kids up and down as if he hadn't seen them in years.

"We really missed you too," Ashley says, getting emotional. Brian sees her eyes filling with tears and puts his arms around her.

"Awww, baby girl. Don't you cry. I'm home now, and we are back together, so you don't have to cry."

"I know, Dad," Ashley says, hugging Brian tightly, "I'm just really glad you're home."

"Me too, baby girl. Me too." The three of them hold on to each other for a while, then Brian breaks the circle of love and says, "Ok, guys. I know you both have homework."

"Yes," they both respond, wiping their eyes and smiling at their dad.

"Go ahead and handle that, and we will catch up."

"Ok, Dad," both kids reply, then head to their rooms to start on their homework. Brian goes into the family room with a feeling of gratitude that he is back home with his kids. It was hard for him not to be around them for those few days, but he couldn't imagine how hard it was for them. He sat down on the couch to relax and watch television, waiting for Stacey to return home, and he falls asleep. It is 6 p.m. when he wakes, and no Stacey.

He looks at his phone. No call and no text. *The routine continues,* Brian thinks. He calls Karen.

"Hey, Sis," Brian greets when Karen answers her phone.

"What's up? Everything ok?" she replies with concern.

"Yeah. Look, I should be ok to get out this weekend," Brian starts.

"Okay, great," Karen replies, listening for Brian to continue.

"So, can you see if your friend can get out?" Brian asks.

"I'm sure she'll find the time," Karen assures him.

"Ok, see if Friday is good for her."

"Ok, let me call her now, and I'll call you back," Karen says.

"Good, do that," Brian responds.

Karen ends the call with Brian and quickly dials Allison's number.

"Hey girl," Karen greets Allison.

"Yeah, what's up," replies Allison.

"Are you free Fri—"

Before Karen can get the rest of the word out, Allison says, "Yes! What time and where?"

"Ok, let me get the details, and I'll call you back," Karen states.

"Ok," Allison says with the biggest grin.

Karen calls Brian back and says, "We're on for Friday."

"Ok, Sis. Sounds great," Brian replies.

It is 7:50 p.m., and Brian notices a glimmer of light from the security camera. It is Stacey.

"Hey, Sis, let me get back to you."

"Ok, baby brother. See you soon," Karen says and ends the call.

A few minutes later, Stacey walks into the house and is surprised to see Brian sitting on the couch. A little startled, she says, "Oh, hey. When did you? How?"

"This afternoon and my sister. I tried calling you, but it appeared that you were busy," Brian answers, looking at Stacey.

"Well, my apologies," Stacey offers.

"No worries," Brian says.

Stacey looks on with concern because she expects an interrogation, but Brian plays it cool. He didn't ask or challenge Stacey about coming home late or her whereabouts. In fact, he is looking forward to the weekend and meeting Allison.

9

Brian continues to get better. He even goes for a check-up on Friday, the day of his big date, and receives a clean bill of health. He is excited to return to work the following Monday for several reasons. One, to get out of the house because he is getting bored, and two, to avoid conflict with Stacey. After visiting the doctor, Brian called Karen to let her know that all systems were a go, and he was looking forward to meeting up with her and Allison that evening.

When he left for his doctor's appointment, Stacey was gone. She left without mentioning where she was going or when she was returning. However, by the time Brian got back, Stacey had returned.

"Oh, don't you look and smell nice," Stacey comments.

"Thank you," Brian replies.

"And where are you going?"

Brian looks at Stacey with a bit of sarcasm and says, "If you can go out without anything being said, then why would you question me?"

"Because this is not like you. And are you even healthy enough to be hanging out?" Stacey asks.

"Oh wow! Funny how you're so concerned now, but while I was laid up in that hospital, you could have cared less. Stacey, I'm not about to go back and forth with you. I'm going out, and that's the end of it. Goodnight," Brian says and walks out. Brian is feeling guilty, but to hell with it.

Stacey has been doing her thing for months, and I've said little or nothing. I need a break, he thinks.

The phone rings, and it's Karen. "What's up, Sis? I hope you're not canceling on me," Brian says when he answers the phone.

"No way. In fact, I was calling to say meet us at Sony's on 8th Ave."

"Ok, I can do that. I'm about 30 minutes away," Brian says.

Karen and Allison were already at Sony's and had chosen a table outside. Whenever a car pulled up, Allison was on guard. Brian pulls into the parking lot. Allison sees a car pull up and says to Karen, "Girl, I can't wait 'til I get my money right. I'ma get me one of them." Karen smiled because she knew the car Allison was referring to was Brian's. The car door opens, and Brian steps out. When Allison realizes it's Brian, she can barely contain herself.

"Wait! Hold on a minute. Damn! Girl, your brother is even finer in person!" she proclaims, hitting Karen on the arm. Allison is so excited that when Brian approaches her, she can hardly speak. Anyone who knows Allison knows it's hard to make her speechless.

"And you must be Allison," Brian says.

"Yes," Allison replies, almost shaking. Brian extends his hand to Allison.

"Oh, you're a gentleman too. Lord have mercy. Chivalry isn't dead," Allison notes as she extends her hand to meet Brian's.

"Excuse me," Brian says with a smile that lights up the area, "You're incredible."

"Well, thank you. You're quite the eye-catcher yourself," Allison returns. Allison is wearing a fitted summer dress that hugs every curve on her body. Brian's eyes examine every inch. So much so that he practically undresses her with his eyes. He wastes no time sitting at the table next to Allison and starting a conversation to get to know her. It is almost like Karen isn't even there. Seeing that her brother is smitten with her coworker, she sits back and ear hustles through the night while Brian and Allison continue to converse and mind fuck each other. After about 30 minutes of talking and laughing, Brian gets up to go to the bar.

"Can I get you another drink?" Brian asks Allison.

"Sure," she responds.

"What will you have?"

"I'll have a Mai Tai."

"Do you want anything, Sis?" Brian asks Karen, finally taking his eyes off Allison to look at his sister.

"No, I'm good. I'll just keep working on this good ol' water," Karen says sarcastically while stirring the straw in her glass.

Brian exits to the bar, and Allison says, "Girl if you weren't here, I would fuck your brother tonight."

"Well, I'm glad you like him, but remember, y'all are just friends," Karen reminds Allison.

"Yeah. Friends," Allison says.

As Brian returns to the table, Allison asks, "Are you bow-legged?"

"Yes. A little," Brian answers.

"Jesus, take the wheel!"

"Excuse me," Brian asks.

"Nothing. I talk to myself sometimes," Allison says.

"I get it. We all do from time to time," Brian responds.

The night is coming to an end because Sony is getting ready to close.

"Well, before it gets too late and I forget, can I see you again?" Brian asks Allison.

"I would love that," Allison answers.

"Here's my number. Put it in a safe place," Brian says.

Allison instantly saved Brian's number under the name Brenda on her phone. "I'll do that. I'll call you sometime during the week," Allison assures Brian.

"That will be fine," Brian responds to Allison with a smile.

"Sis, I love you. Thanks for a great night out. It's been a long time coming, and I certainly needed it."

"You're welcome, baby brother. It was good to see you enjoying yourself tonight," Karen states as she stands up and hugs Brian.

Brian's phone rings. It's Stacey. Brian looks at his phone in disbelief. *Ain't this some shit,* Brian thinks. He ignores the call.

"Is everything alright?" Karen asks.

"It will be," Brian responds.

He then walks over to Allison and hugs her. "I enjoyed this time with you. I look forward to hearing from you soon," he says, looking into her eyes.

"I enjoyed myself too. It was great to meet you, and I will definitely be in touch," Allison responds, feeling like she'd fallen in love tonight.

"Good night y'all," Brian says to Karen and Allison as he walks off.

"Good night," they both respond.

Allison is hooked. Brian looks good, smells good, and drives the car she wants. "Girl! I think I'm in love!" she announces to Karen.

"Girl, that's that alcohol talking. Come on here, let's go," Karen says, brushing Allison off.

Once Brian reached his car, he called Stacey back.

"Hello," Stacey answers.

"Yeah, hello."

"Mr., are you ok?" Stacey asks.

"Yes, I'm fine," Brian responds.

"It's getting late, and I was worried about you."

Oh, really? Now you're worried about me? Brian thinks to himself. *Maybe I need to do this more often to get some attention from my wife.*

"I'll be there shortly," he says to Stacey.

"Ok, see you when you get in."

Brian takes his time driving home. When he arrives, Stacey is sitting in the bed, dressed in his favorite negligee, reading a book by Zane. The negligee is red with spaghetti straps and a pair of laced thongs. Not to mention, she smells good. Brian smiles and ponders. She's *only doing this because I went out. Let's see what else she planned.* Brian plays like he has no interest, even though he instantly becomes horny when he lays his eyes on Stacey. The pipe in his pants is a dead giveaway that even Stevie Wonder could see.

Stacey catwalks across the bed and unzips Brian's pants with her teeth. When she pulls his pipe out of his underwear, it stands at attention, directly in her face. She did her P.I. work and casually smelled Brian's dick before she put it in her mouth. When it passes inspection, she proceeds to lick the head, then spit on it and strokes it. She takes his cock in her mouth all the way to the back of her throat and slightly gags. She massages it fast, then slow, then slow, then fast. Brian can't believe that one night out would have his wife acting like a porn star when he returned home, but he enjoys every second of it. Stacey's sexual escapade ends when Brian releases into her mouth.

"How was that?" Stacey asks

"Aww, umm, that was great," Brian responds.

"So Daddy, you got any more in you for Mommy?" Stacey asks Brian devilishly.

"Sure do. How do you want it?"

"You know how I like it, Daddy," Stacey says, assuming the position on all fours on the edge of the bed. Brian steps out of his pants, walks up behind Stacey, and gives her the pounding of her life. When they both release their love juice, Stacey lies flat on the bed, and Brian stands still, unable to move. When he is finally able to move his legs and walk, he goes into the bathroom to get himself together, then returns to the bedroom and gets in the bed next to Stacey.

Moments later, Brian falls asleep. Stacey is still awake watching television when Brian's phone beeps. Stacey looks at the phone and wonders who would be texting Brian at this time of night. *Should I leave this alone and trust my husband? Or should I see who is texting him?* she thinks, staring at the phone. She decides on the latter and reaches for the phone. She tries to open the phone to see the text message but is unable to because Brian now has a password on it. She repeatedly tries to break the code but is unsuccessful. She tries so many times that she locks the phone. Stacey sits back and wonders all night about that text. She also wonders how she will explain to Brian that she locked his phone.

The following day, Stacey looks as if she had been up all night. "Good morning, beautiful."

"Good morning," Stacey replies.

"Did you rest okay?"

"Ummm, yeah. I did," Stacey responds, waiting for Brian to pick up his phone and realize that his phone is locked. Just like clockwork, he reaches for his phone.

"Hmm, that's strange," he says.

"What?" Stacey asks.

"I'm locked out of my phone."

When Stacey doesn't say anything, Brian looks at her and asks, "Did you touch my phone?"

"Actually, I did. You got a text, and I thought it may have been an emergency, so yes, I did," Stacey retorts.

"So, who was it?" Brian demands.

"How am I supposed to know? I couldn't see the text because you now have a password on the phone, and I couldn't open it!"

"Stacey, please don't start," Brian says.

"I'm not. I just find it odd that your phone was going off at 3:10 this morning, and you have no idea who it may have been," Stacey replies.

Brian senses the hostility in Stacey's voice and immediately tries to defuse it by offering to make breakfast. "We just had a good night, and not even 24 hours later, here you go with the drama. I don't have time for this," Brian says, then gets out of the bed to wake up the kids.

"Good morning. Y'all wanna eat?" Brian asks Malcolm and Ashley.

"Can I help?" Ashley asks.

"Sure, Princess."

Brian and his assistant Ashley go into the kitchen and cook breakfast. Malcolm gets up and turns on his game to play while Stacey sits in the bedroom pouting. Brian serves Stacey breakfast. She is still mean-mugging him about the phone. Brian doesn't care, though, because this is payback for all the BS she had been putting him through.

By 10 a.m., Brian is dressed and leaves the house, and heads to AT&T to get his phone unlocked. While there, he adds a password to the account just in case Stacey gets wise and wants to check phone records. He isn't taking any chances on Stacey flipping this on him and getting any leverage. Once the rep finishes servicing Brian's phone, he is back in business. He immediately checks his text messages and sees that the infamous text message that had come to his phone at three in the morning was from Allison.

He quickly opens the message, which reads, **Hey handsome. Hope you made it home ok. Please save my number. See you soon.**

Brian smiles and immediately erases the evidence. He is thoughtful about everything he does and every move he makes so that he would not get caught. Brian stores Allison's name under Al Work. Once he returns home, he puts on his game face because he knows Stacey might confront him about the text. When he enters the house, Stacey is in the kitchen washing dishes.

"Hey, babe," Brian greets.

"Hey," Stacey responds dryly.

"Can I help you with anything?"

"No, I'm good."

For the moment, Brian thought he was in the clear about the text, so he goes into the bedroom to watch football. Stacey comes in and asks, "Is your phone fixed?"

"Yeah," answers Brian.

"So, did you see who texted you?"

"Umm, yeah."

Stacey turns her head to the side and asks, "Well, who was it?"

"Oh, umm, someone texted the wrong number."

"Oh, what did the text say?" Stacey continued insisting.

"I only read the first part, and once I knew it wasn't for me, I deleted it," Brian returns.

"Oh, you did," Stacey says, looking at Brian like she was seeing right through him.

"Stacey, what's with the interrogation? It was the wrong number, damn! Leave it alone!"

Without saying anything else, Stacey walks out of the bedroom. As soon as the bedroom door closes, Brian's phone goes off. It is a text from Allison that reads, **CUT**. Brian has no idea what CUT means, so he calls Karen.

"Hey Sis, what's CUT?" he asks.

"CUT? I don't know. CUT? CUT what?" Karen responds, seeming as confused as Brian was.

"Umm, your buddy sent it to me," Brian responds.

"Let me call her," Karen says.

"Hey girl, let me ask you something. What's CUT?"

"CUT?" asks Allison.

"Yeah bitch, CUT," demands Karen.

"Oh, CUT! I texted that to your brother. CUT means, can you talk."

"Really?" says Karen.

"Really, what?" asks Allison.

"OMG! Now there's acronyms for cheating! Damn! Who would have ever thought? Ok girl, let me call him back," says Karen and ends the call with Allison.

"Hey silly," Karen says to Brian when he answers.

"Yeah, Dr. Phil. I mean, Miss Phil." They laugh.

"So, enough of the small talk. What's CUT?" Brian asks anxiously, waiting for an answer.

"Yeah, C. U. T. means, can you talk."

"Oh…oh….oh...I get it! I guess I need to brush up on my…" Brian stops talking when Stacey walks into the room. She looks at him with a detestable look. Brian observes the nasty stare, then looks away. To bring attention to who he is talking to, he calls out Karen's name to ease the tension in the room. Once Stacey overhears Karen's name, she immediately says, "Is that my sis-in-law?"

"Yes."

"Let me speak to my girl."

Stacey knew that Karen did not care for her being with her brother, just like their mom didn't like Stacey with her son. But she wants a relationship with Karen. She always felt that she and Karen could have that sister bond, so sometimes, she would confide in Karen about certain issues because she thought that maybe she could trust her. But, at the same time, she would only go so far because she was fully aware of the true nature of their relationship. She takes the phone from Brian's ear.

"Karen. When are we gonna hang out?"

"Shit...girl, you name it."

"Ok, I'ma set something up."

"You do that."

"Ok. Here's your brother."

"Ok."

Stacey returns the phone to Brian and feels confident that she may have blown the whole phone thing out of proportion, but at this point, she doesn't care. She walks out of the room.

"Alright, Sis, thanks for keeping me hip to the game," Brian says to Karen. "I'll talk to you later."

"Ok, baby brother. Be safe," Karen says and ends the call. She is a little confused about the exchange of words she just had with Stacey but brushed it off.

Brian is so glad he was really talking to his sister when Stacey walked into the room. He knew that he had dodged a bullet and was feeling really confident. He lies back on the bed with a smile on his face and texts Allison back to let her know that he can only text at this time. As if she were holding her phone, waiting for the notification, Allison immediately texts him. Their text conversation continues for a good while, and before they both realize it, it is 10 p.m. They say good night to each other and end texting.

10

The next morning

BEEP. BEEP. BEEP.

It is 5 a.m.
Snooze

BEEP. BEEP. BEEP.

5:15 a.m.

Brian gets up to shower. One thing has not changed, his man is still commanding attention. With all the tension between him and Stacey, he knew that attempting to get some early morning lovin' from her would probably be a fight, so he went on and took his shower. Once that warm water hit his body and the soap lined his skin, he closed his eyes and massaged his pipe. Once relieved, he is calm and ready for his day at the penitentiary. He gets dressed, kisses Stacey and the kids, and leaves for work.

Brian drives to work in calm silence. He enjoys being back in the workday routine. He rolls his window down and lets the soft breeze hit his face as he admires the scenery en route to his workplace. At this very moment, he is mentally in a good place, and he will seize the moment.

The morning goes by quickly. Once at work, everyone welcomes him as if it is his birthday. Brian's coworkers greet him and express their happiness about his return. Brian is overwhelmed by his coworkers and tells them that he appreciates all the love and support shown to him while on medical leave. After greeting everyone, he went on to roll call and began his work day.

During lunch, he leaves the building and texts Allison, **CUT?**

She texts back, **Yes**.

He calls her, and the two spend their entire lunchtime talking and laughing, something neither of them has done in a long time. Both of their souls are at peace and finally in a happy place. Could this be love? Or a mirage? Well, whatever it is, they are so glad and show no signs of ever ending it. They end their conversation by promising to speak to each other again on their drive home. They return to work happier than they had been in a long time.

The first thing Brian does when he gets into his car after work is pull out his phone and dial Allison's number. Eagerly anticipating his call, she answers on the first ring. What starts as a general conversation quickly turns sexual. Brian is hesitant about asking specific questions not to offend Allison, but she is very open about her sexuality. On the other hand, Brian is not so open because he does not want the judgment that comes with being honest about his fantasies.

"So, Miss, is there anything that you wouldn't do? Or prefer not to do?" Brian asks.

"Of course. Doesn't everyone have something that they would prefer not to do sexually?" responds Allison.

"Ok, so what then?" asked Brian.

"I don't take it in my ass. That's an exit only!" declares Allison. Brian laughs.

"What's funny? Do you?" Allison asks Brian.

"Absolutely not!" Brian barks.

"So, what's funny?" Allison asks again.

"No, please don't get offended. It was just the way you said it," Brian answers.

"And how's that?" Allison inquires.

"You were dead ass serious!"

"I am! I'm not letting anyone put anything in my ass whatsoever!" Allison retorts. "So, Mr., Do you like having anal sex?"

"I could take it or leave it," responds Brian.

"Uggggh, you're gross! You like a shitty dick! So, if you like anal sex after you've had it, what would you do next? I hope you wouldn't put that shitty dick in someone's vagina."

"Well, isn't that all a part of sex?" asks Brian.

"Hell no! If you're gonna do that, you need to clean it off before putting it in a woman's vagina. Don't you know that could cause an infection?" Allison responds seriously.

"Umm, I never gave it any thought," says Brian.

"Well, should I ever let you into my secret garden, there will be no anal. Understood?"

"Umm…well, yes, I guess so," Brian answers.

"So, Mr. Nasty Man, where else do you like parking your penis?"

"I'm a pretty normal guy. I like oral and vaginal."

"Ok, now you're talking. How's your oral game?" Allison asks.

"I think it's pretty good," answers Brian.

"No. Bad answer," Allison says.

"What you mean?" Brian asks, confused.

"Confident people say it without hesitation. You said it as if it was suspect."

"Ok then, yes! I'm great!" Brian says, trying to sound confident.

"No."

"No, what?" Brian asks, even more confused.

"That sounds phony."

"Ok then, how should it sound?"

"It should sound more like, yeah, I'll eat your pussy 'til your head caves in. Something like that. That's confidence."

"Ok, I'll eat your pussy 'til you pee," Brian says, trying to match Allison.

"Whaaaat? Mmmm, you need to work on that."

Brian couldn't believe the silly words that had just left his mouth. "Ok, ok," Brian says.

"Well, honey, I'm home."

"Ok, sweetie. I'll text you later."

Out of nowhere, Winston appears and knocks on Allison's window, and startles her. "Allison! Who are you talking to?" Winston shouts. Allison quickly ends the call.

"What? Bluntneet!" (Translation, Oh my God, you scared the piss out of me).

"No! Who were you talking to?" Winston repeats.

"Don't ask me any questions, Bumbowhole" (Translation, Asshole)

"Raas?" (Translation, What the fuck is wrong with you?)

"No, raas?" Allison retorts.

"Get in the house!" Winston demands.

"Who do you think you're talking to, rude boy?"

"You! I said get yo' ass in the house!" Winston repeats. Allison notices that her neighbors are watching, and she is embarrassed. She also sees her girls watching from the window, so she gets out of the car, hoping to diffuse the situation, but Winston is on a mission. Allison greets her girls and assures them that everything will be okay. Winston, still on level ten, appears calm while he waits for Allison to come to the bedroom.

"Woman, who the fuck were you talking to?" Winston asks again.

"Don't talk to me like that," Allison responds.

Winston walks to the bedroom door and slams it closed. He shoves Allison slightly to the side and says, "I'm not gonna ask you again!" He grabs her and rips her blouse and her bra. He bear hugs her, throws her face forward on the bed, and rips her panties off. He holds her down while he opens his pants, pulls out his penis, and says, "You need some act right!" Grabbing her by her throat, he chokes her and demands, "When I ask you a question, you answer me!" Allison is not turned on at all. She was dry, and Winston's penis felt like sandpaper scraping her walls. Winston stops, only to spit in his hand and wipe it on his penis.

"Oh yeah. Oh yeah," he says. "You like that? You like that shit, don't you?"

And just as fast as it started, it ended. Winston had cum and calmed down. Allison balls up on the side of the bed and cries. There is a knock on the bedroom door. It is her girls, Destiny and Eleanor. "Mommy, are you alright?" they both ask Allison. She tries to sound normal but chokes up, as one can imagine.

"Yes, girls. I'm ok. Give me a minute." She lies in silence. She cannot believe her husband has just raped her. Winston is asleep, and Allison contemplates getting a knife and cutting his ass. *Never again*, she said to herself. She thought of Brian, and if he had been there or near, he could have whipped Winston's ass. She gets up from the bed to take a shower. She cries silently in the shower. She wants and needs Brian to comfort her. When she finishes showering, she gets dressed and goes into the kitchen to address her kids with the most angelic face she can muster.

"Mommy, you look sad," Destiny says.

"No, baby. I'm fine," Allison tries to reassure her daughter.

"Why was daddy yelling?"

"He had a bad day, and he needed to vent."

"Vent?"

"Yes, let off some steam."

"I'm not sure what you mean."

"Don't worry, baby. When you get older, you'll understand."

"Ok, Mommy."

Allison retrieves her phone from the bedroom and returns to the kitchen. She opens her text messages and initiates a new text. She scrolls through her contact list and finds Brenda, the code name on her phone for Brian. She sends the text, **CUT right now?** Waiting for Brian to reply, she walks back to the bedroom and peeks in on Winston. He is fast asleep and calling the hogs. She quietly closes the door and walks back to the kitchen. Her phone buzzes. She looks at the notification from Brian that says, **Hey, wassup?**

Allison responds and tells him she needs to see him tonight, at whatever cost. Brian replies with a response she doesn't want to read. She is devastated and starts crying hysterically. Her heart drops, and she thinks of ending her friendship with Brian. Instead, she ends the text conversation by just saying, **good night.** Brian looks at the phone and feels terrible that he can't be with her when she needs him.

He makes up an excuse to go to the store. Once he leaves the house, he calls his sister and asks for the address of their job. Once received, he calls the florist and orders two dozen yellow roses to be sent to the office the next day with a note that reads, *I care.* Afterward, he erases all the messages and the most recent call to Karen, then proceeds home.

11

The following day, Brian feels drained. Knowing that he may have blown it with Allison, he can hardly sleep. He would have to wait and see. Usually, they would speak every morning, but this morning, no call, no text. *Damn, I blew it,* Brian thinks to himself. *Oh well, life goes on*. Brian goes on with his morning.

10:30 a.m. Karen and Allison are at work having small talk when Karen notices Allison acting differently.

"Hey, girl. You alright?" Karen asks Allison.

"Yeah."

"Uh-oh. Hell no. I know that look. What happened?"

Before Allison can respond, they both hear a guy's voice say, "Delivery for Ms. Fitzgerald."

"Hmm, delivery?" Allison repeats, confused. She thinks that maybe Winston is having her served with divorce papers. She stands up and says, "Yes. Over here." Allison pulls the card out and reads the words, I care. To her surprise, it was the beautiful yellow roses that Brian had ordered. She tears up.

Karen reaches out and hugs her friend and says, "It's gonna be alright, girl. It's gonna be alright."

"The flowers, the flowers! In all my years of being married, Winston has never sent me a flower," Allison says through her tears.

"You mean Brian sent you these beautiful flowers?" Karen asks, impressed.

"Yes, he did. He is an amazing man!" Allison declares. The idea that Brian had thought enough of her to send her flowers hit a soft spot in Allison's heart, and she was all in from then on. Karen looks at the flowers, then nosily opens the card, and when she reads the words, she assumes that Brian had them delivered because he messed up with Allison.

"So, you wanna talk about it now? Girl, tell me what my brother did. Did he hurt you? That MF! I'ma call him and…"

"No, no. Wait. No, he didn't," Allison says, cutting Karen off.

"Then what?" Karen asks, needing an understanding of what is going on.

"I really needed to talk to him last night, but he couldn't get out of the house. I really needed him."

"Umm, TMI," Karen says, rolling her eyes.

"No, not in that way," Allison explains. "It was Winston."

"Wait. What? You just said Brian," Karen says, confused.

"No, Winston was acting a fool yesterday, and I needed to get away," Allison responds.

"Oh," replies Karen.

"I felt really bad when Brian told me he couldn't get out last night, but this makes up for it," Allison says gleefully. She stands there smiling and smelling them as if Brian had personally picked them from the Garden of Eden. Several of their co-workers walk by, complimenting her on how pretty her flowers are. Feeling like a schoolgirl, she smiles uncontrollably, then seconds later, crying like a baby.

"What's wrong with you?" Karen asks.

Whimpering, Allison responds, "Winston has never sent me flowers."

Karen reaches out and says, "Come here, girl." She hugs Allison and says, "I think I know what you need to do."

Allison looks into Karen's eyes and nods her head, then texts Brian, **Call me when you can.**

During his lunch break, Brian notices the text and is very apprehensive about retrieving it, but he has to. **Call me when you can,** is what he reads. All in all, it isn't bad or good. It makes him think to himself, *what am I getting myself into?* Brian calls Allison, and she immediately picks up. When she hears his voice, it seems to make everything ok. The tears begin to flow, and Brian recognizes the sadness in her voice. "Are you ok?" Brian asks.

"Yes."

"So, why do you sound different? What's wrong?"

"Right now, nothing is wrong. I'm happy, believe me," Allison says, trying to convince Brian.

"Really? Then, why do you sound like that?" Brian asks, unable to let it go.

"You're special," Allison blurts out.

"Oh, so now I'm special?" Brian repeats with a smile. "So, why am I so special?"

"Your flowers, they are beautiful. They said I apologize, and I care, all at the same time."

"Well, I'm glad you like them," Brian says.

"I really do. So listen, when are we gonna see each other again? I'd like to thank you in person."

"Oh, you would?" Brian asks slyly.

"Yes. I would," Allison responds.

"Well, think about it, and I'll talk to you on my way home."

"I'll do that. Talk to you later."

Brian and Allison continue their daily routines, anticipating the end of their workday. Allison continues to get compliments on the beautiful flowers. At the end of her workday, Allison starts packing up her things, anxious to leave so she can talk to Brian. Allison says good night to her colleagues as she anxiously walks out of the office. The call she was waiting on breaks the anticipation she was feeling. It is Brian, of course.

"Hey, babe."

"Babe? Hmm, I'm being upgraded now," Brian answers.

"So, when am I gonna see you again, Mr.?

"When would you like to see me?"

"If it was my choice, I'd say today," replies Allison.

"Hmm, really?"

"Yes, really."

"Ok then, where would you like to go?"

"So, you're gonna let me pick?" Allison asks.

"Yes, give me an idea," Brian responds.

"Oh no, Mr. This one is all on you."

"Ok. Are there any limitations?" Brian asks.

"Limitations?" asks Allison.

"Yeah, one of those things you don't want to do."

"No, I'm pretty open," Allison exclaims.

"Hmm."

"What's hmm?"

"Interesting that you trust me enough to choose," Brian says.

"Yes, I do. Is that a problem?" Allison asks.

"No, it's not. Ok, let's try that new place off Sunset."

"The Tavern?"

"Yes."

"Ok. What time?"

"Let's shoot for 8 p.m. on Saturday."

"Ok."

Brian pulls up to his house and jokingly says to Allison, "Now it's time to say goodbye to all our family."

"Oh, you got jokes?" Allison says, laughing.

"Sure do," Brian responds.

"Alright then. I'll text you before bed."

"Ok. Until then."

Five minutes later, Allison arrives home, and Winston is leaving for work, or at least that's what he says. Those two are like night and day. There is no audible goodbye, just a hand wave gesture when he leaves. Allison had once felt some kind of way, but now Brian had her open, so the loving feeling she once had for Winston was fading fast. She now envisions making love to Brian and how good it would be. That itch was getting so bad that after she spent some time with the kids, she took a shower and masturbated with her toothbrush case. The soap makes it feel sensational as she rubs and squeezes her breasts. She climaxes, rests her hand on the wall, and takes a deep breath. That was just what she needed. Immediately after her shower, she had to call Brian. No answer, so she texted **CUT**. Still, no response. Allison starts to feel some kind of way but then comes to grips with the reality of the situation.

Thirty minutes later, Allison's phone rings, and the name, Brenda appears on her phone.

"Hello," Allison answers.

"Hey, babe," Brian greets.

Allison had to look at her phone briefly because she had completely forgotten that she had listed Brian under the name Brenda.

"Oh, hey, sweetie," she responds as she laughs.

"What's funny?" Brian asks, confused.

"Nothing. I'm having a senior moment," Allison says.

"Ok. We all have those."

"Umm, this isn't like you."

"What do you mean?" Brian responds.

"It's 8 o'clock, and you're calling me," Allison explains.

"Hmm, well, someone isn't here."

"Really," Allison comments.

"Do you know where she is?"

"No, and I'm starting not to care," says Brian.

Allison feels confident that her dreams may soon come true and that the next time she climaxes, it wouldn't be with a toothbrush case.

"I can't wait to see you," Brian says.

"I can't wait either. What are you gonna do with me?" Allison asks excitedly.

"That depends on what you let me do. I wanna… umm…. never mind."

"No, say it." Allison is genuinely curious to hear what Brian has to say.

"I wanna pet that kitten."

"Kitten? I'ma grown-ass woman. No kitten here. I'ma full-grown lioness," Allison says with grace.

"Ok, grrrrrrr. Well, I can't wait to see that lioness."

"Boi, stop talking to me like that. I've already masturbated in the shower thinking about you."

"Oh really?"

"Yes, really."

Brian is aroused. "Girl, stop playing."

"I'm not playing. Hold on, let me check on my girls real quick."

Once Allison returns to the phone, she tells Brian to hang up because she will Facetime him. When Brian answers the video call, he sees Allison in a sheer, colorful wrap on the screen. "This is how I sleep," Allison says, looking at Brian seductively. She gives Brian a peep show, partially showing her pierced nipples, and he becomes even more aroused. Allison notices Brian's eyes glued to the phone. "You like?"

"Hell yeah. You gonna make me have to satisfy myself."

"Is that a bad thing?"

"Not at all," Brian responds with his eyes still glued to the screen as he unbuttoned his pants. For a moment, he forgot that he was home with his kids. Just as he starts to pull his penis out, Ashley walks into the room. Brian jumps when the bedroom door opens. He shoves the phone under the pillow.

"Daddy, what you doing?"

"Oh, hey baby girl."

Allison calls out to Brian, and he fumbles with the phone, trying to turn the volume down.

Ashley asked, "What's that sound?" as Allison started to masturbate on the phone.

To add insult to injury, headlights appear on the security camera. It is Stacey. Brian is in panic mode. As he reaches for the phone, it falls on the floor, and Allison appears on the screen completely nude. He picks up the phone while Stacey is walking through the front door. He is finally able to lower the volume as Ashley looks at him like he is crazy. As Stacey starts walking up the steps, he shuts off the phone.

"Baby girl," he called out to Ashley.

"Yes, Dad."

"What you wanna eat? You want some ice cream?"

"Ice cream? Sure," Ashley responds.

Brian rushed out of the room and downstairs. He passes Stacey on the stairs and says, "Hey."

"Hey," Stacey responds.

"I'm gonna get some ice cream."

"Ice cream this late?"

"Yeah, Mommy. We're gonna get some ice cream."

Brian takes Ashley to the grocery store. While in the store, he powers up his phone and sends a message to Allison indicating the close call. Allison looks at the text and damn near drops the phone. *Oh my god*, she thought to herself. She texted back. We **have to be more careful.** Although she is somewhat embarrassed, she is happy. She feels like a teenage girl experiencing the pure puppy love we all long for. Brian also has that feeling, and their love for one another is getting stronger. There was just one thing left to seal the deal—physical intimacy. The weekend couldn't come fast enough.

Each day, Brian and Stacey continue the same routine, dealing with the daily BS. Stacey is coming in later and later. She claims she is going to start back working out. Somehow, all the exercise equipment in the house just isn't enough, so she bought an expensive membership at Planet Fitness for five days a week, right after work, which she considers her alibi, or at least that's what Brian is thinking. Brian contacts one of his classmates from the academy to do a little spying on Stacey. Becoming aware of his feelings is an excuse to go out and do whatever.

"Hey, Bro. I need a favor," Brian says.

"What's up?" Rodney replies.

"I'm a little embarrassed to say, but I know I can trust you."

"Sure thing. What's up?"

"I need you to follow my wife."

Choked up, Rodney says, "Stacey?"

"Yes, Stacey. I have a feeling that something isn't right, and I just have to know."

"Damn, Bro. You and Stacey always gave me hope that relationships could work. Wow…I can't…I just can't believe, umm…"

"Yeah, yeah, yeah. Can I trust you?" Brian asks dismissively.

"Sure, Bro. I'll get right on it."

"Pictures or anything. If you find nothing, that will be even better."

"Ok, give me a couple days. I'ma need some info from you."

"Like what?"

"I need her license plate number, what she drives, her cell phone number, her address at the job, and any of her close friends' addresses. Hell, I can look up her social media info too, if you have that," Rodney explains.

"Yeah, but I don't have her password."

"Password, I don't need that."

"Hmm, really?" Brian asks curiously.

"Yeah, Bro. Climb from under that rock. This is the new millennium. Everything nowadays is easily accessible."

"Damn, I guess I am behind time."

"Well, give me about a week or so, and I'll get back to you."

Brian hangs up. How did his marriage come to this? He is feeling defeated because he has to go to this desperate length to find out what he already knows deep down. Hiring someone to follow his wife is definitely an all-time low in his marriage. But at this point, he has to know what is going on and if this is the way to find out, then so be it.

12

Friday arrives. It was 24 hours before the date that Brian and Allison had anticipated. The morning drive consists of their regular conversation. However, you can hear and feel the anticipation of what is coming.

"So, babe, did you want to eat anything in particular?"

"No, not really."

"How about seafood?"

"Seafood it is."

As they ended their call, they both had butterflies and smiles beyond anyone's imagination. Karen approaches Allison when she arrives at work.

"Hey, girl. HEY GIRL! Um, hello bitch!"

"HMM?" Allison responds in a daze.

"Where the fuck you at? What the hell you thinking about?"

"Oh, nothing. I was just daydreaming," Allison responds with a huge smile.

"I see. About what?" Karen asks.

"Nothing. I, I, I was making sure that I don't forget what I need from the store," Allison says, appearing to snap out of it.

"Mmmhmm, sure bitch. It looks like you got dick on the brain."

"Uh, umm, no. What would make you say that?"

"Bitch, I know that look. And if it's what I think it is, I don't wanna know shit."

"Girl, you trippin'," Allison says with a slight laugh.

“No, you trippin’. Either y’all have bumped, or y’all about to bump. Which is it?”

“Karen, good girls don’t tell.”

“Are you fucking kidding me right now? You didn’t!”

Allison smiled. “No, silly, we didn’t.”

“OMG! So…so, that means…”

“It means nothing! Stay out of it.”

“Oh, I’m out of it! You just remember what I said. Be careful!”

Allison feels concerned but smiles and says, “Girl, don’t worry. Everything is straight.”

“Mmm, mmm, mmm. Slut.” Allison smiles, and Karen walks away.

The workday ends, and Allison cannot wait to speak to Brian. All day she thought of what she would wear and what perfume she would put on. She wants this night to be special. She treats it like she is a virgin and Brian will be her first.

Brian plays calm and relaxed, although he is nervous as hell. He figures that if he gets liquored up, he will be fine, but it is a wait-and-see game. Saturday rolls around, and Brian stays home and cleans up to kill time. Allison, on the other hand, receives unexpected company. Winston is home, which is shocking because he is never home on a Saturday. Saturdays were money days, so he said. 6 p.m. approaches. Winston sends the kids to Allison’s mom’s house without her knowledge. It was supposed to be a surprise, and indeed it was. Allison takes a shower, and Winston, feeling amorous, decides to enter the bathroom.

“Winston, is that you?”

“Yes. Who else would it be?” he replies as he gets undressed.

“What are you doing” Allison yells out.

“Woman, don’t question me!”

“No! No! Winston stop! Just stop!”

Winston grabs Allison and says, “Let’s not fight!”

“No, Winston! No!”

Winston lines his dick up and penetrates Allison. Knowing she isn’t strong enough to fight him off, she lets Winston do his thing. She thinks about Brian. She is well aware of what is happening to her, but crazily, the thought of Brian instantly turns her on. Instead of Winston taking it against her will, she imagines that it is Brian behind her, and she immediately becomes wet and loosens her vaginal walls. Then, she took all of Winston’s dick inside her. With her eyes closed and still thinking about Brian, she starts bouncing back faster and faster, and two minutes later, Winston explodes. Again, just as quickly as it started, it was over.

"Damn girl, that was good," Winston says, then slaps Allison on the ass as he gets out of the shower. Allison doesn't say a thing. She recoils at the sight of her husband. The only thing that had brought her through this violation was the thoughts of Brian that flooded her mind.

When Winston finally leaves the bathroom, Allison takes a deep breath, rolls her eyes, and continues to wash and remove the stench of hate from her body. Once finished, Allison steps out of the shower, and Winston is lying across the bed, fast asleep. She takes advantage of this situation and hurriedly and quietly gets dressed so she can leave the house before he wakes.

She wears a pair of black leggings with a white shirt and some heels. The perfume of choice is Chloe. Her hair is done in that natural afro that Brian adores. Now all she has to do is to get out of the house. She takes her heels off and quietly exits the bedroom, walking on her tiptoes. She pulls the door shut. She walks through the house and out the door as quickly as possible. Once in her car, she backs out of the driveway and high-tails it out of there. She figures if she is going to argue with Winston, she would rather do it when she returns.

On the other side of town, Brian is also eagerly getting ready. He wears a pair of black pants and a white cufflink shirt. His cologne of choice is Polo Red, which Stacey loves, but now it is time for someone else to love it. Before Brian can get out of the bathroom, Stacey can smell him.

"Umm, Mr., What's up?" she asks Brian.

"What you mean?" he responds.

"I mean, you looking good and smelling good. Umm, where the fuck you think you going?"

"Out."

"What the fuck you mean out? With who?"

"Listen, I don't ask you what you're doing or who you're doing it with, and by my count, you're up five to one."

"Five to one?"

"Yes."

"That's bullshit," Stacey says, rolling her eyes.

"No, what you," pointing his finger at Stacey, "been doing is BS!" Brian retorts.

"Ok, so who you going out with?"

"Why?"

"Because I asked. Is it a bitch?"

"No."

"Ok then, wait for me to get dressed. I'm going."

Brian's eyes get big as he yells, "No, the hell you ain't!"

"Why? Why can't I go? It's 'cause it's a bitch!"

"You can't go 'cause I said so!"

At this point, Stacey is so angry that she grabs Brian's shirt and rips the top three buttons completely off. Brian stands there in disbelief.

"What the fuck is wrong with you?" Brian shouts. "Get your fucking hands off me!"

"No! No! You not going nowhere!" Stacey stands in the doorway, falls to her knees then tries to rip Brian's pants, all while the kids are downstairs.

"Stacey, stop this bullshit!"

"Tell me who you're going with! Tell me, and I'll stop."

"I'm going out with my co-workers. One of the guys is having a bachelor party."

Stacey sits back and ponders the idea. In her mind, Brian had never cheated on her, and for all she knew, he was still madly in love with her. He had never given her a reason to doubt him. She instantly feels terrible. She stands up and says, "I'm sorry, baby. Let me iron another shirt for you."

"No, that's alright. I'll do it."

Feeling horribly about how she'd just acted, Stacey says, "Babe, I'm really sorry."

KNOCK. KNOCK.

"Mommy, is everything ok?" Ashley asks.

"Yes, Daddy and I are playing around."

"Oh, ok."

Brian pulls out a grey cufflink shirt from the closet and sprays it with Polo Red.

"Mmm, you trying to make those strippers come after you?"

"Umm, no."

"Well, when you get back, I'ma have a surprise for you."

Brian looks up at the ceiling and thinks to himself, *Whatever. Guilt sex again. I'm not gonna need any of that. She'll be lucky if I can go another round if all goes well tonight.* "Yeah, ok, Stacey," he says, then grabs his keys and heads out of the bedroom to leave the house. Stacey watches him and wonders if she is sending her man out the door to another woman. She starts to follow him outside but decides against it. *Whatever is happening in the dark will come to light. I'm gonna lay low on this and just wait and see,* Stacey thinks to herself, then grabs the remote to find something to watch on television.

Brian gets in his car, and before pulling out of the driveway, he pulls out his phone and texts Allison, **CUT.** Instead of texting Brian back, Allison decides to give him a call. "Hey, babe."

"Hey."

"What's wrong?" Brian asks.

"Nothing."

"Ok, babe, I know you by now. I hear it in your voice. You don't sound like yourself," Brian states.

"Really? What do I sound like?"

"You sound sad."

"No. Really, I'm good. Just can't wait to see you."

"Well, your man is on his way. I should arrive there in 10 minutes.

"Ok, you'll be there before me," Allison states.

"That's cool. I'll have your Mai Tai ordered and waiting on you when you get there," Brian says lovingly.

Allison smiles. "You really know how to put a smile on my face," she responds.

"Sure do," Brian says confidently.

Allison continues to smile as if Brian could see her through the phone.

"Ok, drive safely, and I'll see you when you get there," Brian says and ends the call.

As Brian pulls into the parking spot, he notices a man on the corner selling flowers. He parks the car and looks in his rearview mirror to make sure he is still on point. He gets out of the car and walks over to the man to purchase a red rose for Allison. He walks into the bar and sits at a quaint little round table for two. When the server comes to the table, Brian orders a shot of patron, along with Allison's Mai Tai, for starters.

The server returns and sits the drinks on the table. Brian places the rose by Allison's glass. He looks around the bar and observes the people drinking, laughing, talking, and having a good time. He looks down at his watch and thinks *Allison should be arriving soon.* Seconds later, Brian looks up and sees her walking through the door. He couldn't move his eyes off of her. She looks like something out of Ebony magazine. *Damn, as fine as she was the last time I saw her, she is looking even better tonight,* Brian thinks to himself as he watches Allison walk towards the table where he is sitting. Two gentlemen approach her as she walks through the club to the table.

"Excuse me. Excuse me," the two men call out to Allison. She looks at them and smiles but never stops walking toward Brian. As Allison approaches the table, Brian observes the attention she is getting from the other men. He thinks that he would interject but decides against it. After all, she is there for him. He admires Allison's style as she gives the men the cold shoulder and sticks his chest out because he knows she only has eyes for him.

"I see I'm not the only one crushing on your beauty tonight," Brian says as he stands up to greet Allison as she approaches the table.

With the biggest smile on her face, Allison responds, "Hey babe," as she gives him a tight hug and a kiss. The two men who tried to pursue her took note of the kiss that Allison had given Brian and kindly walked off.

"Damn, you smell good," they both say to each other simultaneously, then laugh.

"And you look good," they both say at the same time again, now laughing hysterically.

"Hold on, wait a minute," Brian says. "I know great minds think alike, but let's try to speak one at a time."

"Ok," Allison says with a smirk on her face.

Brian pulls her chair out from the table so she can sit down.

"Why, thank you, kind gentleman."

"You are most certainly welcome, beautiful lady."

"I see you've taken the initiative to order my favorite drink," Allison says, looking at her drink, then noticing the red rose beside it. "Aww babe, what a beautiful rose," she says with a blush as she picks the flower up and holds it to her nose to smell it. "Thanks, babe."

"You're welcome, beautiful," Brian says, trying to contain himself.

Allison looks like an angel. She has the perfect skin with just enough make-up to accent her natural beauty and gorgeous light brown eyes, and she wears her hair in a natural bun that Brian had complimented her on the first time he had seen her. Not only is she beautiful, but she is also sexy as hell. Brian wants to take her to the bathroom and lay pipe to her, but he has to be the perfect gentleman. To take his mind off his dirty thoughts, he asks Allison, "So babe, you wanna tell me what was wrong earlier?"

"Oh, nothing. I'm fine," Allison responds, hoping he will believe her and drop the subject.

"Listen, if we're gonna keep it real with one another, I need you to be honest with me," Brian says in a caring tone.

Allison looks at Brian with amazement and wonders, *how does this man already know me so well?*

"Ok, babe, you're right. I was upset before I left home because

Winston and I had words. I guess you picked up on it."

"Yes, I did. I could hear it in your voice. I'm sorry, babe. I wish you didn't have to deal with that," Brian says, reaching across the table and placing his hand on top of Allison's.

"Yeah, me too," she says as she looks into Brian's eyes and appreciates his touch. She thinks about how bad things are with Winston and how she dreads returning home. Her thoughts make her a little withdrawn, and Brian senses it, so he changes the subject. "So, umm..."

"So, umm...what, babe?" Allison asks, wondering what Brian is trying to say.

"I'm just wondering if the rest of you looks that good under those fine ass threads," Brian says, with a devilish look in his eye.

"There's only one way to find out," Allison replies, matching Brian's naughtiness.

Brian is immediately aroused and has to stop his man from leaking pre cum when Allison moves her chair closer to him and places her hand on his lap.

"Mmm, nice," Allison says as she rubs and strokes his penis.

Then, out of the corner of his eye, Brian notices a friend of Stacey's walk into the bar. "Oh shit," Brian says as he turns around and puts his back to Allison.

"What's wrong?" Allison asks.

"The young lady over there," Brian said without turning back.

"Over where?" Allison asks, partially turning to look in the direction she thought Brian was referring to.

"Over there in the red dress."

"Yeah, what about her?" Allison asks, still confused.

"That's my wife's friend."

"Oh," Allison says, now understanding why the woman is looking at the back of Brian's head.

"Listen, neither one of us needs any drama tonight, so why don't we just get outta here before we both end up in court."

"Ok, that sounds like a plan. Why don't you go to your car? Let me clear up this bill, and I'll meet you outside," Brian says as he motions for the server to come to the table.

"Ok," Allison says, grabs her things, stands up, and walks out the door.

Once Brian takes care of the bill, he stands up and discreetly heads toward the door. Once outside, Brian goes to his car. He gets in the car, pulls out his phone, and calls Allison.

"Hey, where are you parked?" he asks her.

"I'm right in front of the fountain," Allison states.

"Oh, ok. You're on the other side of the parking lot," Brian says. They were both glad they hadn't parked next to each other. Before he could say another word to Allison, there was a light tap on his window. Brian looks up, startled, and notices it is Stacey's friend, Teresa. Brian places his phone on his lap without hanging up and rolls down his window.

"Hey," Teresa says.

"Oh hey, what's up?"

"I thought that was you," Teresa says, looking at Brian as if she likes what she sees.

"Yeah, how you doing?" Brian asks, ready to go.

"I'm good," Teresa says, still holding a suspicious look. "So, my girl let you out the house with your fine ass."

Brian looks up at Teresa in total shock. She had never acted like this towards him before. "Umm, yeah," he responds, still in shock.

"Mmm, well, if I were Stacey, your fine ass would be home with me, and I'd be fucking your brains out right about now," Teresa says, looking deep into Brian's eyes.

Brian thought, *oh wow*. Even if Teresa was planning to say something to Stacey about seeing him out, he knew he was safe because she was totally out of pocket with her comments to him. "Umm, yeah. Well, Teresa, I gotta go," Brian says, putting his car into reverse.

"Ok, Brian. I'll see you some other time," Teresa says, backing away from the car because it had already started moving.

"Ok then. Take care," Brian says as he rolls his window up and backs out of the parking space. He immediately picks his phone up to see if Allison is still there.

"Hey, you still here?" he asks.

"Yep, I'm here," she responds.

"Did you hear all that?"

"Yeah, I did. I see I'm not the only one who thinks you look good as hell and wants to fuck the shit outta you," Allison says.

"Hmmm, so you wanna fuck the shit outta me?"

"Isn't it obvious?" Allison waits for Brian's response.

With a slight smirk, Brian says, "Yeah, it is pretty obvious."

Allison chuckles and says, "Mission accomplished."

Brian blushes. He tried to play it cool, but he liked the attention that he was getting from Allison, Teresa, and Cheryl, the nurse at the hospital. It is refreshing to hear these women speak about the qualities that they admire. Not to mention, it is a significant boost to his ego.

"Ok, so what's next?" Allison asks Brian.

"Just follow me," he responds.

"I'm right behind you, Daddy," Allison says and ends the call. Allison can't wait to get her hands on Brian. She hadn't known him long, but she needed to feel his touch tonight!

13

Brian pulls into the Hampton Inn and Suites and parks his car. Allison parks a few aisles over in the parking lot. Brian gets out of his car first, while Allison stays in her car and waits for instructions. They are both anxious and excited because the moment is finally here. Brian goes into the hotel, pays for the room, and gets the key. As he proceeds to the room, he calls Allison and gives her the room number, and tells her to come on in. Brian waits for Allison to get there to get comfortable.

KNOCK. KNOCK.

Brian opens the door. She walks into the room and says, "Hold up. Room inspection."

Brian looks at her and says, "Room inspection?"

"Yes, we have to make sure the room is clean, meaning the bathroom, the floor, and the bed sheets, because we don't want to take anything home that we didn't come with," Allison says, already walking around and inspecting the room.

"Oh, ok," Brian says and looks around the room.

Once the room inspection is complete, Brian goes into the bathroom. When he comes out of the bathroom, Allison goes in. Moments later, she walks out of the bathroom wearing a colorful wrap that is damn near transparent. Brian's eyes could see straight through it, causing the steel pipe to appear in his pants. Noticing that Brian is enamored by what he sees, Allison walks over to him with as much sex appeal as she can and passionately kisses him. The kiss is slow and sensual, turning Brian on. His pipe feels like it is about to burst through his pants. Taking their time to enjoy everything about their kiss, Allison slowly wraps her hands around Brian's back and then slowly moves them down to his crotch. She is amazed when she feels how Brian's man is responding to her touch.

"Damn, is all this for me?" she asks while slowly stroking his penis through his pants. Unable to mutter a word, Brian nods yes.

Allison unbuttons his pants as Brian's hands slowly slide up her wrap and massage her pussy. Allison is Aquafina wet. Her pussy feels like she pissed on herself. However, Brian knew better. This feeling is too smooth to be urine. Brian opens Allison's wrap, sits on the bed, and takes a second to enjoy the beautiful canvas in front of him. He leans into Allison, softly kisses her belly button, then pulls her towards him and guides her to lie on the bed. Next, he takes his hand and caresses both of her breasts, then takes one of them in his mouth and begins to suck it. One of her big hot spots. Allison moans while Brian makes love to her breasts with his tongue and says, "Yes, baby, give it to me."

Not missing a beat with her breasts in his mouth, Brian moves his hand down to Allison's love nest and begins to sensually finger fuck her. Allison can hardly contain herself as her love juices completely cover Brian's hand. Now, Brian's pipe is so hard it hurts. He stands over Allison, pulls his shirt over his head, and throws it on the floor. He is about to give this woman the best lovin' she ever had in her life.

As he stands over her, he admires the beauty before him, then unzips his pants. Allison lies there in great anticipation, almost wanting to yank Brian's pants down herself because he is taking too long to satisfy the ache that is happening down below. Brian finally pulled his pants down, and when they hit the floor, so did his dick. He had gone completely limp! *Oh my god! Not now!* Brian thinks to himself in horror.

"What's wrong, babe?" Allison asks as she sits up and notices Brian's limp penis. *Noooooooooooo!!!,* was what she was screaming in her head, but she didn't want to hurt Brian's already crushed ego, so she quietly and calmly asked, "Is everything ok?"

Brian responded, "Yeah, yeah." He cannot believe the moment of truth has finally arrived, and he has completely lost it! He can't get hard to save his life. Allison begins to stroke his penis as he stands in front of her, but nothing. Brian remembers the kiss they shared earlier that started the ball rolling, so he leans down and kisses Allison in hopes that he can get his mind and his man right, but again, nothing. Brian falls onto the bed in disbelief and closes his eyes in embarrassment.

"Relax, baby," Allison says, feeling bad for Brian and seeing the frustration on his face.

"Umm, yeah, right. This shit isn't normal."

"I understand, baby," she says while rubbing his head, trying to ease the sudden tension in the room.

"Understand? How the fuck do you understand?" Brian asks, still unable to face Allison, so he continues to look straight up at the ceiling instead.

"Hold on one motherfuckin' minute!" Allison says, sitting up and looking directly at Brian. "You gonna get mad at me 'cause you can't get right? I'm sitting here trying to be considerate and understanding, and you're gonna talk to me like that?" She immediately stands up and walks toward the bathroom to put her clothes back on, but before she can get out of Brian's reach, he leans up on the bed and grabs her arm to stop her from walking away from him.

"Hold on, babe, I'm sorry. I didn't mean it. It's just, I've never had this issue."

Allison turns around to Brian and sees the disappointment in his eyes. She feels so bad for him but wants him to know that this does not change how she feels about him. She understands that he has a situation at home just like she does, so maybe his situation is why this is happening or not.

"Babe, I really do understand. It's gonna be alright. We can try again." Allison reaches down and begins to stroke Brian's penis once again. She lies down on the bed, and Brian starts to finger fuck her again, but it is of no use. His manhood is dead. Frustrated and distraught, Brian stops, gets up from the bed, picks up his clothes, and goes into the bathroom. *I have one of the most beautiful and sexiest women in the next room ready to fuck me, but I can't get my shit up! What the hell is going on with me? Why did this happen?* Brian thinks. He stands there looking at his naked body in the mirror, looks down at his limp dick, and loses it. He angrily beats on the walls. When Allison hears the noise in the bathroom, she jumps off the bed and walks to the door to try and console Brian.

KNOCK. KNOCK.

"Babe, what are you doing?"

Brian stops hitting the wall but doesn't say anything.

"Brian, everything is going to be okay. Please open the door."

Brian slowly walks towards the door and opens it. When he sees

Allison standing there, he grabs her and hugs her. When they let each other go, Allison looks in his eyes and says, "Baby, you mean more to me than sex. When the time is right, it will happen."

Brian looks into her beautiful eyes, nods his head, and says, "Okay." They gather their things and leave the hotel. Brian drives slowly down the interstate, still in disbelief about how soft Allison felt and how good she smelled. He fantasizes about how good her pussy felt between his fingers and how wet it was in anticipation of him handling it. He is in deep thought, trying to figure out why his dick wouldn't respond. He is in the perfect situation and has the perfect opportunity with the perfect person. Unable to make it make sense, Brian slams on the brakes and yells, "Whyyyyyyy!!!" But no answer comes to mind.

When Brian arrives home, Stacey is lying in bed, but she isn't asleep. When he walks into the room, she glances at the clock. It is 2:50 a.m.

"Did you have a nice time?" she asks Brian before he can take his jacket off.

"It was ok," Brian responds dryly. Without saying another word, Brian takes a shower. When he finishes, he gets in bed next to Stacey and notices that she is completely nude. He pretends he hasn't noticed, but Stacey is armed and amorous. Before he can ask her what she is doing, she sits up in the bed and straddles him. This movement arouses him, and Stacey can feel him standing at attention, so she sits down on Brian's dick and rides it like she is horseback riding. While Stacey gallops on top of him, Brian closes his eyes and thinks of Allison and how he should have handled her. He figures that he has messed up and his sexcapade with her is now a thing of the past. He decides to make the best of what is happening now with Stacey. He grabs her hips and bounces her up and down on his dick as she screams in pleasure. Then, his volcano erupts almost without warning, and Brian lets out a big moan. *Damn, I needed that,* he thinks to himself. Then his mind immediately goes to Allison.

On the other side of town, Allison's return home wasn't as welcoming. Winston was fast asleep, and he hadn't even noticed what time she had gotten in, so she was safe. She goes into the bathroom, undresses, and takes a shower. The feeling of the warm water beating on her body has her still feeling horny. Her pussy pulsates, and the scent of Brian is still on her skin. She cannot help but fantasize about how his penis felt in her hands and what that pipe would have felt like inside her. As the thoughts consume her mind, she has a strong urge to satisfy herself. As she gently strokes her clit and climaxes, her desire for Brian becomes even stronger. It made her reflect on the reality of the situation. Was Brian the man for her? Or should she try and salvage the disruptive relationship she was currently in? Many thoughts were running through her mind.

Brian is a great guy. He is attentive, patient, caring, and thoughtful, all the things she misses at home. So, in this case, the pros outweigh the cons, which is really just the sex. Speaking of sex, Allison thinks about what happened or didn't happen between her and Brian at the hotel earlier that evening. She wonders what the real reason is behind his dick issue. She understands that sex is only a part of the relationship, but it is clear that he had a dick and a nice-sized one at that, so what could be the real reason for his nonperformance? *Damn, I know I'm good. I'm sexy, I keep my hair on point, I look good in my clothes, my breath doesn't stink, and my pussy cat is fresh, so what is the problem? I hope this isn't an issue of impotence. I would really hate to think about all that good meat going to waste*, she thinks to herself. She tries to put all the thoughts on a marathon in her mind to rest. She concludes that whatever is meant to be will be, so she will slow down and take it one day at a time. With that, she steps out of the shower, dries herself off, puts on her night clothes, and goes to bed.

In the morning, Winston wakes without saying a word to Allison. *This motherfucker is up to something*, she thinks to herself. She slept very little because she had been thinking about her issue with Brian. But now, her mind is directed at Winston and what he is really doing behind her back. Before she knew it, she felt angry and decided it was time to do some P.I. work. As she prepares to do laundry, she checks every pocket of Winston's clothes, looking for anything that would let her know what he is really doing when he stays out late or doesn't come home but finds nothing. She stands in the middle of the room, looks around to see where to check next, and then goes through his closet and dresser. KABOOM! There it is! A receipt for a purchase of wine and flowers!

Before saying anything, she looks around the house to see if he could have possibly purchased them for her but quickly realizes that isn't the case. She decides to hold on to the receipt. She starts a file of evidence to arm herself with an arsenal of Winston's deception. The saying goes, if you look for something, you will find it. Allison is well aware of this, but it does not stop her from being upset. She looks for her phone, and when she sees it, she sends a text to Brian, **CUT.** Allison waits for a response from Brian, and when she doesn't get one, she is even angrier and throws her phone. Unbeknownst to her, when she threw the phone, it dialed Brian's phone by accident.

RING. RING.

The sound of Brian's phone ringing wakes him up. When he looks at it and sees that it is Allison, he doesn't answer because Stacey is next to him. He closes his eyes and pretends to be asleep. Stacey, however, is awake and sees that his phone is ringing.

"Babe. Babe, your phone," Stacey says, shaking Brian to wake him up and answer his phone.

Brian lifts his head off the pillow and says, "Hmm, let it go to voice mail. If it's important, they'll call back." He puts his head back down as if he is going back to sleep, but he is wondering why Allison is calling.

"Well, you want me to get it?" Stacey asks.

"No!" Brian yells.

"What the hell is wrong with you?" Stacey asks, moving away from Brian in the bed.

"Nothing. I just don't want to be bothered right now," Brian says with his back still turned to Stacey.

Stacey wants to know why Brian has an attitude. He told her he didn't want to be bothered, but she wasn't ready to leave it alone. "Well, there's only a couple of people it could be. What if it's an emergency?" she says, still probing Brian.

"Stacey, damn! Enough about the got damn phone!" Brian shouts.

"Ok! Whatever! But you don't have to talk to me like that!" Stacey shouts back, and Brian immediately feels terrible about how he yelled at his wife.

"You're right. I'm sorry," Brian says, softening his tone.

Deciding to let it go and forgive Brian, Stacey says, "It's ok, babe. I'm about to go downstairs and make breakfast. You want something to eat?"

Brian looks at her with a smile. With all that was going on between them, he still admires his wife. "Sure," he says.

Stacey goes downstairs and prepares breakfast. As she walks past Brian to leave the room, he reaches out and slaps her on the ass.

"That's gonna cost you!" she says, holding her ass as if the slap from Brian is hurting.

"I bet it is," he smiles as he responds to her.

Once Stacey walks out of the room, Brian immediately looks at the phone and returns a text to Allison, saying, **My wife is here.**

When Allison receives Brian's text, she responds, **So**. Brian looks at the text, shakes his head, and thinks, *Damn, she is tripping.*

What's wrong with you? Brian texts.

Why is it that whenever I want to talk to you, I can't?

Brian responds and says, **Get a hold of yourself and think about what you're saying. You know I'm married, and you are too.**

So, Allison replies.

Ok, I don't know what's wrong with you, but I'ma talk to you later.

Allison reads the text, then throws her phone. She is already frustrated with her home situation, and now she is frustrated that Brian is unavailable to her. She sits there with a million thoughts racing through her mind, from Winston to Brian, then from Brian to Winston. She has no idea what to do about her crazy life. She decides she needs some retail therapy to clear her mind. *Where is my phone?* She thinks to herself, remembering that she had just thrown it across the room. She finds it on the floor in the corner and calls her girls to see if they are available to go shopping. They all accept her invitation and decide to meet at the mall in an hour.

Brian deletes all the text messages on his phone, then sits and wonders what is next. He always prided himself on being focused and living a decent life. That's how he got his job and his wife. But right now, he is really confused and unsure. This isn't sitting well with his spirit. *What have I done? What have I gotten myself into?* Brian thinks to himself as he sits seemingly in a daze.

Once he realizes that he has been sitting in the same spot pondering for over thirty minutes, he gets up. He needs to make himself useful and do something that will take his mind off his chaotic life, at least for a little while. He looks around the bedroom to see if there is anything that needs to be fixed, but to his dismay, everything is in perfect order. He goes downstairs to see if anything needs to be done, but Stacey has beaten him to it. The kitchen is clean. The laundry is done. Even the bathrooms are clean.

He stands in the kitchen, looking out the window, and notices his yard looks like a mess. *This drama-filled life of mine must have blinded me because there is no way I let my yard get out of control like this,* Brian says to himself, then runs upstairs, gets dressed, and goes outside to tackle his yard. He spends all day mowing the lawn, cutting shrubbery and leaves off the bushes, pulling weeds, and watering the lawn. At the end of the day, his yard is picture-perfect. He is surprised the neighborhood Homeowner's Association hadn't knocked on his door, threatening to fine him if he didn't take care of it.

Brian stands in his yard for a few moments and admires his work. Then, realizing he'd taken a beating while working in the sun all day, he put his lawn equipment back into the shed in the backyard and headed into the house. Brian grabs a bottle of water from the refrigerator, goes upstairs straight to the bathroom, and hops in the shower. Once he finishes his shower, he gets in bed and falls fast asleep.

14

The following day, Brian wakes up and, without thinking about it, grabs his phone to see if Allison has called or texted, but she hasn't. He feels sad that he hasn't heard from her, especially since it had become their ritual to talk in the morning, but he shakes it off. He gets up, gets dressed, and heads to work. On his ride to work, he tries not to think about Allison, but the more he tries not to, the more he thinks about her. *Why can't I shake this woman? What has she done to me?* He asks himself.

He pulls into the parking lot of his job and shuts his car off. He picks his phone up and dials Allison to apologize. The phone goes straight to Allison's voicemail. *Oh well,* Brian thinks to himself, *I guess it's over.* Unbeknownst to him, Allison didn't charge her phone the night before, so it was dead.

Allison sits at her desk, disappointed in herself that she had acted out of character with Brian. She knows she only did so because she had developed strong feelings for him. *I know you really like him, Allison, but you gotta learn how to keep your cool! You can never let him see you sweat!* She gives herself a pep talk. She sits at her desk for a while, seemingly in a daze. She plugs her phone into the charger, sits it on her desk, then walks over to Karen's cubicle.

"Hey girl," Allison says to Karen as she approaches her cubicle.

"Hey," Karen responds.

"How're things?"

"I'm good. What's going on with you?" Karen asks.

"Nothing much."

"Ok, bitch. What's really going on? You're acting strange," Karen says, looking at Allison as if she is looking through her.

"Well, have you spoken to your brother?"

"No. Why? Is there something I need to know?"

"No," Allison says. Allison is nervous and regrets that she had walked over to Karen's cubicle. Karen continually told her to keep it friendly with her brother, but Allison hadn't listened. Now she is walking around, unfocused and confused because she didn't listen.

"No, what?" Karen asks Allison.

"No, no concerns."

"Well, for you to come ask me about him tells me something is up. Hold on. Come outside with me. We need to talk."

Karen and Allison walked to a sitting area outside their building and discussed their weekend. Allison is hesitant about filling Karen in but decides to tell her everything that has happened and what didn't happen. When Allison finally finishes talking, Karen shakes her head and says, "Girl, that is TMI."

"I know, Karen. I really didn't want to tell you because you kept telling me to keep it friendly with your brother, but you're the only one I can talk to right now. Just think of it as me telling you about a regular guy, not your brother, and maybe that will help you to look at the situation differently."

"That sounds good, but unfortunately, I can't think of it as a regular guy because you *are* talking about my brother," Karen says, still shaking her head.

"I knowwwww Karen," Allison says, looking down at the ground, feeling unable to lift her head. "I don't know what to do or where to go from here."

"Well, my brother is very understanding, and I know he's not gonna hold this against you."

Allison finally lifts her head and looks at Karen with a feeling of hope. "So, what should I do?"

"Call him, fool. What else?" Karen answers.

"Ok, but what do I say?"

"Just be honest and tell him how you feel."

"Ok, we'll see how that goes," Allison says, feeling somewhat better. But she knows that she is not going to feel completely better until she is able to hear Brian's voice. Karen and Allison walk back into the office, and Allison decides to do some work. She had been thinking about Brian all morning, and once lunchtime arrived, she decided to call him. She takes the phone off the charger and dials his number. It goes straight to voice mail. Allison is upset and begins to cry. Karen looks up from her desk towards Allison's desk and notices something is wrong with her, so she gets up, walks over to her cube, and sees her in tears. "What's wrong, Allison?"

"I did what you said, and I got his voice mail. He always answers his phone when I call him on our break. I think I've messed up, Karen," Allison says, then bursts out crying even more.

Karen walks around Allison's desk, then hugs her and says, "No, you haven't messed up. Everything is going to be ok. Hold on, let me get my phone and call him." Karen calls Brian and puts the phone on speaker so Allison can hear. Just as when Allison called him, it went straight to voice mail.

"See? He's not sending you to voice mail. His phone is probably dead, just like yours was. Girl, relax," Karen says, trying to make Allison feel better about the situation. Once again, Allison felt a little better but would still not feel her best until she could talk to Brian.

"Ok, girl. It was just a coincidence. Thanks for making me feel better," Allison says with a small smile.

"You're welcome, girl. Can we please get some work done before it's time to clock out?" Karen says, walking from behind Allison's desk. They both laugh. She turns to Allison and says, "And get it together. You know how these bitches in here are. If you don't want them questioning you, clean your face."

Allison takes a moment to get herself together, then puts some music on her computer and dives into her work with Brian still on her mind. It was quitting time, finally, and Allison couldn't wait to get to her car and call Brian again. She grabs her phone and hits redial, but again, it goes straight to his voicemail. She immediately hangs up and calls Karen.

"Hey girl, wassup?"

"Karen! Brian's phone is still going straight to voice mail! I think he has me blocked!" Allison says with great frustration.

"Blocked? Nah, he wouldn't block you. Hold up, let me call him and see if he answers."

Karen dialed Brian's number, and just like Allison, it went straight to voice mail again. Karen ends the call with Brian, then calls Allison back. Allison answers on the first ring. "Did you talk to him?"

"No, girl, it went straight to voice mail," Karen responds.

Allison feels as if she is about to panic. "Karen, do you think something is wrong? Why isn't he answering his phone?"

"No, Allison, nothing is wrong. He probably doesn't have his charger, and his phone is still dead. Just give it some time. He will reach out."

They both hang up and head home. Meanwhile, Brian gets off work and walks to his car. Before he pulls out of the parking lot, he pulls his phone out of his pocket and connects it to his car charger. He forgot his wall charger, so his phone had been dead all day at work. Once he plugs the phone up, he powers it on, and it begins to chirp with voice mail and text messages. After he reviews his messages, he sees that Karen has called, so he returns her call.

"Hey, Sis," Brian says when Karen answers her phone.

"Hey, little brother. Are you good?"

"Yes, I'm good. Why do you ask?"

"I've been calling you, and your phone has been going straight to voice mail," Karen replies.

"Yeah, I left my charger home, so my phone has been dead all day. I'm just getting off, and I plugged it into my car charger and turned it on."

"Oh, ok. Well, I'm not the only one who's been calling you."

"Oh, really?"

"Your new friend is hurt. She thinks you're mad at her, and you're no longer interested in her."

"What? Nooooo, that's not the case," Brian says as he explains the situation.

"Does either of you have any couth?" Karen asks.

"Couth? What do you mean?" Brian asks with confusion.

Karen giggle and says, "You and Allison are meant for each other. Both of you are crazy and crazy about each other. Just call her, please."

"Ok, Sis, I will. Love you," Brian says, then ends the call.

As soon as he hangs up with Karen, Brian calls Allison.

Allison is driving home from work, listening to music, and trying to think of anything other than Brian when her phone rings. She is overjoyed when she sees that it is Brian calling. "Hello? Brian?" she answers.

"Hey, Allison. I am so sorry. Do you forgive me?" Brian says, skipping the formalities.

"Of course, I do," Allison replies with relief, then continues, "I don't know what's come over me. I know I was wrong, but I just couldn't help myself. I think…I think I'm falling in love with you." There is a brief silence on the phone.

"Hello? Hello?" Allison says, then looks at the phone to see if the call disconnected.

"I'm here," Brian finally gets the lump out of his throat and responds.

"Did you hear what I said?"

"Yes, I did."

"Ok, so no response? No comment? Nothing?"

"I'm just a little shocked because I thought after my little issue you wouldn't wanna have anything else to do with me."

"No, no babe. That issue is not enough to make me walk away from you. I understand that the time wasn't right. I know that things happen, but I'm patient. I'm not going anywhere."

Brian, not believing what he is hearing, smiles and lets out a sigh of relief. Before he can respond to Allison, his phone beeps, it is his friend that he had asked to follow his wife.

"Babe, can you hold on for a moment?"

"Sure," Allison responds.

Brian clicks over to the other line and answers the call.

"Hello?"

"Yes, my dude. I got some info for you."

"Well, is it favorable?" Brian asks, not sure if he really wants to hear the news.

"Depends on how you look at it."

"Ok, tell me more," Brian says.

"Well, let me say this. Your hunch was right."

Brian is outraged. "Ok, when can I meet you? Not at my house though."

"I'm on your dime."

"Ok, let me get settled and I'll meet up with you tonight. Be looking for a text from me," Brian says and ends the call. He clicks back over to Allison.

"I apologize babe. It was work."

That's ok. I understand. See, I told you I was patient."

"Yes, you did." Brian is so distracted by the info he just received about his wife that he cannot concentrate on the conversation he is having with Allison. "Babe, I'ma call you a little later. I have a couple of things I need to take care of this evening, but I promise I will call you tonight."

Allison can hear the anxiety in Brian's voice and grows concerned. "Ok babe," she says, "Is everything ok?"

"Yeah. Everything is fine, just fine," Brian responds, ready to flip at the thought of finding out that Stacey really is cheating on him.

"Ok then. I'll talk to you later," Allison says, and they end the call.

Brian races home with all kinds of crazy thoughts running through his head. *Just calm down, Brian. You haven't even talked to him and gotten the news yet. It may not be as bad as you're thinking it is.* Brian thinks to himself as he tries to calm himself down. He pulls into the driveway of his house, and as usual, Stacey isn't home. He walks into the house, goes straight upstairs, takes a shower, and spends a little time with the kids. After about an hour, he texts his P.I. friend, Rodney**. I can meet you at 8 p.m. at Riverside Park.**

Ok, that's fine.

Shortly after, Brian gets ready to leave, and just as he is walking out of the house, Stacey walks in. Brian looks at her with disgust. Stacey notices the weird look on his face and asks, "Is something wrong?"

Without taking his eyes off of her, Brian responds, "I'm about to see."

"What does that mean?"

"Nothing," Brian says as he continues to walk out the door. He gets in his car, but before he starts it, he takes a moment to wind down because he can feel himself getting worked up again. After about a minute, he starts the car, pulls out of the driveway, and races to the park. What is normally a 20-minute drive seems to take 5 minutes, as fast as he is driving. When he arrives at the park, Rodney is already waiting for him. Brian walks over to the bench where Rodney is seated. His mind is overloaded, wondering what the evidence will reveal.

"Well, Bro, there is no easy way to say this, so I'ma just let you see for yourself," Rodney says to Brian as he hands him the folder. As Brian looks through the photos, he quickly realizes Stacey is still up to her old tricks. There are pictures of her kissing, hugging, and even going into a house with a guy. He keeps looking at the pictures thinking that he knows the guy. Then, as he starts looking even closer, he realizes that this guy had been to his house in the past. When he came, he had a female with him, obviously to throw Brian off so he wouldn't think he was really there to see Stacey.

"That motherfucker!" Brian shouts. "This nigga has been in my house once before at one of our cookouts," he says and stands up from the bench he and Rodney are sitting on. He stood in one spot for several seconds, seemingly in a daze, then turned to Rodney and said, "Ok, I've seen enough." Without saying another word, he walks toward his car, and he gestures the peace sign to Rodney. Brian gets in his car and speeds away with only one thought on his mind; to go home and beat the fool out of Stacey. But then he has another thought, an even better thought. He picks up his phone and texts **CUT** to Allison. He sits his phone on his lap with his mind still in heavy thought about what he just witnessed in the photos. He pretty much knew in his gut that Stacey was up to something, but actually seeing it with his eyes was a hard pill to swallow. *I got something for her ass. If you can't beat 'em, then join 'em,* Brian thinks to himself as he waits for a response from Allison.

Allison receives the text from Brian and immediately responds, **Hey babe. Yes, I can talk through text.** She knows something is wrong, and she wants to know what it is.

Brian: Can you get out?

Allison: Yes, for a little while. Why? Is everything ok?

Brian: Yes. I just need to see you.

Allison gets butterflies in her stomach at the thought of Brian needing her. She quickly texts back, **Ok. Where and when?**

Now, at the bar, Brian responds.

Twenty minutes, Allison replies.

Ok, see you there.

Allison is thrilled that she is getting ready to see Brian. She hadn't been able to get him off her mind. She jumps up, runs into the bathroom and freshens up, gets dressed, and rushes out of the house on her way to the bar. Brian waits outside for Allison. As she pulls into the parking lot, he walks to her car, puts his head in his hands, and begins to cry. When Allison sees the tears rolling down his face, she immediately gets out of her car and hugs him. "Babe, is everything ok? Talk to me," she says to Brian as she holds him with as much comfort as possible.

Still holding on to Allison, Brian says, "I finally got my confirmation."

"Confirmation? Confirmation of what, babe?"

Brian feels rage building up inside him as the images of what Rodney had just shown him reappear in his mind. He does not want to be aggressive with Allison, so he breaks the hug between them before he speaks again. "My wife. That fucking bitch!"

"What?" Allison asks, looking directly at Brian.

"That fucking bitch has been cheating on me all this time. Now, I have proof."

Allison is stunned. After a few seconds, she is able to ask, "Wait? What? How?"

"I had a friend of mine to do some P.I. work and he got me all the proof I needed."

"So, what are you gonna do now that you have proof?"

"I really don't know," Brian says, looking directly into Allison's eyes, and her beauty almost takes his breath away. Without taking his eyes off her, he says, "You know what? I'm here with you, and you're all I wanna think about right now."

Allison blushes, "Ok babe. That is fine with me. So, what do you wanna do?"

"Hold on one second," Brian says to Allison, then pulls out his phone and calls Karen.

"Hey, Sis. What you doing?"

"I'm out with Mommy. Why?" Karen answers.

"Do the keys that you gave me still work?"

"Which keys?" Karen asks, feeling confused.

"The house keys, silly. What other keys would I be asking you about?"

"Ohhhh! Yeah, they're good."

"Listen, me and Allison are gonna go over there and chill for a minute."

"Ok, no problem. Just clean up when you're done," Karen says with a cheerful voice.

"Ok, gotcha," Brian says and ends the call. Brian and Allison get in their cars and make a B-line to Karen's place. She has a two-bedroom townhouse all to herself, so it is the perfect place for them to chill for the moment.

They walk into Karen's house, and Brian wastes no time. He pushes Allison against the wall and kisses her passionately. At first, Allison feels a little shell shocked by what is happening but quickly shakes it off as Brian starts to undress her. When he pulls her pants down, he parts her legs and begins to finger her softly and seductively. Allison, now completely turned on, moans softly as her pussy juice slides loosely through Brian's fingers. To his surprise, Allison is even wetter than she was on the first night they attempted to be together. He did not want to think about that night because he did not want to mess up the blood flow that was currently rushing to his pipe. He unzips his pants. His dick is so hard that it feels as if it is trying to bust through his underwear.

He pulls his pants and underwear down and just before he pushes it into Allison's secret garden, he is limp again. "OMG!!! I know this is not happening again!" Brian shouts, beyond frustrated all over again. But before he concedes defeat for a second time, Allison, without saying a word, puts her finger up to her lip and motions for Brian to be quiet.

Brian immediately calms down as she pushes him down on the recliner, then gets down on her knees and gently massages his dick with her hands. Unlike the last time, Brian immediately feels a sensation that makes his dick respond to Allison. Feeling his dick begin to grow in her hand, she leans down and begins to lick the tip. She went from licking Brian's dick to taking it into her mouth and sucking it as she lightly massaged his balls. Brian moans with pleasure. Now his dick is rock hard, and before he has a chance to lose it again, Allison stands up off the floor and straddles him. She slowly lowers herself on his dick and raises her head in complete satisfaction with the piece of meat that she'd been waiting to feel inside her.

"Oh yes, Daddy. I've been waiting for this. Oh this dick is good. Oh my God! Damn!" Allison is overwhelmed with pleasure as she bounces up and down on Brian. After about 5 minutes, Brian stands up from the recliner and walks to the bedroom with Allison still on top of him and his dick still inside her. Once they are in the bedroom, he lays Allison down across the bed and parts her legs wide so he can look at her pussy. He takes his fingers and pulls her lips apart, exposing her swollen clit. Without a second thought, he takes her clit in his mouth and fucks it with his tongue as Allison moans in pleasure.

"Oh shit, I'm about to cum, baby! I'm about to cum," Allison moans out to Brian. And just as she is about to explode, Brian leans up, pushes his man inside her, and fucks her like there is no tomorrow. After a thirty-minute session, Brian collapses on top of Allison, and they both lie there in total satisfaction, drenching in sweat. After about 10 minutes of silence and heavy breathing, Allison realized they did not use a condom.

"Oh my God! Did you…" Allison starts but is unable to complete her question.

"Did I what?" Brian leans up, looks down at Allison, and asks, already knowing where the conversation is going.

"Did you cum in me? Please tell me, for both our sakes, you didn't because I'm fertile Myrtle when it comes to getting pregnant."

Brian rolled off of Allison and then said, "I did."

Allison's heart hits the floor. "Oh my God! Oh my God! Nooooo!"

"Babe relax," Brian says, trying to play down the situation in an attempt to calm Allison.

"I can't relax! Take me to the nearest store. I need to get the morning after pill or something."

"Babe, calm down. Did you forget about the conversation we had about this? I've had a vasectomy, remember?"

Allison gets off the bed and looks down at Brian, who is now lying on his back, looking at her with a smirk on his face.

"Ohhhhh, that's right! Woooo!" Allison says with a sigh of relief.

It was now 10:45 p.m., and both Brian and Allison knew they had to get home before they had to answer questions that neither one of them wanted to answer.

"Babe, this was great, but I gotta get home," Allison says.

"Yeah, me too." Brian gets up and walks to the linen closet to retrieve a rag and some alcohol.

"Umm, what's the alcohol for?" Allison asks.

"It's for me," Brian replies.

"Why do you need alcohol?"

"I'ma use it to freshen up."

"Hold on, what are you trying to say?"

"What do you mean?"

"I mean, is my pussy stink or something?"

"No babe. Soap isn't gonna clear up everything that we've just done, but alcohol will."

Allison stares at Brian with a lost look on her face. "You don't believe me? Let me show you." Brian pours some alcohol into his hand. He wipes it around his penis and below his nut sack. He bounces around, wets his rag with hot water, wipes it over his private parts, and lets them air dry.

"Give me your hand," Brian instructs Allison. She puts her hand in Brian's, and he guides it down to his dick. "Now, run your hand through my nuts and then smell your hand."

"I don't smell anything," Allison says.

"See? I told you," Brian says proudly. "Alcohol will remove any fragrance from your body and hot water will bring your natural body odor back."

Allison takes a few steps back from Brian and asks, "So, why are you so familiar with this method? Hmmm? Who else have you been sleeping with?"

"No one, I swear. I learned this method a long time ago."

"So, now I have to watch out for your slick ass," Allison says, rolling her eyes at Brian.

Brian pulls her into his arms and says, "No babe. If I'm happy with you, then it's only you. I promise. But, at the same time, if Stacey decides to try her little P.I. work on me, I'm covered."

Allison, enjoying how Brian's arms are feeling around her body, softens up and says, "Ok then." Against her will and not wanting to leave the sweet embrace from Brian, Allison goes into the bathroom to freshen up. She calls out to Brian, "Hey babe, your clean up trick should work on me too. Maybe I should try it."

"Nooooo! No! Don't!" Brian shouts.

Allison peeked out of the bathroom and asked, "Why are you yelling?"

"Sorry babe, but that "clean up" trick is not for you."

"I know, silly. I was joking. I'm not trying to get a yeast infection or anything else for that matter," Allison says. She walks back into the bathroom and yells, "We have tricks too, you know."

Brian is intrigued by that statement and says, "Oh yeah? Like what?"

Allison peeked out of the bathroom and said, "A good girl never tells." Then she winks her eye at Brian, and they laugh. Allison finishes getting dressed, and they straighten the place back up.

"Ok, let's get outta here," Brian says as they exit Karen's humble abode. Once they are in their cars, Brian calls Allison, and they talk on the ride home. Brian reaches his home a little before Allison, so he ends the call by telling Allison that he had a wonderful time with her and can't wait to see her again. Allison lovingly reciprocates the feelings to Brian.

"Goodnight babe," Brian says.

"Goodnight," Allison responds and ends the call.

15

Brian pulls into his driveway and takes a few moments to gather before entering the house. By now, it was almost 11:30 p.m. When Brian enters the bedroom, Stacey is sitting in the bed with an angry facial expression. Before he can greet her, she asks, “Who’s the bitch?”

Brian stops in his tracks, looks at Stacey, and says, “What?”

“You heard me! Who’s the bitch? You think you’re slick, but I know you’re fucking around, or you’re about to,” Stacey shouts with fire in her eyes.

“Whatever, Stacey. If you think I’m out there fucking around, then prove it, otherwise, don’t accuse me of shit.”

“Oh, I will prove it! You best believe that!”

“Girl, you’re crazy! You leave this house whenever you want, going God knows where, doing God knows what, with God knows who, and as soon as I go somewhere, I’m with someone else. Get outta here!” Brian says dismissively as he walks towards the bathroom. He stops and turns back around to Stacey. “So, Stacey, tell me, who are you fucking?” Brian glares at Stacey directly in her eyes and can tell his question throws her off.

“Who am I fucking? What the hell do you mean, who am I fucking? I ain’t fucking nobody!” Stacey yells, highly offended that he asked her that question.

Brian keeps his cool and says, “Oh, really?”

“Yeah, really! I ain’t fucking nobody! I go to the gym and work out, and—”

“And? What else?” Brian asks, cutting her off.

“There is nothing else! That’s it!”

Brian, still keeping his cool, calmly responds, “Ok.”

The idea of Brian being so laid back about the situation is driving Stacey crazy. Unable to let it go, she lashed out at him, “So, what are you saying, Brian? If you think I’m doing something, then prove it!”

Brian stands quietly with his eyes still on Stacey. He thinks about going to the car, getting the pictures, and spreading them all over the bed for Stacey but decides against it. He wants to gather more evidence to build an even stronger case against her. So instead, he says, “Forget it. Just forget it.” Then walks into the bathroom and closes the door.

On the other side of town, as Allison walks into her house, she and Winston pass each other like two ships in the night. Unlike Stacey, Winston does not give Allison a bit of grief about coming home so late because he is leaving as she is coming in. *What a joke*, Allison thinks.

“I’ll see you tomorrow,” Winston says as he rushes out of the house.

“Whatever,” Allison replies as she walks upstairs, straight to the bathroom. She turns the water on in the shower and removes her clothes. She looks at herself in the mirror and imagines how much better her life would be if she and Brian were together. She washes the makeup off her face and steps into the shower. The hot water flows over her body, and she thinks about her encounter with Brian. She remembers every place his hands had touched her. She remembers how he smelled, how his dick tasted in her mouth, and how he felt inside her melting pot. She shakes her head as she thinks about how good it felt and how wonderful their next session will be.

Hmm, that dick. I can’t get over that dick, she thinks to herself. It had been nearly a year since she had good sex, but now that she’d had it, she knew she’d been spoiled because she was yearning for more. After her shower, she gets in bed and sleeps like a baby for the rest of the night.

The following day, on their way to work, Brian and Allison have their usual morning call to each other. They enjoy talking and laughing with each other throughout their drive in. Allison walks into work with a smile on her face that even the devil cannot wipe away.

“Good morning, girl,” Allison says as she walks past Karen’s cubicle.

“Morning,” Karen replies as she watches Allison bounce past her.

She gets up from her cubicle and follows Allison to hers. "Umm, bitch. You're in a good mood today," Karen says with her hand on her hip.

Allison looks up with a huge smile and simply says, "Yep."

"Yep? Yep what?"

"Just yep," Allison says and smirks at the look on Karen's face.

"So, my brother called me and told me y'all were going to my place to chill," Karen says, still grilling Allison.

"Yes, we did, and girl your place is nice as hell! How the hell…who the hell helped you decorate it?"

"What you mean who helped me decorate it? I decorated my place! Me and only me!"

"Wow! I never envisioned your place to look like that. Not saying that I thought it would be trash, it's just that, umm, damn, it's really, really nice!"

"Umm, well, I don't know if that was a compliment or an insult," Karen says, unsure how to feel about what Allison said.

"Oh, stop it girl. It was definitely a compliment."

"Thanks, I guess," Karen says.

"No girl, really, it's a nice spot."

"So, umm, did you and my brother talk and clear the air?"

A devilish smile appears on Allison's face as she slyly responds, "Ohhhhhh yes, we did."

Karen takes a few steps back and gazes at Allison for a few moments, then says, "Hold on, bitch! Did y'all…"

Trying to look as if she doesn't know what Karen is talking about but doing a terrible job at it, Allison responds, "Ummmm, did we what?"

"I know good and well y'all didn't fuck in my house," Karen fusses, and Allison smiles. "You did! Bitch, really? In my house?"

"No! Who said that? Not me," Allison says with a straight face.

"Bitch, you ain't fooling nobody! It's written all over your face!"

Before Allison can continue with her lie, a delivery guy walks into the office with a dozen red and a dozen yellow roses and announces, "I have a delivery for Allison Fitzgerald."

"Hmmm, another delivery?" Karen says as they both look on in shock.

"I'm Allison Fitzgerald."

The delivery guy walks the roses to Allison's desk and places them down. She gives him a tip and thanks him. She stands there for a few moments admiring the beauty of the flowers. She leans in and smells them. Her heart is so overwhelmed as she pulls the card and opens it. The words,

thanks for being understanding, make Allison tear up. She feels so loved and appreciated.

"Aww, this is so sweet," Karen says, still admiring the beautiful roses.

"Mmm Hmm," is all that Allison can manage to get out as she is still really overwhelmed.

"So, now are you gonna tell me the truth?" Karen asks, letting Allison know that the flowers are a confirmation of what she already knew.

Allison looks at Karen and says, "There's nothing to say."

Karen rolls her eyes at Allison, "Oh ok. That's your story and you're sticking to it, right? Ok good. I don't wanna know your sexual escapades with my damn brother anyway. Yuck!"

Instead of responding to Karen's rant, Allison seems to drift off into another world. She is staring at one spot, her eyes become glassy, and she has a massive smile. Karen looks at her, trying to figure out what is going on. "Hellooooo, earth to Allison," Karen says as she snaps her fingers in Allison's face.

Without blinking her eyes, Allison says, "He's so sweet. He's everything I've always wanted in a man and in a relationship. He just makes me feel complete. I feel safe and I feel feelings with him that I don't feel with Winston."

"Damn, bitch. It sounds like you're in love!"

"Umm, maybe."

No, this bitch did not just say maybe! I told her ass not to let it get to this point with my brother. Damn, I shouldn't have introduced them, Karen thinks to herself. "Allison, have you forgotten that you are married? Remember what I said about you and my brother getting too close? About y'all just being friends and having some fun? What happened? Where did this love come from? Nooo! No mam!"

"Yes, I know what you said, Karen, but I can't help how I feel."

"Damn, I knew this was going to happen," Karen says, then stands directly in front of Allison. "Allison, look at me. I said this before, and I'ma say it again. Please be careful. I care about you, and I care about my brother, and I don't want either of you to get hurt, or worse, killed. People are crazy nowadays."

"Karen, Winston is not a killer."

"Girl, you never know what people will do when they're in love or infatuated with someone. Don't forget, Brian has a wife, too."

"And?"

"And? Don't ever take anyone for granted, Allison. I know you watch Lifetime with all those love-gone-wrong killer movies. And what about Snapped? Girl, that's some real shit! We see the tv episodes, but it happens all the time, and it happens right near us, but we take it for granted like it can't happen to us."

"I really don't think either of us will have to worry about anything like that," Allison says dismissively.

"Ok, Allison. Be careful."

"I will. But on another note, I can't wait 'til lunch time so I can reach out to him and thank him for my beautiful, beautiful flowers."

"Oh my god, she is sprung."

"Whatever," Allison says, then giggles.

"Yeah, ok. You just remember what I said. Be careful," Karen reminds Allison.

"Ok. Ok, Mama Karen. I will be careful. I promise." Allison watches the clock for the rest of her morning. She picks up her phone at precisely noon to dial Brian's number.

RING. RING.

Brian answers on the second ring. "Hey, you."

"Hey, my sexy man. I'm just calling to say thank you."

"Okkkkkk, what are you thanking me for?"

"Those beautiful flowers."

"What flowers?"

Allison sits back in her chair quietly and wonders if she has spoken too soon.

Brian notices her silence, starts laughing, and says, "I'm just kidding, babe. You're welcome. I was hoping they would make your morning special."

"Babe! Don't play with me like that! I thought I'd put my foot in my mouth!" They both laugh. "Aww babe, they have made my day extra special! The girls in the office are jealous, even your sister."

"Really? Karen saw them?"

"Yes, and she reminded me to be careful."

"Careful about what?"

"Our relationship. She reminded me of the show called Snapped. Do you watch that show?"

"I sure do."

"Well, she's concerned about us seeing each other and she feels that one of our counterparts could find out about us and snap."

"I don't see how they could snap when they both seem to be doing their own shit, so I see it as us leveling the playing field."

"Yeah, me too."

"So, what else is on your mind?" Brian asks.

"Nothing, but I'm missing you and your friend," Allison says.

"My friend?" asks Brian.

"Yeah, that mini bat in your pants that has my kitty cat throbbing and wanting more."

"Ohhhhhh, that friend," Brian says, blushing.

"When can we see each other again?" Allison asks, praying that he will say soon.

"Soon, babe. Very soon!" Brian says. "Stacey drilled the hell outta me last night," Brian continues.

"Really?"

"Yes. She asked me who I was fucking and told me I was being slick. Blah, blah, blah."

"Hmm, maybe your sister is right."

"About what?" Brian asks, wondering what Karen has said to Allison.

"Your wife."

"Stacey? Please. She's no killer. She's more like a roach when the light comes on. She's out!" Brian says, and they both laugh.

"Well, I'ma get back to work. I'll talk to you later, my sexy man."

"Ok," Brian replies while blushing from ear to ear.

As Allison goes on with her day, she gets a text from Anita, which reads, **call me when you get a free moment.**

Allison responds, **I sure will. I got some tea for you too.**

Anita responds, **Ok. Can't wait.**

At quitting time, the first person that Allison wants to call is Brian, but before she can call him, her phone starts vibrating. When she pulls it out of her bag, she smiles when she sees it is Brian. "Heyyyy, babe. I was just about to call you," she says, answering the phone.

"Well, now you don't have to because I've beat you to it," he says. They talk briefly then Allison's phone beeps, letting her know that another call is coming in. When she sees that it is Anita calling, she apologizes to Brian and explains that the other caller is Anita and she needs to speak to her.

"Ok, babe. I understand. Call me when you can. Better yet, text me when you can," Brian says.

"Ok, I will," Allison says, then switches the call from Brian to Anita.

"Hey, Nita. Girl!" Allison answers with enthusiasm.

"Hey girl. What's up?" Anita responds.

"Let me tell you, me and Brian, umm," Allison says, skipping the preliminaries and jumping right into the subject.

"You and Brian did the nasty? Girrrlll! Tell it!"

"Well, we kinda did and didn't."

"Kinda did and didn't? What the hell does that mean?" Anita asks in confusion.

"The first time, we tried, but it didn't work," Allison says, softening her voice as if she were embarrassed.

"It didn't work? Bitch no! He impotent?"

"No, I think he was scared."

"What you mean? Aww shit, he on the DL?"

"The DL? Oh, hellllll no! I think he was feeling guilty about having sex with me being that he and his wife are still together."

"Ohhhh, ok. Now I understand. Awwww, he's a keeper. Girl, if you and Winston don't iron out your differences, you better lock him down. Hell, it seems like he's half-trained."

They laugh.

"No, girl. He's a complete man and a gentleman. I can't think about anything or anyone else."

"Bitch, you're in love," Anita says with a big smile. She is happy for her friend.

"Nita, I think I am."

"Good for you. I'm glad, but where does all of this go from here?"

"That's the thing. I don't know. I really don't know," says Allison.

"Sooo, are we missing something?"

"Something like what?" Allison asks, trying to figure out what Anita is referring to.

"Bitch, did y'all ever fuck or what?"

"Well, we tried a second time, and he still couldn't get it up, so I decided to take matters into my own hands."

"Awwww, shit! That sounds juicy! Do tell!"

"I was determined that I was gonna experience his magic, so when he had his mishap this time, I sat him down in the chair, then got on my knees in front of him and went to work."

"Ooooooh, bitch! Tell me more!"

"Well, I pulled his penis out and started massaging it. As soon as I started, I felt it getting hard, so I went for the gusto and gave him head that made his eyes roll back in his head!"

"Yesssss, bitch! Yes!" Anita says excitedly into the phone. "And girl, he's not too big and he's not too small either. He's just right! That thing felt like a piece of vibrating metal in me. He had my kitty cat purring, even long after we'd finished. Winston hasn't made me feel like that in years."

"Damn, girl. I'm getting turned on just listening to you tell the story," Anita says.

"Umm, no. Change the channel. You don't need to get any visuals thinking about my dude," Allison says matter-of-factly.

"Ohhhh no, girl. I don't want your man. I'ma pull my electric man out and let him ease this tension."

"TMI, mam. TMI," Allison says to Anita.

"Oh, so you can tell me your whole x-rated story with your man straight out of Pornhub, but when I say something about my man, it's TMI," Anita says.

"Ok, ok. You're right," Allison responds, and they laugh. Allison pulls into her driveway. Winston isn't home. She heads to the bedroom, kicks her shoes off, sits down on the loveseat by their bedroom window, and gets comfortable. Anita is still on the line.

"So, what's his ultimate fantasy?"

"His ultimate fantasy? I don't know. I haven't asked yet," Allison says, kicking her feet up on the ottoman and looking out the window.

"Don't you think you should?"

"Ummmm, I guess. I'll get around to it sooner or later. Why?"

"Because you know you're a freak!"

"A freak? Who, me? Girllll shut up!" Allison says, and they laugh.

"Nah, but seriously, he seems like he's the type of guy that you can let your hair down with and be yourself. I am really happy for you, friend."

"Thanks, Nita."

"Girl, you know I got you," Anita says to Allison.

"Yes, friend, I know you do," Allison responds. Just then, she hears the alarm ding, letting her know the front door is open.

"Hold on a minute, girl. It sounds like someone is coming in."

As soon as the words left her mouth, Winston walked through the bedroom door. Without acknowledging Allison, he takes his jacket off, then his shirt, and heads straight into the bathroom. Allison notices the distinct smell that is in the air. When she realizes the smell is coming from Winston's shirt, she picks it up and tells Nita to hold on for a minute. She smelled the shirt, and it smelled of a woman's perfume. She also notices that Winston left his phone in his jacket pocket. "Nita," she whispers when she puts the phone back up to her ear.

"Yeah, girl."

"This mother fucker came in here smelling like some bitch and I got his phone."

"What? Where is he?"

"He's in the shower, probably trying to wash that bitch off him."

"Al, calm down."

"Nah, fuck that," Allison says, feeling herself about to erupt like a volcano. She swipes his phone and sees it is locked and needs a password. She tries several obvious passwords to unlock it, but none of them work. "Damn, Nita, this nigga got a password on his phone, and I can't figure out what it is to get in." Just then, she thinks of using her birthday. "Bam! Girl, I just used my birthday and that was it! I'm in!"

She goes straight to his call log to see who the last call was made to, and she sees the name Daniel repeatedly. She goes to his text messages and sees messages from Daniel. Not only text messages but nude pics of her breast, her clean shaved pussy, and her manicured fingernails, which held her pussy lips open, along with the words, **this is all yours, baby**. Allison immediately goes into a rage. "That mother fucking rassclout! I'ma kill him!"

"Allison! Allison!" Anita tries to calm her down.

"Stop it! Think about what you're doing!"

"No! No, Nita! This mother fucker has some nerve!" Allison yells.

"Al, listen to me. Don't fuck this up. You have to be smarter than him. Remember, you just had your night with Brian. Two wrongs don't make a right. And I'm not saying what you're doing is wrong or right, I'm not your judge, but he's doing what he's doing and now you're doing it too. I need you to be smart and think of your next move."

Before Allison can respond to Anita, she hears the shower stop. "Girl, hold on. Let me put Winston's phone back before he catches me with it," Allison says. She places the phone back in Winston's pocket. As he walks out of the bathroom, Allison listens to Nita's advice and doesn't say anything just yet. So, she sat back on the ottoman and looked out the window while she continued her conversation with Anita. "You're right, girl. I don't know what I was thinking," Allison says to Anita.

"Allison," Winston calls out. "Did you cook?"

"Hold on, Nita," Allison says, then puts the phone down and turns towards Winston.

"No, I didn't cook, so if you're hungry, you're on your own tonight."

"Damn. What a man gotta do for some food in this house."

Oh, no, the hell he didn't, Allison thinks to herself as she turns around to look out the window. She does not respond to Winston.

"What did he say? Anita asks.

Speaking almost in a whisper, Allison responds, "You're not gonna believe what the fuck he just said."

"Girl, what?" Anita asks.

"He had the fucking nerve to ask what he gotta do to get some food around here. Girl, this Boombaclout got my blood boiling. He's really trying me. I don't know how much more of this shit I can take."

"Girl, you have to remember that we are the smarter species. Stay right there for as long as you have to and save your money and his money. Then, when you have enough to bounce, leave and never look back."

"Yeah, you're right, Nita. You know you're like my good angel and my voice of reason, which I truly need. Otherwise, I probably would have killed this mother fucker in his sleep by now."

Nita started laughing and said, "Girl, I know. Stay cool and I'll talk to you later."

"Ok, girl," Allison says and ends the call. Once she hung up with Anita, Allison sat back on the ottoman and watched TV while Winston was downstairs cooking.

16

Allison picks up her phone and texts Brian **CUT.**

He immediately responds, **Hey babe.**

Allison: **What are you doing?**

Brian: **Going over travel arrangements.**

Allison: **Travel arrangements? Really? Where are you going?**

Brian: **A trip that Stacey and I booked a while ago.**

Allison is enraged and texts, **WTF!**

Brian: **Babe, don't act like that. We always take trips, despite our problems.**

Allison: **How the fuck can you make love to me and then go anywhere with that BITCH? Especially when you KNOW she's sleeping with someone else!**

Brian: **Allison, please don't do this.**

Allison: **Don't do what? Keep it real? I guess all I was to you was a new piece of pussy. I need to leave you alone.**

Brian: **Babe, stop.**

Allison: **Good night.**

Allison is so mad that she can hardly think straight. She turns her phone off and looks at the TV, but she has no idea what is playing because she is zoned out. Brian, not knowing that Allison turned her phone off, texts her back twice but gets no response. Winston returns to the room and notices something is wrong with Allison. "What's wrong with your face," he asks.

"Nothing," she responds dryly. "I was looking at this show on TV and I can't understand why a mother fucker who has a good woman at home, would fuck it up by fuckin' around with another bitch."

"Really?" Winston responds. "What's the name of that show?"

"I don't know. Something on Lifetime." She then looked up from the tv at Winston with a cold stare and said, "I see how people can get fucked up or even killed when they keep playing with someone's heart."

She looks at the TV and envisions getting a knife and stabbing Winston, especially after Brian had just hit her with the vacation shit with his no-good-ass wife.

"Do you need anything for the house?" Winston asks.

"No. We're good," Allison responded without taking her eyes off the TV.

"How about my girls?"

"They're good too."

Allison remembers the conversation she just had with Anita about saving money so she can bounce. "You know what, Winston? I almost forgot that the girls have been asking me about going back home."

"Oh ok, to see our parents?"

"Yes. You know it's been a while since they've seen them."

"No problem. How much do you need?"

"Enough to enjoy ourselves."

"Ok, will four be enough?"

"Yeah, that will be fine."

"Ok, it will be in your account first thing in the morning," Winston says, then walks into the bathroom. Allison thought getting the money would make her feel better, but it didn't. She gets up from the ottoman and gets in bed. Maybe she could sleep her mix of emotions off, and she will feel better in the morning. As soon as she lies down, Winston walks out of the bathroom, gets in the bed, and wraps his arms around Allison. He rubbed her inner and outer thighs, and before she knew it, she felt his dick brush against her leg. Allison looks up at the ceiling and thinks, *this nigga has a lot of nerve fucking some bitch, then coming back to me.*

Allison turns to him and says, "Get a condom."

"A condom? Where the fuck am I supposed to get that from? And why would I need one?"

"Winston, I'm not saying no, I just—"

"You just what?" Winston snaps, cutting her off.

"Nothing. Come on." Knowing that she is now taking a chance with her life and the uncertainty of losing her marriage, she decides to go ahead and honor her commitment to being a wife and have sex with Winston. Winston lies back while Allison leans on his chest and strokes his penis. As Winston's soldier stands at attention, all she can think about is Brian. She climbs on top of Winston and slowly rides his dick. As she moves her body back and forth, she closes her eyes and thinks about Brian. This dick didn't feel nearly the same. Nevertheless, the more she thinks about Brian, the harder she fucks Winston. Allison knows that if she keeps twirling her ass and bouncing up and down the way she is, Winston will nut, and this assignment will be over. However, she wants more. When she feels Winston is about to cum, she eases up and then drills his ass some more.

"Oh, yes! Yes! Oh my god, Brian."

Everything comes to a screeching halt! Winston pauses for a second, looking at Allison, who is so caught up in the moment that she does not even realize what she has done.

"What the fuck did you say?" Winston asks.

Still on top of Winston and clueless about what is happening, Allison says, "Huh?"

"Who the fuck is Brian?" Winston asks her as he grabs her waist and shoves her to the side. "Who the fuck is Brian?"

"Brian? You're tripping. I never said nothing about no Brian. What are you talking about, Winston?" Allison is terrified of what she has done but has to play it cool for her life's sake.

"Allison, I know what the fuck I heard, and you clearly just said Brian."

Still keeping her cool, Allison responds, "No I didn't. You're hearing things, babe."

She reaches over and begins to work her magic on him. "Come on, babe. Relax," she says as she pushes Winston back down on the bed and strokes his dick again. Just as fast as the argument had started, it ended. Allison has a special thing she does for Winston every once in a while. She would shake her ass like a G-String diva. It always does the trick. To ease his mind, she straddles him backward, and while looking back at him, she begins to bounce one ass cheek left to right, then down on his dick. It drives Winston crazy.

"Oh shit, babe. Yesss, bounce that ass. Bounce that ass," Winston moans.

Allison is in a zone, and before she knows it, Winston climaxes. She slows down but does not stop moving up and down on his creamed dick and says, "I know you're not done."

"What?"

"I know you're not done."

"Why? You didn't cum?"

"Umm, no, I didn't. So, now that you've started this, finish it," Allison demands, making Winston feel like he can go for round two. He gets up, retrieves a wash rag, cleans up his nut, pulls Allison to the edge of the bed, and kneels on the floor. He spreads her legs as wide as they can go and eats her pussy as she moans in complete satisfaction and busts in his mouth. He thought he was finished, but when his dick got hard as a rock again, he took advantage of his second wind. He stands up, pulls her to the edge of the bed, and pounds her pussy like a champ. When they finish, Allison takes a shower while Winston falls asleep.

The following day, Allison wakes up with Brian on her mind. She really wants to talk to him, but she is hesitant to call after he tells her about the vacation getaway that he had planned with his wife. On the other hand, Brian was thinking about Allison just as much as she was thinking about him and had no reservations about calling her to clear the air. He picks up his phone and dials her number. Allison hears her phone and sees that it is Brian. Her heart drops. She ponders if she should answer, only because she knows that their conversation could lead to an argument that they may not be able to come back from. The fear of losing Brian is imminent, and Allison isn't ready to imagine her life without him. Before she answers, she says a quick prayer and asks God to see her through her anger, frustration, and uncertainty. She answers, "Hey, babe."

"Hey, can we talk?" Brian asks.

Dreading what he is about to say, Allison responds, "Sure. What's on your mind?"

"Babe, I just want you to know I care about you a lot and I don't want to hurt you. I just thought we had an understanding about our situation."

"We do have an understanding, babe. I know we aren't doing right because of our situations, but Brian, I love you."

Brian pauses, not because of what Allison had just said, but because he feels the same way about her. "Babe," he says, trying to figure out how to tell Allison that he loves her too.

"Yes," she answers, anxiously wanting to know what he is about to say.

Those three little words felt feels a huge lump in Brian's throat. He tries to get them out of his mouth but can't. Instead, he says, "Let's talk later."

Let's talk later? I know good and damn well that's not all he has to say to me, Allison is screaming in her head. "Later?" Allison repeats.

"Yes, later," Brian confirms.

"So, you don't have time for me? You know what? Just forget it. Forget it!" Allison growls and hangs up on Brian.

"Damn!" Brian yells out. He knows he has to do something, and he has to do it quickly. He calls into work and informs his supervisor that he will not be in due to a family emergency. He calls Karen and gives her a heads up that he will stop by.

"Is everything ok?" Karen asks.

"I need to talk to Allison in private," Brian answered.

"Is there somewhere in your office that we can talk privately, without interruption, for twenty minutes or so?"

"Sure. The conference room," Karen says.

"Ok. I'll be there in fifteen minutes," Brian says and heads toward Allison and Karen's job.

Brian enters the office and is greeted by the receptionist. "Good morning, Officer. How may I help you?"

"Good morning. I'm here to see Allison Fitzgerald."

"One moment. Let me call her. It will be just a second," the receptionist informs Brian. "In the meantime, you can have a seat."

"No, I prefer to stand. Thank you," Brian states.

The receptionist is curious about why an officer is there to see her colleague. She dials Allison's extension, and when she answers, the receptionist announces, "Mrs. Fitzgerald, there is an Officer here to see you."

"A what?" Allison asks curiously.

"An Officer," the receptionist repeated.

"Ok, I'll be there shortly," Allison states to the receptionist, trying to sound cool, calm, and collected. She makes a B-line to Karen's cubicle. Karen looks up and sees the look of nervousness on Allison's face. "Girl, there's an Officer here to see me."

Karen keeps the secret to herself, knowing that the officer is her brother. "An Officer? Why would an Officer be here to see you?"

"I don't know!" Allison says, now looking more scared than nervous.

Karen gets up from her desk and says, "Well, there's only one way to find out. Come on." Allison nervously proceeds down the hall with Karen, only to be surprised by the sight of Brian standing at the door.

"Mrs. Fitzgerald," Brian says as soon as he sees Allison.

"Yes."

"May I have a word with you in private?"

"Yes. Come this way," Allison responds, not knowing what to expect as she turns and starts walking to Conference Room B with Brian right behind her.

"I'll make sure that no one bothers you," Karen says and winks at Brian as he walks past her.

As Allison and Brian walk through the hall to the conference room, all eyes are on them.

"Did the receptionist send out an email blast to the entire office letting everyone know that I'm here?" Brian whispers sarcastically to Allison. Allison snickers as she keeps walking but does not respond. When they make it to the conference room and walk in, Brian closes the door and locks it. He turns around, and Allison is standing in his face.

"What is the meaning of this? Why would you come here and embarrass me like this?"

Brian calmly says, "You know one thing that I've noticed about you?"

"What?"

"You talk too damn much!"

Allison looks at Brian in disbelief and responds, "I what?"

Without saying another word, Brian grabs her by her outer thighs, picks her up, and sets her on the conference table. Allison, with very little effort, pretends to put up a fight by lightly pushing him away. Brian then kisses her passionately, and she does not hesitate to return the kiss. Allison squeezes him tightly as he reaches up her skirt and pulls her panties down. Brian gently places her back on the table and proceeds to french kiss her pussy until there is no anger or fight left within her. Everything on the table flew as Allison moaned, forgetting where she was.

Karen is standing outside the door with her head down in her hand. She cannot believe she is hearing the sexual gratification that her brother gives her friend in the conference room at their place of employment. Several climaxes later, Allison and Brian emerge from the conference room, looking both calm and sneaky. Karen looks at them both in disbelief, shakes her head, and walks away. Allison smirks but keeps a straight face as she walks Brian to the door.

"Thank you so much for your time, Mrs. Fitzgerald. I'll be in touch," Brian says when they return to the front office. The receptionist is sitting with her eyes glued on the two of them.

"Ok, great. Thank you, Officer."

Brian walks out the door, and Allison nonchalantly walks back to her cubicle floating on Cloud 9. If she had any doubt, she knew for certain now that she loved Brian and wanted him. She is not only dickmatized, but she is tonguematized. *I can't believe he just turned me all the way out on the table in the conference room at my job!* Allison thinks as she smiles, still feeling that slimy, slippery sensation she felt in the conference room. She yearns for more of Brian. However, she knows she has to get to the bathroom and clean herself up.

After she cleans up, she calls Brian and thanks him for being such a great and understanding man. Brian assures her how much he cares about her, but he still cannot bring himself to tell her that he loves her. They continue to talk and enjoy their conversation as Brian drives toward his house. When he arrives home, he notices Stacey's car in the driveway. Not wanting to start World War III with Allison at the mention of Stacey's name, Brian tells her that he needs to make a call to his job and that he will call her back. Totally unaware of the real reason Brian is ending the call, Allison agrees, and they end the call.

Brian sits in his car for a moment wondering why Stacey is home so early. She isn't supposed to get off from work for another few hours. He gets out of the car and approaches the door in total silence. He figures if Stacey is on the phone or even entertaining someone in their home, he can sneak up on them. He puts his key in the door as quietly as he can and opens the door. When he walks into the house, he doesn't see or hear anything out of the ordinary. He goes to the bedroom, where he hears the shower running.

"Stacey," Brian calls out.

"Ummm, hmmm."

"What the fuck are you doing home?" he asks as he walks into the bathroom.

"Umm, I wasn't feeling well, so I left early," Stacey responds.

"You work in the hospital," Brian retorts.

"Yeah, and?"

"I don't get it. I really don't get it."

"You don't get what, Brian?"

"You don't feel well, so you leave a place that can cure you and come home," Brian says with a slick tone. By this time, Stacey had turned the water off, grabbed her towel, and stepped out of the shower.

"Did it ever occur to you that after a doctor has seen their patients, they go home? Stop being an asshole!"

"Asshole? Really?"

"Yes! Really! And let's switch gears here. What the fuck are you doing home so early?"

"Well, I umm."

"Mmmhmm, just like I thought. You're on some bullshit," Stacey says and walks past him into the bedroom.

Brian turns around, walks into the bedroom behind her, and says, "Listen, you know what? I'm not even gonna get into it with you. Whatever."

"No, you started this, so let's finish it," Stacey says, not letting up on Brian. She continues to press him about his whereabouts, but Brian remains calm and quiet. Several times he thought to bring out his evidence, but he held back because he wanted to get that dagger. He watches Stacey's mouth moving but is completely zoned out as he lets the bullshit she is speaking go in one ear and out the other. Once he had enough, he walked out of the room and downstairs to call his P.I. friend, Rodney, to see if he had any more information.

"Hey, man. Tell me something good," Brian says when Rodney answers the phone.

"Well, I'm actually on it as we speak. My tracker indicates that she is currently at your residence." Knowing Stacey is at home, Brian feels confident that Rodney is giving him accurate information.

"Ok, man. Thanks for the update," Brian says.

"No problem, man. I should have some more info in about a day or two. Is everything ok?" Rodney asks with concern.

"Yeah, yeah. I was just checking in," Brian confirms.

"Ok, I got some good updates and some bad, but I'll fill you in with everything," Rodney said.

"Ok. I'll wait," Brian says with a sardonic grin and ends the call. Brian sits in silence. Everything that is currently going on around him, from the argument he just had with Stacey to hearing Rodney tell him that he had more evidence to share of his wife's indiscretions. The only person he can think about is Allison. She is the only person he wants to think about at this moment. She is the only person he wants to be with. His phone rings as he continues in deep thought with a big smile. It's Karen. "Hey, Sis. How are you?"

"I'm good. Still feeling some kind of way about you and Allison today, though."

"Sis, don't be upset. I typically wouldn't have come to your job, but I really needed to see her. It couldn't wait," Brian says.

"Oh, I could tell it couldn't wait! I still can't believe the BS y'all pulled in that conference room. What were you thinking?"

"I know, Sis. No one in the office knows what happened besides you, right?"

"No, I'm the only one who has been traumatized by the events that took place today."

"I'm really sorry about that, but I have something I need to tell you."

"Yeah? What is it?"

"I'm in love," Brian says, hearing himself say it for the first time.

"You're in what?" Karen shouts, then looks around the office to ensure no one hears her.

"You heard me, Sis. I'm in love with Allison."

"Oh my God! No, Brian! This wasn't supposed to happen!" Karen says, feeling disappointed.

"I know, Sis. I know, but she is everything that Stacey isn't, and so much more."

"So, what are y'all gonna do?" Karen asks. She sees her supervisor walking in her direction and says, "Wait a minute. Don't say another word. Let's revisit this later when I get off from work. Come to my house around 6 or 7."

"Ok. Will do," Brian says, and they end the call.

Karen's workday couldn't end fast enough. After clocking out, she races home to hear all that Brian has to say about him and Allison. Brian shows up at her house around 6:30. As soon as he walks in, he sits down and gets straight to the point. Karen listens intently to everything he says and is shocked that his relationship with Allison has grown so deeply. She knows all the hell that he has been going through with Stacey. He has been frustrated about his marriage for a long time. She watches him talk about Allison and notices how jubilant and excited he is about her. She has not seen her brother like this in a long time, and it really makes her happy to see him so happy. At the same time, she wants him to proceed with caution. No matter how happy he feels with Allison, the fact is that he is still married, and so is she.

"Wow, little brother. It's been a long time since I've seen you smile this hard," Karen says as Brian's smile widens. "I truly want to see you happy, but I have to remind you not to forget your situation and Allison's. Please be careful, Brian."

"Come on, big Sis. You know I will definitely be watching my back, front, and side," Brian says to Karen, still smiling.

They visit a while longer before Brian leaves for home. He pulls into the driveway and is not surprised that Stacey's car isn't there. He walks into an empty house. He is surprised that the kids are not at home. His first thought is that something may have happened. His children are usually in the house when he gets home. Trying not to panic, he calls Stacey.

RING. RING.

"Yes, Brian. What is it?" Stacey asks when she answers the phone.

Damn, can I at least say why I'm calling before you serve all this attitude? Brian thinks to himself. "I just got home, and the kids aren't here. Are they with you?"

"No, I let them go to the neighbors' house while I'm at the gym. I will pick them up when I get back."

"The gym?" Brian asks.

"Yes, the gym. Did you forget that Planet Fitness is open 24hrs?"

"Hmm, yeah," Brian says as he scratches his head.

"Don't worry about them. I'm home. I'll get them."

"Ok. Do what you will," Stacey says, then hangs up abruptly.

Man, whatever, Brian thinks to himself as he leaves the house and walks next door to get the kids. After thanking the neighbors for their hospitality, Brian and the kids walk back home. When they get in the house, he sends them upstairs to take their showers while he cooks dinner. They eat, and he sends them to bed. He sits down on the couch and texts Allison, **CUT.**

She texted back, **No, but I can text.**

Brian knew her response meant that Winston was home. He also knows he must play it safe with the texts he sends her. He is sure to make the conversation Rated G. The Rated G text conversation is going good until Allison tells Brian that she is still tingling from the conference room encounter they had earlier that day. The temptation that he is fighting to keep the conversation Rated G is over, and Brian expresses to Allison how much he enjoys being with her. He lets her know how much he loves the excitement of being on the edge and how great the sex is. Spontaneously he texts the words. I **think I'm falling in love with you.**

Allison's mouth drops when she reads the words she longed to see, just as much as she longed to hear them be said. **You don't know how much I have wanted you to say those words to me, Brian, because I truly love you too.** This new revelation of how they feel about each other is the beginning of days, weeks, and months of their quietly kept escapades. Brian and Allison are growing so close. They both wonder why they couldn't have met before meeting their spouses. They spend so much time talking, laughing, and just enjoying their new love for each other. They both are receiving information, almost by the bag loads, about their spouses' extramarital affairs.

Information had gotten back to Brian's mom about Stacey, but she hadn't talked to Brian since their fallout when he was in the hospital, so she decided to remain quiet about what she'd heard. But, make no mistake, she wanted nothing more than to see an end to her son's marriage with Stacey. Karen continued to play the middleman and intervened whenever she could.

17

TWO YEARS LATER

Brian's children notice that their parent's relationship is falling apart. Allison is experiencing the same. This realization causes the children's grades to drop and makes them isolated, wanting to be by themselves. They begin to speak out about what they see and how it makes them feel. Brian definitely does not want his indiscretions to affect his kids. Allison also does not want her children to suffer for her choices.

Brian assures his kids that no matter what is going on in their marriage, they still love each of them and will always be there for them as their parents. Allison reinforces the same sentiments with her children. Separately, their marriages are going downhill fast. Verbal fights are getting close to being physical, and both couples know they have to do something. Separation is imminent.

The first to make a move is Brian. He moves to a home left to him when his grandparents died. Although it is nothing like the home he had made with his wife and kids, he knew this was the best decision for all parties involved, so he made the best of it. He and Allison continue to see each other discreetly. Brian hates being separated from his family, but he loves being with Allison. He still had not released the information he had collected on Stacey's extracurricular activities. In his mind, he is holding on to it for leverage if he needs it, when, or if that time ever came.

Brian keeps his promise and is active in his kids' lives as often as time allows. Stacey, who now has the freedom to come and go as she pleases, still has no clue about Brian's information from his P.I. friend. Rodney consistently updates Brian on the findings of his investigation into Stacey's activities away from home. He recently came upon some new findings. She is not just dealing with one guy anymore. She added another to her repertoire. And in between those two, she continued to offer sex to Brian. He usually turns her down, but for some strange reason, he still feels obligated to be with her. Every once in a while, he would bump her off, with a condom, of course. However, his rendezvous with Stacey was short-lived.

Brian's love for Allison had become so intense that the last time he tried to get a quickie from Stacey, he could not perform. Stacey thinks that Brian is getting older and is starting to lose it, but nothing could be further from the truth. He didn't see Stacey the same anymore, and the love was no longer there. Brian has everything he wants and needs in Allison.

Meanwhile, on the other side of town, Allison is dealing with her own issues when one of her girls becomes ill, and Winston is nowhere. One night, while getting ready for school the next day, Destiny starts complaining about a pain in her stomach. The pain quickly worsens, and Allison rushes her to the Emergency Room. On the way there, Allison calls Winston and receives no answer. She leaves a message on his voicemail to inform him of what is going on with their daughter.

Once at the Emergency Room, the doctor informs Allison that it is Destiny's appendix and that she must be admitted for surgery the following day. Allison panics. She fears everything that could go wrong when her daughter goes into surgery. She calls Winston repeatedly. No answer. Call after call and text after text. No response. Winston is missing in action, and Allison does not know what to do. One needs to be at the hospital with Destiny, and the other needs to be with Eleanor to ensure she gets to school the next day.

Allison stays with Destiny until she is admitted and checked into her room. The nursing staff administers medication to calm her and help her get some rest in preparation for her surgery. Once Destiny is asleep, Allison and Eleanor go home to try and get some rest. The house seems empty with Destiny at the hospital. Eleanor falls asleep as soon as her head hits the pillow.

On the other hand, Allison's attempts to get some rest are to no avail. She lies there looking at the ceiling while thinking about and praying for her baby. She keeps thinking, *what if Destiny wakes up and realizes she is alone in a cold, unfamiliar hospital room.* Allison sits straight up in the bed and calls the nurse's station on the floor where Destiny is on. The nurse assures her that Destiny has been sound asleep since she left. She appreciates that but is still devastated that her baby girl is alone in the hospital.

2 a.m., Allison is still wide awake when she hears Eleanor enter her bedroom. "Mommy, I can't sleep without Destiny. Can I get in bed with you?"

"Of course, baby girl. Come on in," Allison says, holding Eleanor in her arms for the rest of the night as she sleeps on her chest. The following day, Allison gets up and calls her job to let them know what is going on and that she will not be in the office. She calls Winston's job, only to find out that he has been out on vacation all week. *So, all fucking week, this nigga has been laid up with some bitch. What the hell am I gonna do?* Allison thinks to herself. Emotionally wrecked and confused, Allison picks up her phone and calls Anita.

RING. RING.

"Come on, come on. Please answer," Allison mutters.

"Hello," Anita answers.

"Anita, girl! I'm so damn scared! I don't know what to do!" Allison responds in a panic.

"Hold on, girl! Wait! What's going on?" Anita answers, now in a panic herself.

"It's Destiny. She's in the hospital about to have her appendix removed this morning and I can't find Winston. He's not answering his phone, so I called his job and nothing! Just nothing!" Allison responds nervously.

"Ok, ok. Calm down and just breathe, Allison. We're gonna get through this. Don't we always?" Anita asks, trying to reassure Allison that everything will be alright.

Allison pauses.

"Don't we?" Anita repeats.

"Yes," Allison responds weakly.

"Ok, so let's come up with a game plan. What do you need me to do?"

"Umm mmm, I can't think. I can't think!" Allison shouts, now walking around in circles in her bedroom.

"Ok, what would you have Winston do if he were there?"

"I would get him to make sure that Eleanor gets off to school and I would stay at the hospital with Destiny."

"Ok. Go ahead and get dressed, get Eleanor ready and I'm on the way to pick her up and take her to school. Do you need anything else?"

"Umm, no. Thank you so much, Nita. I don't know what I would do without you."

"Don't mention it. You're my sister for life and I will do whatever I can for you. You already know that, so cut it out, girl."

"Yes, I know. I love you," Allison says with tears streaming down her face.

"I love you, too. Now, stop crying and get off my phone. I'm on my way."

Allison hangs up with Anita and then calls Karen to inform her of what is going on and that she will be out of work. When Karen hangs up with Allison, she calls Brian and tells him about the situation. Without hesitation, Brian rushes to the hospital. When he arrives, he sees Allison in the hall pacing the floor.

"Babe. Babe, are you ok?" Brian asks as he walks up to Allison and hugs her. Allison is so happy to see Brian.

Allison has been an emotional wreck since Destiny left for the operating room. "Oh Brian, no, I am not ok. My baby. Oh my god, my baby," she tries to whisper.

Still holding Allison, Brian squeezes her even tighter and assures her that everything will be alright. Allison welcomes his embrace as she tucks her head in his chest and begins to cry. "My baby, Brian. My baby," she repeats as the tears flow from her eyes.

"It's ok, Allison. It's ok. Just let it out."

They stand in that position for a while as Allison purges her broken heart, with Brian patiently holding and encouraging her. Brian's presence and support help to calm her, and she pulls herself together. Her broken heart quickly turns into a heart of rage as she thinks about the fact that her daughter is in the middle of a medical crisis, and Winston is still missing in action. She lifts her head from Brian's chest and blurts, "That mother fucker!"

Brian, thrown off guard by her outburst, responded, "Hmmm?"

"I have been continually calling that mother fucker since last night, and he hasn't answered his phone or called me back, but I got a trick for that ass!" Allison stood there looking as if she had gone into a trance. She thinks about all the evidence she has collected over the years and how it is about to come full circle. When she is done with Winston's ass, he will need Kevlar to protect him from the massive onslaught he will endure. As she stands in that hospital waiting room, scheming revenge, the call that she'd been waiting on for hours comes through. Winston.

"Hello," she answers calmly, knowing she is getting ready to brutally slice him up in just a few moments.

"What is going on? Why are you blowing my phone up?" Winston asks, sounding irritated.

"I'm blowing your phone up because your daughter is here at the hospital having emergency surgery and you are MIA!" Allison shouts.

"Emergency surgery?" Winston yells. "What's wrong with my daughter? What's going on?"

"Destiny is having her appendix removed because it was about to rupture. I brought her here without any help from you and thankfully, the doctor caught it in time. So, don't waste your time worrying now. Everything is being taken care of now," Allison responds and then abruptly hangs up on Winston before he can say anything else. Brian, who is sitting quietly right next to Allison, knows that it is time to leave.

"Babe, I'm gonna head out before he gets here. But I will be just a phone call away if you need me," he says as he stands up from the chair.

"Thanks so much, babe. I really appreciate you being here," Allison says as she stands up. Brian kisses her on her forehead, tells her he loves her, and leaves the hospital. Allison watches him go with a slight smile on her face. His presence is just what she needed to comfort her during this difficult time. She really didn't want him to leave, but they had been extra careful with their relationship up until this point, and there was no need to fuck up now.

Unfortunately, things aren't going to get any better with Winston on his way to the hospital. She knows he is doing a sprint trying to get there, so she sits back down and gathers her thoughts as she anticipates his arrival.

"Allison! Allison! How is Destiny?" Winston asks as he nervously walks into the hospital.

Allison looks at Winston with fire in her eyes and says, "Had you answered your mother fucking phone, you'd know how she's doing."

Without saying anything, Winston gives Allison a look as if he didn't want to get into it with her.

"Who's the bitch, Winston?" All these years. All these mother fucking years, you've been playing me!"

"Playing you? What the hell are you talking about, Allison?"

"I'm not speaking French! You know exactly what the fuck I'm talking about! For years, you have had a whole other life, while I've been home playing wife. You really must think I'm a dumb bitch."

"What? Woman, all I do for this family, when do I have time to have another life?"

"All you do? All you fucking do is pay all the bills. I guess you figured that's how you could buy my silence."

"I don't know what you're taking about," Winston says dismissively.

"Oh, really?"

"Yes, really."

"Who the fuck is Daniel?" Allison asks, looking directly at Winston. She notices how his face is quickly going from dry to sweaty.

He stutters and says the obvious, "I don't know a Daniel."

Allison rolls her eyes, and before she can say anything else, the doctor approaches them. "Mrs. Fitzgerald, is everything ok over here?"

"Yes, sir. Everything is fine," Allison responds as she and Winston stand up to greet the doctor.

"Well, I just want to let you know that everything went well with surgery and your daughter is fine."

"Thank God!" Winston states. "Can we see her?"

"Are you Mr. Fitzgerald?" the doctor asks, turning his attention to Winston.

"Yes. Yes, I am."

"She's resting right now, Mr. Fitzgerald. You can go in, but she probably won't know you're there."

"That's fine, doctor. I just wanna see her."

"That will be fine. She's in Recovery Room 10."

"Thank you so much!" Allison says.

When the doctor walks away, Winston holds his hand out for Allison, but she pushes it away. He reaches out and tries to pull her close to him, and she refuses.

"Keep your hands off me," she says to him and walks off towards the recovery room with Winston following behind her. Allison opens the door and walks in. It is dark and cold. They both walk up to the bed. Destiny is lying still, sound asleep. Allison stands on one side of the bed holding Destiny's hand, and Winston is on the other side holding her other hand. The sight of the machines hooked up to Destiny is a bit much for Allison to witness, and she begins to cry.

"I'm sorry, baby. I'm so sorry," Allison says and kisses the top of Destiny's forehead and wipes the tears that had fallen on Destiny's face. Winston stares at Destiny and whispers, "Daddy's here, baby girl. Daddy's here."

Allison looks up at Winston and wishes she could make him disappear. She wonders what could have made her fall in love and have kids with a man who does not appreciate her. Inconsiderate bastard. She decides not to focus on Winston. She cannot afford to become stressed about her issues with him because her baby needs her. She turns her attention to Destiny and says a silent prayer as the tears begin to flow once again.

After being in the hospital for several days and showing signs of recovery, Destiny is released and sent home. Focusing on both of his girls and making sure that Destiny makes a full recovery, Winston stays around the house. He does not make any moves during this time that would cause Allison to be on his heels. However, letting his guard down, he makes a crucial mistake by leaving his phone out while he is showering. Allison sees the phone and takes full advantage of his negligence. When she picks the phone up, she retrieves detailed messages, as well as new photos of Winston and his female companion in some compromising positions. As she looks through the pictures, she is intensely frustrated because of the drama surrounding Winston and the women that he has been or is involved with.

All Allison wants is to leave, but because of her fear of not being able to survive on her own, she has to stay a little longer. She does not want her girls to miss out on the lifestyle that they are currently living when she leaves. Her objective is to get her income to a place where she can support herself and her girls without missing a beat. Now, she was on a mission to collect all the overwhelming evidence against Winston and feed it to a bloodthirsty lawyer. That crucial information would help her to clean Winston's pockets.

In the meantime, she still craves her American boy candy, which could do no wrong in her eyes. Feeling confident, Allison takes more chances that most would consider risky. However, she does not care because she is no longer in love with Winston. The sight of him makes her sick, and everything he does aggravates every fiber of her being. She continues to discreetly feed her appetite with her American boy toy.

18

One morning, while sitting at her desk at work, Allison texts Brian, and surprisingly, he is off from work for the day. Eager to take advantage of an opportunity to get a snack of human hard chocolate, Allison decides to go to Brian's house on her lunch break. When she arrives, he opens the front door wearing his boxer briefs and a wife beater. The pipe in his pants indicates clearly that he is ready to pile drive the softest place on earth. To his surprise, Allison has something else in mind. She wants to be in total control, so she pushes Brian against the wall and pulls his wife beater over his head.

"Damn, girl," Brian says, liking where this is going.

Allison remains silent as she rubs her hand over his washboard stomach, then kisses his nipple as she pushes his boxers down just enough to expose his chocolate pipe. She moves over to his other nipple and sucks on it as she takes his dick in her hand and strokes it. Brian is mesmerized as he places his head against the wall, closes his eyes, and moans softly.

Knowing she has Brian right where she wants him, Allison slowly moves down and gets on her knees with Brian's pipe in her face. She takes him in her mouth and sucks his dick like a kid with a lollipop. Allison's mouth felt like her pussy but with a lot more suction. She sucks his dick so well that Brian must stop her because he is about to bust. The only place he wants to bust is in her secret garden.

He takes control back from Allison, stands her up, then guides her to the sofa and lays her down. He pulls her legs apart, then gives her clit some much-needed attention with his lips and tongue. After Brian makes

Allison climax twice, she abruptly interrupts him and says, "No more, Daddy. Give me the dick."

"Your wish is my command, beautiful," Brian says, then pushes his hot pipe into Allison's garden as he sensually tongue kisses her. Allison is in pleasure heaven as she moans, "Oh my god. Oh my god, Brian. You feel so good inside me. Damn, I love you, baby. I love you so much."

Sensing that Allison is emotional, Brian wants nothing more than to show her that he loves her by making love to her body and her mind. Allison, however, realizes that once again, she told Brian that she loves him, and he did not respond. She pauses and pushes him up by his shoulders.

"Do you love me?" she asks, looking into his eyes.

"Yes, baby. You know I love you," Brian responds.

"Then why is it that when I tell you I love you, you don't respond?"

"Babe, I—"

"I, what?" Allison asks, cutting him off.

"I love you, Allison. I think about you every day, and no one else. I swear."

"Are you sure? It's easy to say you love me when you're in the middle of getting the goods. I hope you're talking from here," pointing at Brian's heart, "and not from here," pointing at Brian's dick that is still hard.

"No, babe. I know I've been a little laxed lately. The truth is, I'm scared."

"Scared? Of what, Brian?" Allison asks out of concern.

"Of what we're doing and where we're going," Brian admits.

"You don't think I think about that too?"

"Yes, I'm sure you do."

"You know what? I get it. I really do understand, but it's ok, babe. Everything is gonna work out," Allison says.

She pushes Brian off her and sits him down on the sofa. She straddles him and rides him like a horse in a rodeo. As she bounces up and down on his hard rod, the thought of her secret weapon that she uses on Winston comes to mind. She needs to know if her weapon only worked on Winston or if it would also work on Brian. She stands up, turns around, and slides down on the dick again. She looks back at Brian, leans forward, and puts her hands on the floor as she bounces her ass left to right and right to left.

"Ahh damn, baby. Oh shit. I love you, Allison."

Allison smiles and thinks to herself, in the words of Lil' Kim, *I got that ill na.* Moments later, she comes so hard that she loses her breath for a second. Brian climaxes right behind her. Allison collapses on top of Brian on the sofa and lies there for a few minutes before saying, "Babe, I need to go."

She gets up, walks to the bathroom, and freshens up. She gets dressed, kisses Brian, and says, "I'll call you later."

"Ok, babe," Brian says.

Allison returns to work like a bat out of hell. She does 90 m.p.h. and is still five minutes late. She tries to focus on work but is preoccupied with the love fest she just had with Brian. *Damn, that was the best 60 minutes of my life,* she thinks. Remembering how many times she climaxed causes her legs to shake, and her pussy starts throbbing. As she thought about how perfectly Brian had just deep stroked her and pounded her pussy, she crossed her legs tightly to stop her body from reacting, but it did not work. It is like crack, and she cannot shake the itch. *I have to stop this,* Allison thinks to herself. She closes her eyes and is seconds from touching herself when Karen walks up to her. "Umm, what the hell are you doing?"

Allison jumps as Karen's question interrupts her daydream. "Girl, my brother got you tripping. You are at work, or did you forget?"

Nodding her head, Allison responds, "Yeah. Oh yeah, I'm good."

"Well, I advise you to go clean yourself up before someone other than my nosy ass sees you and figures out what you're over here doing with yourself," Karen says, looking at Allison and shaking her head.

"What do you mean? I'm not doing anything."

Without saying anything else, Karen continues to shake her head and walks off. Allison does not think that what she is doing is obvious, but Karen has just proved otherwise. She is totally gone over Brian. She hasn't been back from lunch for an hour yet, and she already wants to call Brian to let him know how much she enjoyed herself. *Get yourself together, girl,* she thinks.

She signed into her computer in an attempt to do some work, but Brian was heavy on her brain. *Girl, go ahead and call this man,* she mumbles, then picks up her phone and dials his number. When Brian answers the phone, he is laughing.

"What's so funny?" Allison asks.

"You," Brian answers.

"What about me?"

"You haven't been back at work for 30 minutes and you're calling me already? Daddy put that thing on you."

Allison smiles and says, "Well, apparently it's written all over my face. Your sister just walked up to my desk and almost caught me getting ready to masturbate."

"She what?" Brian shouts.

"Yeah, you got my kitty cat purring and wanting more."

"Well, you can have it whenever you want it."

"I'ma hold you to that, Mister," Allison says with a massive smile. "On another note, we really need to talk and figure out what we're gonna do about our future."

"I know, babe," Brian responds, recognizing the change of tone in their conversation.

"It's just, you know…"

"Yeah, I know. The kids, our families…"

"Yeah," Allison interrupts quietly.

"Allison, I really do love you and I wanna be with you. I just want it to be right. I don't want another failed relationship."

"Neither do I, Brian. I love you and I can really see us enjoying each other for the rest of our lives."

"Damn, you got a crystal ball or what?"

"No, but I know what I want, and I believe you can provide it. Winston is a good provider, but you're the entire package. I want you and I need you, Brian. You're the one," Allison says lovingly.

Brian is in shock while listening to Allison express her needs and how she feels he could provide them for her, unlike Stacey, who never did anything but take from him. "Sweetie, I promise, we are gonna work on it. I'ma do whatever I need to do to make sure we are together."

"I'm damn sure gonna do what I have to do as well because I really want this," Allison replies. "Well, I'ma get back to work."

"Ok, babe. I'ma take a nap."

"Hmmm, looks like Momma put that thing on you," Allison chuckles.

They both laugh and end the call.

Later in the day, Allison checks her calendar and realizes it is almost time for her menstrual cycle. Normally, her body would give her warning signs that it was coming, but she hadn't received any signs. *I wonder why I haven't had any premenstrual symptoms. Well, my cycle should be here in the next two days, so we'll see*, Allison thinks. She had been very sexually active lately and hadn't used any birth control, but there was no possible way that she could be pregnant. Both Winston and Brian had vasectomies, or so she thought.

Three days pass, and she has not seen a drop of blood. Allison is now nervous, scared, and confused. She has no other choice but to call her lifeline, Anita. She always knows what to do.

RING. RING.

"Hey girl, what's going on? Is Destiny ok?" Anita asks when she answers.

"Oh yeah, she's ok. It's just..." Allison could hardly get her words out.

"Bitch, it's been a minute since we last talked, so what's up?"

"I think," Allison trails off. She is trying to release the words from her throat, but before she can, Anita blurts, "Oh, hell no! Bitch, I know you're not pregnant!"

"Umm, I don't know, Anita."

"What you mean you don't know? You're not using any protection with these niggas?"

"I didn't think I needed to. Both Winston and Brian are fixed."

"Fixed? What the hell?"

"Yeah, they both had vasectomies."

"Well, who the fuck else are you fucking?"

"Nobody," Allison answers, starting to feel more nervous because of Nita's questions.

"Well, have you taken a test?"

"No. I'm scared, Nita."

"Girl, I'm gonna need you to become unscared and... You know what? Never mind. I got it. I'll be over in 30 minutes," Anita says, then races to CVS to pick up a home pregnancy test.

When Anita gets to Allison's house, she meets her at the door.

"Girl, let's go," Anita says as she pushes Allison towards the bathroom.

Allison takes the test from Anita's hands, goes into the bathroom, and pees on the stick. When she finishes, she walks out of the bathroom and stands in the hall with Anita until the test is complete. Neither one of them say anything while waiting. Finally, when time is up, Allison looks at Anita and says, "Moment of truth." She walks into the bathroom. Seconds later, Allison walks back into the hall and calmly gives Anita the test. When Anita looks at the test, she sees two pink lines, which means the test is positive. Anita looks at Allison with her mouth wide open. Then she said, "Hold on, bitch. Drink some more water."

"Why?" Allison asks Anita in confusion.

"Because I bought two tests. Maybe this one is defective. Just take it again."

Allison runs into the kitchen and gets two bottles of water. She goes back into the hall with Anita and drinks them, one behind the other. Then they both sit on the floor in the hall and wait for Allison to get the urge to go. After about 20 minutes of talking, Allison gets up and takes the second test. After waiting for the test to complete, Anita walks into the bathroom for the results this time.

"Bitch! Double lines, again!" Anita shouts.

"Oh my god! Oh my god!" Allison yells and bursts into tears like she just lost her last meaningful dollar left on earth.

"How can this be?" she asks while holding her head in both hands.

"Are you sure Brian had a vasectomy?" Anita asks.

"That's what he said," Allison responds, trying to get herself together.

"Well, you need to call him and tell him what's going on. And you need to ask him again if he had that vasectomy, 'cause baby, we got a problem."

"You're saying I need to tell him I may be pregnant?"

"Yes, ma'am! You need to call him and you know what? Give me the got damn phone," Anita says and snatches the phone from Allison, who is visibly shaking.

RING. RING.

"Hello," Brian answers on the first ring.

"Hey Brian, this is Anita. I'm here with Allison and she has something to tell you."

Brian can tell by Anita's voice that something is wrong. Allison is very apprehensive about taking over the conversation with Brian, but she knows she has to because Anita has not given her any other choice. She takes the phone from Anita and says, "Babe, I'm pregnant."

Dead silence. After a few seconds, Allison says, "Babe, did you hear me?"

Shaking his head in disbelief, Brian responds and says, "What? How? Winston?"

"No, Winston had a vasectomy ten years ago."

"So, what are you telling me? You're fucking someone else?" Brian asks, trying to make this situation make sense.

"No! You know I'm not, Brian!" Allison cannot control her emotions any longer and begins to cry.

Anita snatches the phone from her and yells at Brian, "You insensitive bastard!"

"What? Anita wait a fucking minute! I've had a vasectomy and she just told me that Winston had one too, so how the fuck can she be pregnant?"

"I don't know, but y'all need to figure it out," Anita responds to

Brian.

"I don't need to figure shit out. Y'all running game, but I'm not stupid. Goodbye," Brian says, and before Anita can say anything else, he hangs up the phone.

"Oh no, that mother fucker didn't!" Anita says. She redials Brian's number, but Allison snatches the phone from her and says, "No, wait. I'ma call and make an appointment so I can get a definite answer."

Allison calls her OB/GYN and schedules an appointment for three days later. "Ok, so I have three days to find out if I really am pregnant or not, so let's just stay cool and take it easy until we know for sure," Allison says to Anita, trying to calm her down. She is just as upset about Brian's response as Anita is, but for now, she will try to keep it together until her appointment.

19

Time seems to stand still as Allison waits for her appointment day. She is on an emotional roller coaster because she does not know what to expect. All week she had done her best to avoid Winston. He did try to sneak a piece, but she was prepared. She armed herself with a maxi pad, so when he crept his hand between her legs, he felt the pad and left her alone. Right now, sex is the last thing on her mind, especially with him. Her mind is boggled with so many thoughts. Is she really pregnant? If so, is Winston the father? Or is Brian the father? If Winston were the father, what would that mean for their marriage? Too many questions and not enough answers.

Allison's appointment day arrives. She walks into the office and to the receptionist's desk. When she checks in, the receptionist gives her some paperwork. Allison fills the paperwork out and returns them to the receptionist. Allison sits with nervous anticipation. She looks around the waiting room and sees several pregnant women waiting to see the doctor. Her mind is going one hundred miles per minute. She pulls out her phone and scrolls social media to try and distract herself. She looks through her phone for about two minutes when the nurse opens the door and calls her name.

Allison nervously stands up and almost sprints to the examination room. The nurse takes her weight and her vitals, gives her a cup with her name and date of birth written on it, and instructs her to provide a urine sample. Allison fills the cup with urine, places it on the window in the bathroom, and returns to the examination room.

"Ok, Mrs. Fitzgerald, you can have a seat, and the doctor will be in to see you momentarily," the nurse states before she walks out of the room. A few minutes later, there is a light knock on the door, and then it opens.

"Mrs. Fitzgerald, how are you this afternoon?" the doctor asks once entering the room.

"I'm doing fine, doctor," Allison responds with her emotions all over the place.

"Well, you're here to find out if you are pregnant, correct?"

"Yes sir," Allison responds while nervously twiddling her thumbs.

"What makes you think that you're pregnant?" the doctor asks, sitting down on his stool and giving Allison his undivided attention.

"My menstrual cycle didn't come on this month," Allison says, wondering why the doctor is asking all these questions when she knows he already has the results of her pregnancy test in the folder he was holding. The doctor glances at Allison, then says, "Ok, I see that you've taken a pregnancy test, and I know you want to get to the results." He opens the folder and reviews the paperwork that is in it. "Mrs. Fitzgerald, it looks like you are definitely pregnant. Congratulations."

Allison stares straight ahead as if she were frozen and cannot move.

"Mrs. Fitzgerald," the doctor says.

Allison continues looking straight ahead. The doctor stands up, walks toward her, and leans down in front of her. "Mrs. Fitzgerald, are you okay?" he asks while waving his hand in front of her face. Allison snaps out of the trance she appears to be in. She looks directly at the doctor and asks,

"Did you say I'm pregnant?"

"Yes ma'am, it appears that you are."

"I can't believe this."

"Excuse me?" the doctor says, standing in front of Allison.

"I'm pregnant? It...it...just can't be. There's no way this could have happened."

"Mrs. Fitzgerald, you seem to be an intelligent woman. I'm sure that you're well aware of how this could happen, and I certainly hope you're not questioning my ability to do my job."

"No. No, I'm…I'm just so confused," Allison says, now holding her head in her hands.

"I thought this would be good news for you and Mr. Fitzgerald. What are you confused about?"

Allison sits with her head still in her hands for a few minutes, then looks up and says, "See, my husband had a vasectomy over ten years ago, and we have been having sex regularly, and…"

"Ok, now I understand," the doctor says, cutting Allison off. "Let me see if I can clear the air a little. First, let me ask you, you said it's been ten years since your husband had his vasectomy, right?"

"Yes, that's right," Allison confirms.

"Has he been back to the doctor to have his sperm count checked since he's had the vasectomy?"

"I doubt it. Why would he need to?" Allison asks curiously.

"Let me see the simplest way I can explain this. It's kinda like a woman who's had a tubal ligation, or has had her tubes tied, as we commonly say. It's a very effective method of birth control, however, in some cases, over time, the tubes may grow back together, and the woman can become pregnant. It is very rare for a vasectomy to fail, but it can happen, so I would suggest that you go home and speak to your husband about making an appointment to have his sperm count checked."

"Ok. I see," Allison says, still confused.

The doctor gives her instructions on her next appointment and what to expect during her pregnancy. After he consults with Allison, he asks if she has any other questions.

"No, sir. I think I've gotten all the information I need for one day. Thanks," Allison says, feeling like she is in the twilight zone. The doctor chuckles and responds, "Ok, I'll see you back in one month."

Allison makes her return appointment and then walks outside. She gets in the car, starts it, puts her hands on the steering wheel, and sits there. *How the hell did I get here? How the hell am I gonna explain this to Winston? He's gonna kill me. She* thinks to herself as she runs the words that she will say to him through her head. She puts the car in gear and pulls out of the parking lot. The drive home was the slowest and longest ride she had ever taken. The longer it takes to get home, the more time she will have to figure out exactly what she will say to Winston when she gets there.

She finally pulls into the driveway, and just her luck, Winston is home. *Damn,* she mutters to herself. She says a small prayer before she gets out of the car. When she walks into the house, Winston is in the kitchen looking through paperwork that he has spread over the table. He is fully dressed and seems as if he is about to leave the house. She sits her bag and keys on the counter, then asks, "Winston, can we talk?"

"About what? I'm kinda in a rush," Winston says without looking at her.

"It's important."

"Hold on just a minute. Let me get this paperwork together."

"Ok, when you finish, can you come up to the bedroom?"

"Ok," Winston says, and Allison walks upstairs.

She kicks her shoes off when she gets in the bedroom and sits on the love seat. She feels like she is in a court of law, and her life is on the line. She replays in her mind how she is going to present her case. Just as she pleads her case in her mind, Winston brings her back to reality when he walks into the room and asks, "Ok, what's up?"

This is it—the moment of truth.

"Ummm, so what I'm about to say is gonna shock you. I know 'cause it did a hell of a number on me."

Winston's facial expression goes from calmness to a look of concern. "Ok, what? What is it, Allison?"

At that moment, she could not remember any of the preliminary jargon she had rehearsed. No legal counsel, no opening statement, no evidence. Everything had gone out the window, and she blurted, "I'm pregnant!"

"You're what?" Winston shouts as he takes a couple of steps toward her. "Who the fuck?!"

"Wait a minute! Just wait a minute!" Allison yells. She throws her hands in front of her as if to tell Winston to stop walking in her direction. "It's yours, you sorry ass bastard!"

"What the fuck you mean it's mine?" Winston asks, needing an understanding of what Allison is saying.

"If you would calm your ass down, I can explain!"

"Ok, well, start!" Winston shouts.

"I went to the doctor, and it's confirmed, I'm definitely pregnant. I'm just as shocked and surprised as you are right now."

Winston is staring at Allison, eyes ablaze, nose flaring. She is still talking, but he zones out, trying to figure out how all of this has happened. *How the hell was she pregnant when I had a vasectomy? Who the hell has she been fucking?* He thinks to himself as he watches her lips continue to move.

Allison sees Winston becoming agitated about what she just revealed to him, and she knows exactly what is going on in his mind. He is trying to figure out how she got pregnant when he had a vasectomy and who she is cheating on him with. She wants to try and get the attention off her, so for a moment, she considers the idea of pulling out the pile of evidence she stacked up on him and all his hoes. She decides against it because she does not want her bedroom to turn into a war zone. As she attempts to devise a plan B,

Winston blurts out, "You better make this shit make sense, Allison! How the hell are you pregnant when I can't get you pregnant?"

"The doctor explained to me that because you had your vasectomy so long ago that you need to go back and have your sperm count checked."

"Say what? What the fuck are you talking about?" Winston shouts, becoming even more agitated.

"Winston, I'm telling you what the doctor said to me. You need to have your sperm count checked! Before you flip your lid, can we just make the appointment so you can have it done?"

Winston glares at Allison for a few moments, then says, "Yeah, go ahead and make the appointment, and I'll show up."

Allison calls the doctor's office immediately and schedules the appointment. "Ok, the appointment is set for day after tomorrow at 10am."

"Bet. I'm there," Winston says, then walks out of the bedroom and leaves the house.

20

Two days had gone by. Allison has not seen Winston since he left after she had given him the news of her pregnancy. He arrives at the doctor's office well before Allison. She arrived just in time for the appointment. Winston had already checked in with the receptionist and was seated in the lobby. Allison sits next to him. She attempts to have small talk with him. However, he ignores her. The nurse shows them to a waiting room, and the doctor enters the room almost immediately.

"Good morning, Mr. and Mrs. Fitzgerald. How can I help you guys today?"

Winston skips the preliminaries and gets straight to the point. "Doctor, I need you to check and see if I have any swimmers."

"Swimmers?" the doctor asks, looking confused.

"Yes, sir. Can you please check my sperm count? I need to know if it's high or low."

"Yes, we can do that, but may I first ask why you're wanting to have your sperm checked?"

"Well, my wife is pregnant."

"Congratulations to you both," the doctor says, looking at Winston and then at Allison. He notices the tension between the two of them. The room becomes uncomfortably silent. After a few seconds, the doctor breaks the silence by saying, "Ok, Mr. Fitzgerald. We can take the sample from you today and have your results within the next 36 hours."

"That will be fine," Winston responds.

"Ok, do you know how this works?"

"Umm, no," Winston says, looking at the doctor. "I've never had a sperm count done before."

The doctor chuckled a little and said, "Ok, so how this works is you will go into a room, and you will have to get aroused so that we can get a sample of your semen."

"Get aroused?"

"Yes, sir. You can take your wife with you to help you." Winston doesn't even look at Allison. The look on his face tells the doctor, loud and clear that he does not want her to go with him. Before Winston can respond, the doctor intervenes and says, "We do have magazines that you can view, or you can take your phone with you and pull up one of those sites to help you out."

Winston responds, "Yes, I'll take my phone with me." Allison rolls her eyes.

"Ok, well give me a few minutes and the nurse will come back to lead you to the room."

"Ok. Thanks, Doc."

The doctor leaves, and a few minutes later, the nurse returns and escorts Winston to the room so that he can give them the sperm sample. Once he submits his sample, he makes the return appointment for three days later, and he and Allison leave.

The three-day wait time for the results seems so far away. Allison attempts to converse with Winston several times, but he does not engage. He knows they need the conversation, but he takes advantage of an opportunity to take the spotlight off him and all the wrong he was doing for once. He treats her like she does not exist.

Their appointment for the test results finally arrives, and they return to the doctor's office. This is the moment of truth! *She is always trying to catch my ass, but now she is about to be put on blast. Her ass was out here fucking around the whole time, and now she pregnant,* Winston thinks to himself as he and Allison sit in the examination room, waiting for the doctor to walk in. He knows he has done his dirt, but what the doctor is about to reveal about his grimy wife will supersede all of his dirt. A few minutes later, the doctor gives them the test results.

"Mr. Fitzgerald, it appears that there is a 5% chance that you have the ability to fertilize an egg."

"Hmm? How?" Winston asks in great confusion.

"Well, it is a bit surprising because you've had your vasectomy, but it has been 10 years now, and over time, the body has a natural way of healing itself. It rarely happens, but obviously, this is what is happening in your case," the doctor explains. He notices the shocked look on Winston's face and the smile on Allison's and asks, "Is there a cause for alarm?"

Feeling great relief from the news that the doctor had just revealed, Allison looks at Winston and begins her Oscar-winning performance. "Yes, doctor. There is a cause for alarm. I am pregnant with my husband's child, and instead of him believing that I am being faithful to him, the first thing he did was accuse me of cheating on him because he's had his vasectomy. So, I had to bring him here to prove that he could still get me pregnant because it's been over ten years since he had the vasectomy," she says to the doctor without taking her eyes off Winston.

Winston feels smaller than an ant. He had been fired up and ready to shoot his shot at Allison, but the whole time he was wrong. Now he had to beg for her forgiveness. "Babe, I'm sorry. I'm so sorry. I love you. Please forgive me," he says, feeling lower than low.

"No! You don't love me! You swore I was cheating and gave me your ass to kiss, even after I kept telling you I wasn't," Allison says, kicking Winston while he is already down.

"Babe, I'm sorry. I should have believed you. Please forgive me and let's work this out."

Allison looks at Winston with disgust and says, "Work this out?" She stands up and repeats, "Work this out? I ain't working shit out with you! Let me outta here!" she says, then bolts out of the examination room. She zips past the receptionist's desk, straight to her car, and speeds out of the parking lot. When she gets on the interstate, she pulls out her phone and calls Anita to give her the news. "Girl, I'm safe," she says when Anita answers.

"Safe?"

"Yes! The doctor just told Winston that he has a 5% chance that he can fertilize an egg so the possibility is definitely there that he got me pregnant."

"Damn, girl! You have a rabbit's foot in your pocket! So, what are you gonna do?"

"I'ma abort this baby. Think about it, the doctor said Winston can be the father, but the truth is, I have been with Brian, and he could be the father. I can't run the risk of this being Brian's baby."

"Yeah, girl. I get it," Anita says.

"Nita, I need you now more than ever. There is no way that I can do this without you."

"Girl, I have never let you down before and I won't now, so just calm down. Whatever you need, I got you," Anita assures Allison.

"Thanks, girl. Seems like I've been saying this a lot lately, but I appreciate you so much. I swear I do."

"And I've been saying a lot lately that no thanks is necessary. That's what friends are for girl."

There is a brief silence on the phone then Allison starts crying. "I think I may have lost Brian.

"Awww, man, I'm so sorry. I may have made things worse, but I'll fix it," Anita says, feeling bad for her friend.

"No. I know him. He's too mad to talk to you or me. Then, he has some issues going on with his wife that has probably damnaged him even more, so I'ma give it some time. For now, I need to work on me."

"Ok, I understand," Anita says. "Just let me know how I can help."

"I definitely will," Allison says and ends the call.

Allison makes the earliest appointment possible to terminate her pregnancy. Winston offers his support, but she refuses. She wants nothing to do with him. However, she needs Brian more than ever. Anita comforts her as much as possible, but she also knows that Allison is yearning for Brian. Anita took Allison to the appointment. During the procedure, she calls Brian to tell him what is happening and that Allison needs him. No answer.

After the procedure, Anita drives Allison home. It is a quiet ride as Allison tries to sort through her feelings regarding what she has just done. She is ashamed of herself, but at the same time, she is relieved that it is over. Anita has gospel music playing low in the car. Allison closes her eyes and thinks. *Is this a message from God? I know that two wrongs don't make a right, but why allow this man to come into my life if he isn't for me? Everything about him is so right, so how can he be wrong? God, I'm turning this situation over to you. If he comes back, I'll know it's a sign for us to be together. If he doesn't come back, then I'll know it was you who removed him.* Anita sheds a tear as she watches the tears fall down her friend's face. Without saying a word, she grabs her hand and holds it for the rest of the ride to Allison's house.

"Are you going to be ok, Allison? Do you need anything?" Anita asks.

"Yes, I'll be fine. You've been such a great help to me. Thanks again, Nita."

"You're more than welcome. I will be checking on you. If you need anything, I'm just a phone call away."

Allison opens the door, and Winston helps her into the house.

"Thanks so much Anita for taking care of my wife today," he says before closing the car door.

"Yeah, whatever," Anita says and drives off.

Not at all surprised by Anita's response, Winston walks Allison into the house and upstairs to their bedroom. He helps her down on the love seat and asks, "How are you feeling? Is there anything I can do?"

"No. I'm ok," Allison says, wishing he wasn't there.

"Ok, Al. If you need anything, just ask. I'm here."

Allison sits back on the love seat and thinks, *Winston has rarely shown me this much attention. He's actually home right now, which is not the norm. God, I know you don't make mistakes. Is this your way of straightening my husband up?* Allison is taking sick leave for three days. While she is home, she pays close attention to Winston. He went to work, came home, cooked, cleaned the house, and helped the kids with homework while she relaxed and healed. He had become very attentive to her and had actually begun to act like a real husband. Allison is impressed because it seems that the man she had fallen in love with is back.

21

Allison returns to work. Karen approaches her and expresses concern about her absence from work. They sit in Karen's cubicle as Allison fills her in on all the details. Karen is infuriated. She calls her brother and gives him a piece of her mind, but Allison stops her and tells her to let it go. "If it's meant to end this way, then so be it," Allison says to Karen.

"Ok, I'll respect your wishes, but my brother is dead wrong!"

Karen suggests a girls' night out to unwind and relax. Allison accepts the offer, and they select Friday night.

"Bring Anita with you," Karen says.

"I'm already ahead of you. I'll call her today," Allison responds.

By Friday, what started as a party of three had turned into a party of ten. The ladies meet at a popular hangout in the city and enjoy a night of fun letting their hair down, relaxing, getting drunk, and of course, bashing men the entire night. The more they drink, the more they laugh and find every reason to criticize the male species. However, one young lady in the group isn't going for it. Nicole defends the men and quickly shuts the discussion down. "Listen, y'all are being extra hard on the men tonight, but if these same men walked in here right now, y'all hot and horny asses would be leaving with them. Now, tell me y'all don't want that wood tonight. I'll wait."

A thick silence falls over the group as they each think about Nicole's words. Karen is the first to cut the silence. "Hell yeah, I want me some dick tonight. I'm about to send a booty call text right now." She picks up her phone and scrolls through her contact list to see who the lucky man will be tonight. She isn't the only one. All the ladies have their heads in their phones making dick plans for the evening. One by one, they excuse themselves to go and be with the very same men they were just complaining about. Nicole shakes her head. "These bitches just sat here and talked all this shit about these men and look at their weak asses. Running to the dick."

Those that are left at the table laugh. Karen says, "Well, I just got the text I was waiting for, so let me get my weak ass outta here too. Later, gators."

"Hold up, I'ma walk out with you, Karen." Karen and Nicole exit the building.

"Damn, their horny asses got outta here quick, didn't they?" Anita says.

"Shit, Nicole acting like she setting us straight, but I bet her ass ran outta here just now looking for some dick too," Allison responds, and they both laugh. Allison thinks about her situation and feels left out. "Man, just a week ago, I had two dicks to choose from, now I don't have any. What a difference a damn week makes," she says and takes another sip of her drink. "I mean, I can go home to Winston. He is still breaking his back trying to make things right with me, but I don't want him anymore. I want Brian!" she says and puts her head down on the table.

Anita, sipping on her drink the whole time Allison is talking, suggests they call Brian. Allison refuses. She lifts her head from the table and says, "I've been waiting to hear from Brian since the night I told him I was pregnant, but I haven't heard anything from him, so I'm not calling him tonight." She puts her head back down on the table.

Anita picks up the phone and dials Brian's number. "You don't have to call him tonight. I will," she says as the phone starts to ring. Allison lifts her head off the table and tries to grab the phone from Anita. Anita jumps up from the table so that Allison cannot reach her. Allison jumps behind her and tries again to snatch the phone. Brian answers. "Hey! Brian! Hey, it's Anita."

Allison stops in her tracks.

"Oh, hey, what's up?" Brian responds.

"Listen, I don't know what the issue is between you and my girl, but I do know y'all need to fix it."

"I don't have a problem. I'm just confused about what's going on," Brian says.

"I know. Let me first apologize for how I came off on you. I know it was wrong. I just love my girl and I don't wanna see her hurt."

"I understand that. I'm not trying to hurt her. I love her, too."

Anita smiles. Allison will give her right arm to hear what Brian is saying.

"Well, that's good to hear. Now, do you mind telling her?"

"Sure, but she already knows this."

"Yes, she does, but I think she really needs to hear you say it right now," Anita says, then passes the phone to Allison.

"Hello," Allison says softly in the phone.

"Hey, babe. Listen, I love you and I apologize for hurting you."

Allison feels relieved as the tears slowly run down her face. *Finally*, she thought to herself. "I love you too, babe," she whimpers.

"I know you do. We both handled this situation incorrectly," Brian says.

"I agree."

"Can we make it right?"

"I would love to try."

"Good. Hello, my name is Brian. It's a pleasure to meet you."

Allison smiles and says, "Hi, my name is Allison and it's a pleasure to meet you."

"So, tell me Ms. Allison, is there anything I can do for you tonight?"

"Hmmm, let me see. Right now, I would love more than anything for you to make love to me, but I have some issues."

"That's understood. However, I could come over and let my tongue make love to your pussy cat."

"Damn," Allison blurts as her pussy twitches. "That would be nice. I guess that can be arranged," she responds.

"Ohhhh shit, my girl is about to get some dick!" Anita shouts, laughing and drunk dancing by herself.

"Shhhhhh," Allison gestures to Anita by putting her finger over her mouth. But instead of being quiet, Anita asks her, "Did you ever ask him what his fantasy is?"

"No," Allison answers, covering the phone so Brian cannot hear what they say.

"Bitch, what better time to ask him than now?"

"What did she say?" Brian asks.

"Her drunk ass is in here telling me to ask you what your fantasy is."

"My fantasy? Hmm, what's every man's fantasy?"

"Let me guess. Two women," Allison says.

"Yes lawd," Brian responds.

"Well, if you ever decide to put a ring on it, I promise I'll make that happen."

Brian drops the phone.

"Umm, hello. Hello," Allison calls out.

Brian picked the phone up and said, "Really? What? Did you—"

"I didn't stutter," Allison says, cutting Brian off.

Brian cleared his throat, "You'd really do that for me?"

"Yes, I would. Babe. You complete me, however, I would approve of a third party in our bed, if that's what you want. But it will only happen one time."

"Wow! You're an amazing woman."

"I know," Allison says, grinning from ear to ear. "Now, enough of the chit-chat. We're about to get out of here. Can you meet us at Anita's house?"

"Wait. You wanna do this at Anita's spot?" Brian asks.

"Yeah, why not? She doesn't mind. Do you?"

"I mean, I'm ok with it if you are."

"Ok. I'ma text you her address and we'll see you there shortly."

Going to Anita's house is a surprise. Brian didn't think that Allison would be ok with this, but if she was cool, then so be it. Twenty minutes later, he heads to Anita's house. He knocks on the door. Anita greets him. She is wearing a white satin robe looking sexy and elegant. *Damn,* Brian thinks as he looks her up and down.

"Hey," Anita says.

"Hey," Brian responds, trying to keep his pipe under control.

"Your girl is waiting for you."

"Ok," Brian says as he smiles and tries to keep his cool.

It was evident to Anita that Brian likes what he sees. She knew because of the way he looked at her. *Damn, it's about to be a good night tonight,* she thinks and smiles at Brian. "She's down the hall. Second door on the right."

Brian walks down the hall, slowly opens the door, and sees Allison lying on the bed in her bra and matching boy shorts listening to Trey Songz, On Top. Brian walks into the room, closes the door, and sings, *make your love come down*, as he unbuttons his shirt. Once the shirt is off, he spins around and grabs the first thing he sees, a brush, and uses it as his mic. He gives Allison a show while continuing to sing the chorus of the song. Allison lies there in amazement. She cannot take her eyes off him. When the song ends, he smiles and says, "Hey babe. Don't you look nice."

"Only for you," Allison replies.

Brian makes his way to the bed, grabs Allison by her hips then slowly tugs on the bottom rim of her boy shorts until they come down. He rubs her legs with a gentle massage as he kisses and licks the inside of her legs and thighs. Allison moans in pleasure as Brian moves up from her thighs and licks and sucks her clit. After her third climax, Allison's eyes roll back in her head. Her legs shake uncontrollably, and her entire body trembles. She had never experienced this amount of pleasure and almost felt as if she could not handle it. She tries to move away from Brian, but he locks his arms around her legs so she cannot escape. She is officially tongue-matized.

"Ohhhhh baby, I don't ever want us to argue again. I missed you so much. I missed your tongue so much. I want your dick so bad," Allison moans. As tempted as she is, she knows she can't. She does the next best thing. Brian finally lets her up. Allison pushes him down on the bed. She pulls his dick out and strokes it lightly. She goes from stroking it with one hand to massaging it with both hands. Allison is mesmerized by Brian's pipe. She wants to feel it inside her but does not focus on that. Instead, she massages his nuts as she licks the shaft of his dick up and down. She then focuses on the head and slowly circles it with her tongue.

Brian is watching her work her magic. It feels so good that he has to close his eyes and concentrate on holding his nut. He knows he will bust a good one, but he does not want to let it go quite yet. Allison makes it extremely hard for him to hold it. She swallows his dick down to her tonsils, then, in a circular motion, strokes his penis with her tongue and lips, up, down, and around, then fast, then slow, up and down. Brian loses all control. He moans and nuts on her face. She puts half of Brian's dick in her mouth and sucks all the cum out.

"Ooooh, shit! Girl, you are a beast," Brian says, now officially tongue-matized himself. They both lie back and reminisce on this sexual escapade, which had them both desiring each other in the worst way. Brian was totally relaxed and had no worries, but it was late, and Allison either needed to get home or call Winston and advise him of her whereabouts. The choice is clear, she needs to get home, but she does not want to leave the spot where she is lying in the arms of the man who had captured her heart.

Brian is drifting off to sleep. She quietly gets up from the bed and walks into the bathroom to call Winston to tell him that she is drinking at Anita's house and may stay for the evening and sleep it off. To her surprise, Winston agrees and tells her to get some rest.

Winston's response was unexpected. Allison's excitement is overflowing because she is about to have a whole night with Brian without any worries or concerns. She walks back into the room and thinks, *I wonder if he's being so cool about me staying out because he's got something going on tonight too?* The thought quickly leaves her head as she looks over at Brian, sleeping peacefully.

She can smell the fragrance of his cologne. She gets in the bed next to him, under the covers, and puts her head on his chest. He feels her lay on him and puts his arm around her. There is no other place she would rather be than right where she is with the man of her dreams. She lies there for a few moments, feeling completely loved, then falls asleep with a massive smile on her face.

Not long after falling asleep, Allison hears a soft tap on the door. Allison wakes up and opens the door. Anita is standing there. Allison steps out into the hall, so she does not wake Brian up.

"Hey, girl. Wassup?" Allison asks.

"Hey, do you see what time it is? Winston is gonna kill you staying out this late," Anita says with great concern.

Allison chuckles, then says, "Girl, I'm straight. I told him I had too much to drink and needed to stay here tonight and sleep it off."

"He went for that?" Anita asks in shock.

"Yeah, girl. With no questions."

"Ok, well you're straight then," Anita says. She peeks in the room and says, "Damn girl, you must have put it on him. He sleeping like a baby." They laugh.

"I think we outdid each other tonight," Allison says.

"Yes, girl. I hear that!" Anita says, still eyeing Brian with a sly smile on her face. Noticing Anita's gaze on Brian, Allison says, "Anita, I'm not trying to be rude, but I'm sleepy as hell. Can we talk in a couple hours?"

"Yeah, girl. Y'all get some rest," Anita says and walks back down the hall to her bedroom.

When Allison returns to bed, Brian is still sound asleep. She slides the covers back as quietly as possible, and when she does, she notices that Brian has morning wood. Allison's excitement is apparent as she notices the river between her legs. *Damn, he's still thinking about me in his sleep,* she smiles. Unable to take her eyes off it, she thinks, *I wonder how he would respond if I put his pipe in my mouth while he's asleep.* Allison is no stranger to being adventurous.

She slides under the covers, and without wasting time, she devours Brian's dick with her mouth. Much to her surprise, his dick gets even harder as she begins to stroke it with her lips and tongue. *Damn, damn, damn, I want this shit in me,* Allison thinks to herself as she continues to move up and down on Brian's pipe, all while he still appears to be asleep. Having intercourse this soon after her procedure is a considerable risk, but it is a risk that she is willing to take. Her body yearns for that dick inside her. She pulls the covers back. She gets on top of him and straddles his dick, allowing it to slide in her juicy, succulent pussy.

Allison closes her eyes and exhales as she slowly bounces up and down. She is trying to take it easy on herself, but it is feeling so damn good. Her head goes from side to side as she moans with pleasure. Brian can hear and feel everything happening but thinks he is dreaming. He is more than excited when he wakes up and realizes it isn't a dream and that it is happening for real. He grabs Allison without pulling out, lies her on her side, and pounds her pussy from behind. He raises her right leg over his leg and pushes his dick all the way inside her.

The headboard is hitting the wall. As their sexual rhythm increases, the bed hits the wall harder and with more of a bang. They are both concerned that Anita will hear them, but the sex is so good that they can't stop, even if they tried. After a few more minutes of nonstop gratification, they both climax all over each other and fall asleep in each other's arms.

22

The following day, Brian and Allison wake to the scent of coffee. When they walk downstairs, they discover that Anita has prepared a meal fit for a king and queen.

"Good morning, love birds," Anita says as they enter the kitchen.

"Good morning," they both reply in harmony.

"Anita, girl you shouldn't have," Allison says as she sees the big spread Anita had prepared for them.

"It was no problem, girl. I figured you two needed some fuel after all that hard work you did last night."

Damn, she did hear us, Allison thinks, feeling a little embarrassed. "What do you mean?" she asks Anita as if she didn't already know.

"Chile, all that banging, cat squealing and dog grunting that went on last night, I figured y'all needed a good hearty breakfast to get y'all energy back up," Anita responds, and they all laugh.

"Dang Anita, I'm sorry girl," Allison says, feeling embarrassed again.

"Oh girl, it's no problem. I just gotta make sure y'all have plenty of energy to put in that overtime at work."

"Overtime? Work? Wait, what?" Allison says, trying to figure out what Anita is talking about because it's Saturday, and all of them are off from work.

"Yeah, overtime because after y'all get my bill from whatever damage y'all did in my room, I figure y'all gonna need some extra cash to cover it," Anita says, and they all laugh.

"But seriously, I'm really sorry about us disturbing your peace," Allison says.

"Girl, stop. I'm just kidding. Y'all didn't bother me one bit last night," Anita assures.

"Seriously, Anita. If we did mess up anything, I'll fix it," Brian says.

"I know, Brian. I was referring to Allison, silly."

Brian sits down and turns his head to one side.

"Aww, don't look at me like that. Me and Allison are friends and you're the man."

"Hmmm, the man?" Brian replies.

"Yes. You're her man and I expect nothing less from you."

The room is quiet. Anita looks at Allison, then at Brian, and breaks the silence, "Wait a minute, now. Don't go getting all serious on me."

Brian and Allison look at each other but remain silent.

"Awww, come on now. Y'all are way too serious," Anita says. She waits for a response from Brian and Allison. When she doesn't get one, she blurts, "Oh my god! Just eat, you two! Just eat!"

Brian gets up and walks back to the room.

"Oh my goodness. What is he doing?" Anita glares at Allison. Allison returns the glare with a blank face and shrugs her shoulders. She knows he is checking the room for damages. A few minutes later, Brian returns to the kitchen and sits in his chair.

"Well?" Anita says anxiously.

"Oh, nothing. I just went to get my watch," Brian says with a straight face. Anita turns her nose up at him because she knows he is lying. Brian smirks and says, "Gotcha!" The awkward silence from a few minutes before eases into a shared laugh between the three of them.

"Nah, I really went to check the room," Brian admits.

"I knew it! I knew it!" Anita says. "You two have to lighten up. Especially you, mister. Me and Allison are friends for life and there isn't much that we don't share with each other." Brian is lifting his fork to eat some eggs but stops in his tracks with his eyes dazed over. He glances at Allison and thinks, *Is she saying she knows everything about me? Like my situation at home, how big my dick is. Oh shit! I know good, and damn well, Allison didn't tell her about that time I couldn't get my dick up!* He immediately feels embarrassed.

He replays the session that took place last night and how well he pounded the pussy, and feels redeemed. The conversation is casual and light, sprinkled with laughter. Anita reaches over the table to get some cream, and her boob pops out of her robe. Brian picks up his coffee cup to take a drink but spills it upon seeing Anita's flesh flip out right in front of him. He tries to play cool like he didn't see it but can't unsee what he has seen. He focuses on his coffee cup when Allison breaks the awkwardness in the room by saying,

"Hey bitch, I saw that. No peepshow for my man," with a smile on her face.

"Girl, damn! That was an accident," Anita replies.

"I know. It's no biggie. My babe has seen tits before," Allison says. Brian feels he is in the twilight zone because they are downplaying it like it isn't a big issue. Allison notices how uncomfortable Brian is and reaches over to him and says, "It's ok, babe. I've seen them a million times, too." Brian turns his head to Allison and looks at her with a blank stare. "Babe, really. It's ok."

"Ok," Brian says, puzzled as hell. He asks Anita for a towel so he can take a shower. She gets up, walks out of the kitchen, and returns with a towel, wash rag, and several choices of body wash. "Damn, aren't you prepared," Brian says.

"I try," she says with a smile.

He gets up from the table and walks to the bedroom. Allison waits until she hears the water running and knows that Brian is in the shower, then excuses herself. "Girl, I'ma go get some of that morning dick."

"Get it, girl," Anita says with a devilish grin.

Allison quietly enters the bathroom and creeps into the shower. She stood there in awe as she looked at Brian's body, covered with soapy lather. She realizes that she isn't just sprung anymore. What she is feeling for Brian isn't just about sex anymore. She is in love with him. After removing her clothes, she slides into the shower with Brian. Tears are pooling in her eyes.

"Babe, what's wrong? Why are you crying?" Brian asks.

"Nothing is wrong, Brian. I just…I just love you."

Brian lightly wipes the tears from her eyes and says, "Oh babe, I love you, too." They embrace each other, feeling the love filling the bathroom.

"What do we do now?" Allison asks. The water is cascading over their bodies and intertwined in each other's embrace.

"We do what our heart feels," Brian responds.

"I need you," Allison whispers.

"I need you, too," Brian says, releasing Allison from his embrace.

"So, what do you want for us?"

"I want you in my life, Brian. I want to be your wife."

Brian pauses with a blank stare. He is slow to respond as they stand there looking into each other's eyes. Allison eagerly awaits his response. She notices a tear roll down Brian's face as he says, "I would love to be your husband." He kisses her passionately.

Allison feels a calm reassurance. Her dream is coming true, and matrimony with Brian is in their future. They both agree that the first thing they have to do is to rid themselves of their toxic marriages. Brian has already moved out of the house with Stacey, so he is halfway there. Allison is still in the house with Winston. She has all the ammo against him that she needs to initiate her plan. They linger in the shower a little longer, talking about their future. They get dressed and walk out of the room.

"I take it y'all's shower was good," Anita says with a smirk.

"Yeah, it was," Allison responds.

"We were able to clear some things up," Brian says. He puts his arm around Allison's shoulder and kisses her forehead.

"We have some news we wanna share," Allison says with a massive smile.

"Well, well, what is it?" Anita asks eagerly.

Allison glances at Brian and says, "Do you wanna tell her?"

"Go ahead, babe," Brian responds.

Allison turns her attention to Anita and exclaims, "We're getting married!"

Anita takes a huge breath, holds her chest, steps back, and says, "Hold on! Wait! How the hell?"

"Hold on, Anita. We know we have to clean up our shit first, but that's exactly what we're about to do because we are going to spend the rest of our lives married...to each other," Allison trails off. She glances at Brian, "I love this man."

"I know that silly. I just want to make sure y'all do it right," Anita says.

"We will and we are counting on your support."

"Of course, I will support you. We may not have come from the same vagina, but we are joined together for life. I'll always support you," Anita says. Group hug!

"Ok, ok. I need details," Anita says once they release their embrace.

"Hang on now. We haven't gotten that far, yet. Remember, we just had this discussion in the shower," Allison retorts.

"I know," Anita says with a slight chuckle. "Oh, I have an idea!

Why not do it back home?"

"Back home? Hmm, that would be nice. But you know Winston's people probably won't be happy about it," Allison says.

"And?? By then, they all should have accepted the fact that y'all are Done! Over! Finished! End of story!" Anita says, matter of factly.

"You're right, girl. The truth is, if Winston been doing what he was supposed to and not parking his dick in other bitches, this wouldn't even be a conversation."

"Ain't that the truth," Anita says, giving Allison a high five.

"Umm, ladies. I am standing here," Brian says, getting annoyed at where the conversation is going.

"Yeah, we know," Anita says sarcastically.

"Awww, I'm sorry babe," Allison says and kisses Brian on the cheek.

"Ok, ok. Enough of the lovie dovie stuff," Anita fusses.

"Girl, stop hatin' on black love," Allison says.

"I'm not hatin' on it, I just don't wanna see it, especially when there's no dick here for me," Anita replies.

"Umm, excuse me. I think I better be going, so y'all can talk y'all women's talk openly and freely," Brian says as he gets up to leave.

Allison walks Brian to the door and kisses him before saying good-bye. She watches him drive off.

23

"Damn, girl. You must have a bionic pussy," Anita says when Allison returns to the table. Allison blushes at the idea.

"Bionic pussy? Girl, you're crazy," Allison says.

"I'm serious. You got this man wanting to marry you. I mean, wow!"

"Nah, it's not the na, even though it is good," Allison says, laughing.

"See! I know what I'm talking about. You and Brian are both whipped!"

"No, girl. Really, it's not just that. I'm not built to be alone and Brian's the perfect guy for me. I know this is not the holiest way to go about it, but I swear this is God's doing."

Anita observes her friend glowing in love, putting a smile on her face. "Well, they say people come into your life for a reason or season, so I guess he's your reason. I'm really happy for you, friend."

"Thank you, friend," Allison says as she grabs Anita and hugs her.

"So, I get to plan your bachelorette party! Mmm, Mmm, Mmm!"

"Let's not get carried away. Both Brian and I have a long road ahead of us before we will be able to walk down the aisle."

"I know, but I can't wait!" Then Anita eyes Allison seriously and asks, "Do you realize this could be your last dick?"

"Yes, I do, but I'm fine with that because this dick is all I need."

"Yesss, girl! I hear that! So, what about him?"

"What about him?" Allison asks.

"Have you asked him how he feels about you being his last?"

"No, I haven't."

"Mmm, ok," Anita says with a square look on her face.

"What's that face about?"

"My face is about you asking the right questions when necessary."

"I know. I guess I've just been so caught up with what I want, I forgot to ask."

Instead of saying anything in response to what Allison said, Anita raises her eyebrows. Allison knows that the raised eyebrows mean Anita is telling her she needs to call him. She plays as if she doesn't know. "What? Why are you looking at me like that?" she asks Anita.

"You know why."

"Ok. Ok," Allison says. She reaches for her phone to call Brian. Just as she does, her phone rings. It's Brian. "Hey babe, your ears must have been ringing," she says when she answers the phone.

"Why? Were you thinking about me?" Brian responds.

"I'm always thinking about you, but I was just talking about you, too."

"Oh, really? So, what were you saying about me?"

"Well, I actually need to ask you something."

"Ok, babe. What is it?" Brian asks curiously.

"Are you gonna be happy with me for the rest of your life? I'm asking because I don't wanna go through this again. I'm in this for life." Silence. Allison says, "You can take some time and think about it because I want you to be sure before you answer."

"I don't have to take time to think about it. I've already thought about it and I know exactly what I want. You are what I want, Allison. I am totally in love with you and I'm in this for life," Brian responds.

Allison blushes. "Thanks babe. That's all I wanted to hear. And don't forget what I said about giving you your one night. Maybe it can be your bachelor night."

Brian smiles widely and says, "Oh yeah, I almost forgot about that." The truth is, he didn't forget about that. He thought about it several times since Allison promised it to him.

"Ok, babe. I'll let you go."

"Ok, talk to you soon. Love you," Brian says.

"Love you, too," Allison responds and ends the call.

Before Allison can sit the phone on the table, Anita blurts, "Ok, bitch! What kinda deal did you make?"

"Damn, you all in my conversation!"

"Girl, you know my nosy ass can hear like a bat."

"Well, I kinda agreed on having a threesome."

Anita knocks over her coffee. "You did what?" she says in disbelief.

"Yeah, I did."

"Wow! I guess you're coming out of your shell."

"Yeah, I guess so. He's so different from Winston. I feel free with Brian. We can talk about anything, and I feel we can do just about anything."

"Hmm, ok. So, this threesome, is it gonna be two dicks? Or two va jay jays?"

"Girl please! Two dicks? Hell no!"

"Wait! Hold on, bitch. You're gonna entertain another woman in your bed? With your man?"

"Yep," Allison says.

Anita shakes her head in disbelief.

"So, ok, ok, ok. Details. I need details."

"I don't have any yet. All I know is I get to pick the woman."

"So, he has no say so?"

"Nope. It's my party and my gift to him."

"Ok, well make sure whoever you pick gets tested."

"I'm way ahead of you, girl."

"I see that. I'm shocked, but not really surprised."

"Well, hold on to your emotions, because I have a question for you," Allison says.

"Ok, I'm listening." Anita is all ears.

"I was hoping you'd be the third wheel."

Anita is puzzled. "Hmm? Wait! What? Are you serious??"

"Yeah, I am."

"Ok, now I'm shocked and surprised!"

Allison watches Anita pace back and forth in shock.

"So, you're saying you want me and Brian to umm..."

"Yes. I know you, I trust you, and I know this secret will be safe with the three of us."

Anita tries to imagine being in a sexual triangle with Allison and Brian. She had always thought her friend was beautiful and admired her sexy body but never considered having sex with her. "Umm, I don't know about this one, Al. You're my girl and all, but this is a lot to ask, especially considering the circumstances."

"Yes, I know it's a lot to ask, but I've been thinking about this since

I had the talk with Brian, and honestly you're the only one I want to share my man with. You're perfect."

"Really? I didn't know you looked at me like that."

"Girl, please. I know you have it in you. And besides, didn't you just tell Brian that we share everything?"

"Yeah, I did, but I was talking about everything as in information, clothes and food. Not dick!"

"So, I guess you forgot about your little situation back in college," Allison says, staring at Anita with her arms folded.

Anita's eyes open wide. "Oh, my god! You remember that?"

"Yes, I do. I remember all the details too," Allison says, still zoned in on Anita, whose tone starts to change.

"Hmm, let me think about it."

"Ok, you do that," Allison says as she gets up from the table. "I'ma get on outta here and see about my other life. Thanks for everything."

Anita, seeming shaken up about the blast from the past that Allison just revealed, says, "Don't mention it."

24

When Allison arrives home, she is happier than she has ever been. She now has the promise of the man of her dreams. All she needs to do is end the mess she is in with Winston. So many thoughts run through her mind. She needs to come up with a plan of escape. However, she has no idea where to begin. As fate would have it, she didn't have to be in the dark for long.

As soon as she walks through the door, she hears Winston talking on the phone. The way he is talking, the tone of his voice, and the things he is saying let Allison know that he isn't talking about work, nor was he on the phone with a man. She stands outside the room and listens to as much as she can. When she cannot stomach it anymore, she busts into the room. "Good morning, husband," Allison says calmly when she walks through the door. Winston looks like a deer caught in headlights.

"I know you hear me, mother fucker," Allison says calmly with a slight smile. Knowing that he has been caught red-handed, Winston fumbles with his phone, says, "Let me call you back," and hangs up before whoever is on the other end can respond.

"So, honey, who were you talking to?"

"Oh, um, that was my job."

"Your job? Really? So, tell me, who exactly on your job were you talking to?"

"Ted. It was Ted."

"Ted? Well, tell me. Did Ted have a sex change recently?"

Winston smirks at Allison as if she has lost her mind and asks, "A sex change?"

"Yeah, because I just heard you saying that you couldn't wait to eat that pussy and I can't imagine you saying that to a man."

Winston clears his throat. He knows he's busted, but he has to play it down for as long as possible. "What are you talking about, Allison?"

All the cool that Allison had maintained was out the door. She tries to allow Winston to come clean, but now he is playing on her intelligence. She does not appreciate that. "Don't play with me, Winston! I've been standing outside this door the entire time you were on the phone and heard everything you said!"

"Oh, so now you're eavesdropping on my calls?" Winston shouts, trying to divert the attention off of him and onto Allison.

Allison realizes what he is doing and yells, "You must be outta your fucking mind! You think I'm stupid!"

"No, I think you don't know what the fuck you're talking about!" Winston shouts back.

"You really think I'm stupid, but I'ma show you."

"Show me what?" Winston says.

Without saying anything else, Allison retrieves her phone from her bag in the kitchen. She returns with pictures on her phone and shows them to Winston. "So, Mr. Slick Ass, since I don't know what I'm talking about, tell me who this is."

Winston looks at the picture and, in his mind, screams, *Damn*! But out of his mouth, he lies and says, "I don't know who that is."

"Oh, you don't? Hmm, ok. So, how do you explain the screenshots of you and her together?"

"What screenshots?"

Allison scrolls through the pictures, puts the phone in his face, and yells, "These screenshots, mother fucker!"

Allison swipes through an enormous amount of pictures proving Winston's infidelity. Winston is speechless. He is busted. There is nothing he can say to get out of it because the proof is right there. Since he cannot lie his way out of it, he grabs the phone and attempts to get rid of the evidence. When he takes the phone from Allison, a struggle ensues. Winston runs around the room with Allison on his tail, beating on his back and demanding her phone back.

Winston attempts to break the phone by throwing it across the room but is unsuccessful. Allison beats Winston to the phone. When she picks it up, she is glad to see that the phone is still intact. Allison pulls up the screenshots of Winston's text messages. She reads them out loud. He listened to his inappropriate text conversations with other women and wondered how she got them. Once Allison finishes reading the texts, she says, "I'm done."

Winston, really not knowing how to respond to everything he just heard, responds, "Be done then. None of that matters or proves a thing."

"Mmmhmm, it may not matter to you, but I bet my lawyer will make sense of it."

"Your lawyer?" Winston asks with a confused look on his face.

"Yeah, mother fucker. My lawyer!"

"Oh, so you're gonna take it there?"

"Yeah, I'ma take it there! You've been doing this shit for years! I thought you would change because you had a good woman at home, but you are a fucking dog, and you will never change. I'm done!"

Winston is stunned and unable to articulate a cohesive sentence. He knows he is caught. As he opens his mouth to speak, Allison yells, "Get out!"

The tone of her voice and the hurt in her eyes let Winston know it is over. There is no need for him to continue his charade. Without saying anything else, he packs up some of his things and walks out the door.

Shortly after Winston leaves the house, Allison takes off to Lowes to get new locks for the front and back doors. She gets to the service counter to purchase the locks and asks if anyone can change the locks for her. Because it is so late in the afternoon, no one is available. She calls Brian and asks if he can change the locks for her. She doesn't know if he knows how to do it or if he is available, but she doesn't know who else she can call. She knows she will not feel comfortable at home if the locks aren't changed.

RING. RING.

"Hey, babe," Brian greets her when he answers the phone.

"Hey, can you do me a favor?"

"Sure, sweetie. What do you need?"

Allison pauses for a moment, then says, "I know it's a long shot, but I was wondering if you could come over and change my locks."

"You mean, the locks on your house?"

"Yes."

"Allison, are you serious right now? You know I can't come to your house."

"Yes, I am serious, babe."

Brian remains quiet as he takes a moment to try and understand Allison's request. But there is nothing about this request that makes sense to him. "Ok, am I missing something?"

"Yeah, kinda," Allison responds.

"Babe, talk to me."

"When I got home from Anita's house, me and Winston had a big fight because I overheard him talking on the phone with some bitch. When I confronted him, he got belligerent with me like I didn't know what the hell I was talking about. So, I pulled out the receipts that I've had in my back pocket and when he saw my proof, he had to back down. Long story short, I put his ass out and now I need my locks changed."

Brian paused to take this new information in. "Wow, babe! Are you ok?"

"Yes, I'm fine. I'm just finally at my breaking point with him and I'm not taking his shit anymore!" Allison says.

"Ok, I understand and I'm glad you're ok, but I really don't feel comfortable coming to your house and changing your locks, given our situation."

"I figured you would say that," Allison says in disappointment.

"Hold on, babe. I may have someone who can do it for you." Before Brian pulls up the information of the person he is referring to, his phone beeps with another call. It's Ashley. He tells Allison to hold on for a moment and clicks to the other line.

"Hey, baby girl. What's up?" he greeted when he answered the call.

"Hey, Dad. I don't feel good," Ashley says.

"Oh, no baby girl. What's wrong?"

"I have a fever and chills. I called Mom, but you know she's at work and didn't answer. Can you pick me up and take me to her job?"

"Sure thing, princess. Give me a minute. I'm on my way."

"Ok, Dad," Ashley says.

Brian clicks back over to Allison. "I'm sorry, babe. That was Ashley. She's not feeling well.

"Oh, no. I'm sorry to hear that," Allison says with concern.

"Yeah, I'm getting up now to go pick her up and take her to the ER. Her mother can have her seen right away since she works there."

"Ok, if you need anything, just let me know," Allison assures.

"Thanks, babe. I appreciate that. Meanwhile, I'ma check on those locks for you."

"Don't worry about it. Take care of your baby."

"Babe, remember who I am. I got you," Brian says.

Allison smiles. "Ok, babe."

"I'll talk to you in a few," Brian says and ends the call. He rushes to get to Ashley. When he arrives at the house, he checks her head for a fever. She is burning up.

"Princess, how long have you been feeling like this?"

"It started last night," Ashley responds weakly.

"Ok, well we're gonna get that fixed. Where's your brother?"

"At Carlos' house."

"Ok, text him and let him know that you're with me and where we're going."

"Ok," Ashley says as she gets in the car with Brian.

They proceed to the hospital. Stacey meets them at the entrance. She already has a room ready for Ashley. It is one of the many perks of being employed at the hospital. The tension between Brian and Stacey is thick. However, they remain cordial for the sake of their daughter. On the way to the room, several of Stacey's colleagues notice Brian and speak to him. He is sure Stacey has not told them they are currently separated, so he keeps the conversations light. While waiting in the room to be seen, Ashley hears a voice outside her room door that she recognizes.

"That voice sounds familiar to me," Ashley says out loud.

Brian asks Ashley, "What do you mean?"

"That voice, it sounds like Mommy's friend, Keith," Ashley states.

"Keith, hmm? What does he look like?" Brian asks.

"Umm, he's light skin, with a low haircut and about your height."

The image of the person that Brian had seen in the photos came to his mind. Brian walks to the door. When he looks out, he notices three people standing just outside the door. Two women and one man who fits the description. When he realizes that it is, in fact, the dude in the incriminating pictures, Brian tells Ashley, "I'll be right back."

Brian steps out of the room and walks toward the gentleman, Keith, who is walking out of the building. Stacey is standing at the nurse's station and notices Brian heading to the door behind Keith. She sees the crazed look on Brian's face and instantly becomes nervous. Her secret is about to come out, and she does not know how to stop it.

Brian puts a pep in his step as he follows Keith out the door and catches up with him. Before he says anything, he takes a good look at the man who has possibly been the cause of his marriage ending.

"Excuse me," Brian says calmly.

Keith responded, "Yeah."

"Is your name Keith?"

"Yeah, why?"

"I wanna know what the situation is with you and my wife," Brian says, standing directly in front of Keith.

"Your wife? I don't know your wife."

As they stand there staring at each other, the tension elevates because Brian knows who Keith is, and even though he is acting otherwise, Keith definitely knows who Brian is. Without saying anything else, Keith moves closer to his vehicle in an attempt to leave the scene, but Brian is just two steps behind and is closing in on him fast. Keith knows his only way out of this situation is to get in his vehicle, so he keeps the conversation minimal as he picks up the pace to his car.

Once he got close to his car, he pulled his keys out, opened the door, and gets in the car, and locked it. Before Keith starts the car, Brian walks up to the window, pulls out his gun, and taps on the car door. Keith, however, refuses to lower the window or open the door, which intensifies the situation even more.

Without looking in Brian's direction, Keith shouts, "I don't know your wife, man!"

Brian knows he is lying. He knows that Keith is having an affair with his wife, and he wants answers. Keith sits there looking straight forward.

"Man, open the door, and let's talk about it, man to man," Brian says, with the gun in plain sight. Keith knows he has to get away from him, so instead of responding to Brian, he starts the car and attempts to drive off. Brian uses the gun to bust the driver's window out. Keith, in a panic, speeds off, nearly hitting two cars and a pedestrian. Brian watches him swerve out of the parking lot. As soon as Keith is out of Brian's sight, he calls Stacey. Stacey is still standing at the door and has witnessed everything that happened between her husband and her boyfriend. When she sees that Keith is calling her, she walks into the bathroom and locks the door. "Keith, what the hell just happened out there?" she asks when she answers her phone.

"Your husband is a maniac! That's what happened!" Keith shouts into the phone.

"I saw what he did with his gun. I'm so sorry," Allison says.

"Fuck your apology! What is that crazy nigga gon' do next?" Keith asks, clearly afraid of Brian.

Stacey remains calm but has no answer for Keith. For the first time, she feared Brian and what he might do next. Brian walks into the hospital. Now that the secret is out, his next move is to confront Stacey about her affair with Keith. Before he can say anything to Stacey, she confronts him and says, "Not here."

"Not here? Don't you think you've done enough?" Brian barks.

"Ashley!" Allison shouts. "Remember, we're here for Ashley!"

Brian wants to kill Stacey but realizes that Ashley's exam room is nearby. He does not want to upset her. He drops his rage level of ten down to a high five. He calms down as much as possible and then walks back into the room with Ashley. "Dad, is everything ok?" she asks.

"Yes, princess."

The doctor enters the room with a look of concern after hearing about an incident in the parking lot.

"Is everything ok?" the doctor asks.

"Yes, everything is fine," Brian responds.

Stacey enters the room with the same look of concern as the doctor. Brian meets her facial expression with his own, saying, "I know what you've been doing and who you've been doing it with." The doctor recognizes the tension in the room and attempts to direct their attention back to Ashley.

"Well, Mr. and Mrs. Phillips, it appears your little angel is gonna be fine," the doctor says. Brian and Stacey nod with relief. "I'm gonna write her a prescription, and the princess will be ok in a couple of days," the doctor says as he smiles at Ashley and squeezes her cheek. "If you need anything else, just let me know," the doctor says, leaving the room.

As soon as the doctor exits the room, the attention immediately shifts from Ashley to the incident that had just taken place in the parking lot. Brian looks at Stacey with the utmost disgust while she shrinks in shame. Ashley had known for a while that things weren't good between her parents, especially when Brian moved out of the house, but now was not the time for them to hash it out. When Brian addresses Stacey, Ashley intervenes and asks her dad to take her home.

Brian understands that his daughter is trying to put the small fire out before it becomes a blaze. He follows suit. Once they receive Ashley's prescription and discharge clearance, they leave the room. As they walk down the hall toward the exit, hospital security confronts Brian. Stacey pulls Ashley to the side while Brian follows hospital security. Keith has not filed a formal complaint, but one of the security officers watched the entire incident on the surveillance camera. The two officers spend several minutes grilling Brian in an attempt to get a confession out of him, but he remains silent with a sardonic grin on his face. He knows that without a formal complaint from Keith, they cannot make an official charge against him.

"Officer, is there anything else I can do for you?" Brian asks sarcastically, knowing that he is in the clear.

Both officers look defeated. They are forced to let Brian go. Once Brian exits the office, he walks up to Stacey and whispers in her ear, "This shit ain't over."

Stacey quietly watches Brian and Ashley leave the building. Just before they walk out the door, Brian turns around and gives Stacey a look to let her know that he means business. Stacey feels a wind of fear brush against her but tries her best to shake it off as she continues her work shift.

25

Brian drives to the pharmacy, picks up Ashley's prescription, takes her to her favorite restaurant, and then takes her home. Brian is feeling many different emotions. He is happy that his daughter is okay, concerned about her making a total recovery, and pissed about the discovery of the other man at the hospital. He is trying to work through his mountain of emotions while still keeping a smile on his face so that Ashley does not pick up on what is happening with him. But Ashley knows her dad, and she knows that the tension between him and her mother has nothing to do with her. She feels responsible because she told Brian about Keith, so she asks the million-dollar question. "Dad, did I get Mommy in trouble by mentioning Keith?"

"What? Oh no, baby girl. What makes you think that?"

"It just seems like everything changed after I said I knew who that voice was. Then you walked out of the room and was gone for a long time. I was scared that something happened between you and him."

Brian does not want Ashley to feel responsible for anything that has happened at the hospital. If anything, she did him a favor by revealing who Keith was to him. "No, honey. Your insurance card was in the car, so I went to get it. You didn't do or say anything wrong," Brian lies to try and reassure his daughter, but Ashley, still not convinced, continues with her questioning.

"Well, why did the police ask you to come with them?"

"Oh, they told me that there was an incident that took place in the parking lot around the time that I'd gone to get your insurance card and wanted to know if I'd seen anything."

"Oh, well, did you?"

"No, I didn't. Whatever took place happened before I got out there."

Ashley sat in silence as she looked at her father's face and searched for any forehead lines, eye twitches, or nervous blinks that would let her know he was lying to her. Before she can say anything else, Brian asks, "I do have a question for you. How do you know Keith?"

"When Mommy had 'bring your child to work day' at her job, she introduced us and asked me if I thought he was cute."

Brian is enraged inside but cannot allow Ashley to see it. He calmly asks, "Oh. Well, do you think he's cute?"

"No, Dad. You're cute," Ashley says with a girlish smile that makes Brian blush.

"Aw, that's really nice to say, baby girl. You know how to make your old man smile." Ashley leans over to Brian and kisses him on the cheek.

"Thanks, baby girl. I needed that."

"You're welcome, Dad. I love you."

"I love you too."

Ashley's cell phone rings. It's Stacey calling to check on her. Once Ashley confirms to Stacey that she is fine, Stacey asks if her dad is still around. Ashley informs her that he is. Brian, ear hustling the conversation, quickly advises Ashley to tell her mother that he will leave shortly. Ashley, hearing the sound of distress in her mother's voice and seeing the look of pain on her father's face, tries to defuse the situation before it gets out of control by asking them to please be cordial with each other. Brian is stunned as he sits back and notices the maturity in his baby girl's voice. For the first time, he realizes that his little girl is growing up and coming into her own.

After a few moments of silence, Brian responds to Ashley and says, "Yes, baby girl. I can do that for you."

On the other hand, Stacey is on ten and feels Ashley is being disrespectful by telling her parents to calm down. Ashley tries to explain to her mother how it makes her feel to see the tension between her parents, but Stacey is not trying to hear her. Ashley becomes very upset and wants to end the call with her mother.

Brian intervenes and takes the phone from Ashley. "Look, I get it. I realize that you don't want me here, and honestly, I don't wanna be anywhere that I'm not wanted. However, please be mindful that you have a very impressionable child who is quite emotional and is feeling some kind of way right now. If you don't want this issue between you and me to have an adverse effect on her, then it will be best for you to calm down and rethink your actions," Brian says very calmly to Stacey.

Stacey realizes that what Brian is saying is true. She knows that responding carelessly out of her emotions could cause her to lose Ashley's love and respect for her. That idea brings her back to reality and calms her down. "You're right, Brian. Ashley, I apologize, sweetheart. You are our top priority, and we love you very much," Stacey says to Ashley, and Brian confirms. He lets Stacey and Ashley know that he is leaving. "Princess, if you need anything, you know my number. I'm only a phone call away."

Ashley remains silent. She is still in her feelings, and Brian recognizes it. Not wanting to make a bad situation worse, he apologizes to her again, kisses her on the forehead, tells her he loves her, and says good night. As he pulls out of the driveway and drives off, he thinks about how his baby girl had been affected by his and Stacey's actions. He believes that maybe their actions are having a more significant effect on Ashley than they thought, and perhaps that's what landed her in the hospital. *I need to do something to cheer my baby up and put a smile back on her face,* Brian thinks to himself. He remembers who her favorite music artist is and goes to the mall to purchase a Nicki Minaj CD. He puts the CD in a nice gift bag, returns to the house, and leaves it at the front door with a note that says, **I'm sorry, Princess. Daddy loves you.**

Brian drives off and texts Ashley to look outside for the gift he left for her. Once Ashley retrieves the CD, she is all smiles. She walks back into her bedroom and texts Brian. **Thanks, Dad. I love you.** She includes several smiley faces. Brian feels as if a load has been lifted off him once he receives the text from Ashley. He smiles for the rest of the ride home.

Once he arrives home, he stops in his living room and sits in silence. His mind replays the day. From the scare of his daughter being sick to finding out who his wife has been stepping on him with, to confronting the culprit. It was a lot. *Come on, man. You gotta shake this off,* he says to himself, then jumps up from the sofa and moves around as if he is shaking the pressures of the day off of him. He stops dead in his tracks at the thought that comes to mind, and a big smile appears on his face. *I know who can help me shake this off. Who better than the new love of my life,* he thinks to himself.

He picks up his phone and texts Allison, **CUT**. He is anxious to receive a response from her. He holds the phone in his hand and waits for it to vibrate. Two minutes later, Allison responds and says **ten minutes**. Brian responds, **okay**, then sits back down and waits. The ten minutes seem like forever. After about seven minutes, he goes to the bedroom. He places his phone on the nightstand and sits down on the bed. Every 30 seconds, he picks up the phone to look at it. He even turns the ringer up to make sure that he does not miss her call. After another five minutes, the phone rings. *Finally!* Brian thinks with a massive smile on his face.

"Hey, babe! You won't believe how hard I was trippin' waiting on your call," Brian starts. He notices that Allison is sniffling as if she were crying. "Babe, what's wrong?" he says, now really concerned.

"I don't know what I'm doing," Allison responds softly.

"What do you mean?"

"You, me, us," she responds simply.

"So, now what? You're having second thoughts?"

"No, that's not what I'm saying. Don't get me wrong, I love you to death and I wanna be with you. I guess I'm just getting nervous."

There is a moment of silence between them then Allison continues. "I've been thinking a lot about what people are gonna say and how they're gonna look at me, you know?"

"Yes, I get it. But remember, it was you who convinced me that we are doing the right thing. As long as we both love each other and know that we are meant for each other, who gives a fuck about what other people think. The only thing that matters is what we think," Brian says, reassuring Allison of their love for one another.

"I know, babe. You're right," Allison responds, already starting to feel better.

"Okay, enough of the sad talk. Let's go to a happy place," Brian says.

"What do you mean?" Allison asks.

"Let's talk about the wedding. How many people do you want to be in the bridal party? What colors do you have in mind? Where do you want it to take place?"

"Well, I want something small, just me, you, Nita, your best man and our immediate family."

"Okay, that's a start. What about the colors?"

"I was thinking peach," Allison replies.

"Hmmm, that's soft and cute, but I don't know if I can pull that off."

"Trust me, babe. How you look is a direct reflection on me, and I'll never have you looking bad. Besides, I don't think you could look bad in anything. Just leave it up to me," Allison says with a smirk.

"Awww, thanks babe. Okay, you're in charge of the attire," Brian says with a smile.

"Babe, I made an appointment to see the lawyer on Monday. I'll keep you posted on what she says," Allison says, changing the subject.

"Okay. My appointment is in two weeks, so we are moving in the right direction," Brian responds.

"Yes. I just can't wait for all of this to be over."

"I know. Me too," Brian agrees.

"One day, we will be completely happy. That's all I pray for."

"You're right, babe. So do I," Brian says. His daughter crosses his mind, and he says, "Babe, I'm gonna call and check up on my baby girl."

"Okay, we'll catch up later," Allison says, and they end the call.

Brian hung up with Allison and called Ashley. She answers on the first ring. "Hey, Daddy!" she says with excitement, happy to hear her dad's voice.

"Hey, princess! What are you up to?" Brian asks, meeting her excitement.

"Not much. Just listening to my CD. Thanks again, Dad."

"You're welcome. Anything for my princess," Brian says.

"Dad, is there any way that you and Mommy can work things out and get back together?"

"I don't think so, Princess," Brian responds sadly. He can hear the sadness in his daughter's voice.

"Well, did it have anything to do with me and Malcolm?"

"No, baby girl. Your mom and I have been unhappy for some time now, but our problems have nothing to do with you or your brother. We love you both, and no matter what happens between your mom and I, that will never change."

"I just feel like y'all should be able to work anything out," Ashley says and begins to cry.

Brian's heart breaks. He has to take a moment to get himself together because he does not want to break down crying and make his daughter feel even worse. "Sweetie, don't be sad. I will always be here for you and your brother. I promise."

Ashley takes a moment to get herself together. "Okay, Dad. I love you."

Brian feels terrible about the separation and upcoming divorce, but this was it. Nothing is salvageable from his marriage except his love for his children. He will always support them, but Stacey had broken his heart for the last time. Brian keeps hearing his mother say, *don't you marry that girl. She is no good,* etc. The more he thinks about his mom, the more he figures he needs to call and let her know about his failed marriage. He will probably regret calling her, but it is what it is now. As he musters up enough intestinal fortitude to call his mom, the only words he can hear her saying was, *I told you so*, but regardless of the outcome or response, the call is necessary.

RING. RING.

"Hello," Barbara greets.

"Hey, Mom."

"Hey, my son."

"You got a minute?"

"For you, I have hours. What's up?"

Brian figures there is no need to beat around the bush about this. He takes a deep breath and says, "Well, me and Stacey, umm…"

"Umm what?" Barbara asks. "Y'all breaking up?"

"Yes."

"Hmm. Well, are you okay?"

"Yeah, I've finally begun to see my marriage for what it really is, and I can't do it anymore."

"Son, I'm so sorry that you're going through this, but I definitely understand. How are my grandbabies taking it?"

"Ashley is taking it kinda rough. Malcolm is just Malcolm. If it isn't a video game, it really doesn't faze him."

"Yes, I know he's quiet and nonchalant, but I think you should talk to him and see where his head is. We don't wanna lose him to the streets."

"I know, Mom. You're right. I will."

"Okay, Son. Let me know if you need anything."

"Thanks, Mom. I love you and I'll talk to you later," Brian says.

"Okay. I love you too," Barbara returns, and they end the call.

Brian is amazed at how well the conversation had gone with his mom. She responded the total opposite of how he thought she would, and he was grateful. He walks down to the den and turns his Bose system on to the tunes of Sade. While he let the music soothe his soul, he reminisced on all the good times he and Stacey had shared. The idea of it all coming to an end brings him to tears. He thinks about the birth of their children and realizes that he will miss out on seeing his children every day, which is another depressing thought. But as depressing as this situation is, the positives outweigh the negatives. Instead of dwelling on the situation, he changed his focus to the positives of his new situation with Allison. The thought of spending the rest of his life with Allison brings joy to Brian that he has not felt in years. He anxiously welcomes the new life and happiness with Allison.

26

Brian thinks about the terms of his divorce. Money isn't an issue. However, he does have to be smart because he doesn't know what tricks Stacey may have up her sleeve. He is not stupid enough to think she is going down without a fight. He prepares for war.

In the divorce proceedings, Stacey conjures everything from faking a disability to false and misleading accusations of threats and misconduct. Brian is suspended from his job and almost terminated. After paying nearly ten thousand dollars in legal fees, the onslaught ends with Brian giving Stacey the house and one thousand dollars a month in child support. He is sad but also relieved that it is finally over.

On the other side of town, Allison was also dealing with her fair share of drama. She tried to reach a reasonable resolution with Winston, but he was not budging. He fought for the house, kids, kitchen sink, soap, and the water. Allison, drained, lets it all go and gives it to Winston. The material things he'd fought so hard for were of no value to her anymore. She took a bold stand in the courtroom and told the judge to let him have it all—everything except her kids. The judge felt that Allison's proposal was fair and granted her full custody with Winston having the kids every other weekend. Winston was fine with that. In his mind, as long as he could see them and they knew that he was their dad, nothing else mattered.

Allison and Brian are both legally single again. Given the circumstances of their divorces and the drama surrounding them, they kept in contact but decided to use wisdom and keep it minimal. They did not want their relationship to harm their future. Even though they still hadn't officially come out yet, they enjoyed some freedom post-divorce, such as no longer needing the code text before calling each other. It felt odd when Allison made the first call without having to hide her phone, feelings, or actions.

RING. RING.

"Hey, babe."

"Hey, how are you holding up?"

"I feel great. It's finally over."

"Yes, it's finally over." On cue, they both say the same thing at the same time.

"I wanna see you," they say in harmony.

"Me too," they both respond and laugh at each other.

"When?" Allison asks.

"Now," Brian answers.

"Okay, I'm on my way," Allison says with a jubilant smile, and they end the call.

Allison rushes over to Brian's place. He meets her outside. She could not get out of the car fast enough to get to him, and they embraced each other with tears of joy and happiness when she did. The BS of their past is over, and true love is finally in their reach. After standing outside holding each other and basking in their love for several minutes, they go inside the house and spend the rest of the evening planning their wedding. It is to be held in September, a year from now. They both agree that the ceremony will be in Jamaica. Their bridal party will consist of one bridesmaid, one groomsman, a flower girl, a ring bearer, and a soloist on the beach with their closest friends and family.

They book their travel arrangements, flights, and hotel rooms for themselves and their guests at a discounted rate, thanks to Allison's friends who works in the hospitality industry. A wedding vacation sounds like a great plan. There is one last minor detail to address. Allison is excited and anxious to grant Brian his wish of having his fantasy fulfilled. She knows he will enjoy it but wonders if he would object to who she has chosen to fulfill it.

"Babe, I have a surprise for you," Allison says with a slight smile.

"Really? What?" Brian responds, blushing.

"I found someone to entertain our request for your threesome."

"Oh, really?" Brian's eyebrows raise high. He is surprised and intrigued about Allison really being serious about going through with this.

"Yes, I do. Would you like to meet her?"

"Sure, babe," he says, trying to play it calm. Inside he is jumping up and down.

"I hope you approve of my choice."

"I'm sure I will," Brian says as he reaches for Allison's hand and rubs it softly, "You're the best."

Allison smiles and says, "Well, if you trust me that much, then why don't we wait until the day-of for you to meet her."

"Sure, I don't mind. It adds to the excitement," Brian says, now losing his calmness and letting his excitement show.

Allison noticed he was smiling a lot wider now and said, "Don't forget that this is gonna be a one-time event. This is something that we both have a desire to do, so we will share this experience together."

"Okay, babe. I get it. You don't have to worry about me. It's just about us from here on out," Brian says.

Time moves quickly. The year had gone by like months. The months went by like weeks. The weeks went by like days, and before Brian and Allison knew it, they were thirty days from their wedding day.

Business continued as usual, and Brian maintained his relationship with his kids. He visits them as often as he can and maintains his every other weekend visitation schedule. Ashley is now a gorgeous and intelligent, fully developed young woman. While Malcolm, who at one time couldn't do anything besides play video games, is now an All-American, All-Star athlete in high school. Not only is he gifted in sports, but he also overachieves with his academics and maintains a perfect GPA. Although Brian is not as involved in the day-to-day facets of their lives as he desired, they seem to be turning out fine from the exterior.

What cannot be seen is a different story. Emotionally, they were both facing anxiety and trust issues, which they both developed as a result of the separation of their parents. Brian made himself available to them as best as he could, but their parents were no longer together, and it tore at the fibers of their souls. Ashley, who was once Daddy's baby girl, was now seeking an emotional connection from older men instead of guys her age. Malcolm, on the other hand, controlled his emotions through sports. Malcolm's resentment against his parents for not working through their issues made him an All-Star. When he wasn't on the field, and his mind wasn't on sports, he'd break down mentally.

Brian and Stacey had tried endlessly to get into his mind. Stacey even considered getting back with Brian for the sake of the kids, but Brian wants no parts of that. They would both have to find another way to help their son.

Allison was also dealing with a rough patch. Her girls are now budding young ladies. Through the years, they'd seen their mother crying and distressed because of their father, but he is still their father, and they love him. Now that they are older and have a better understanding of how their mother had been mistreated, they both had anger issues, and they dealt with it by fighting each other. It is so bad that they attack each other for no reason. And sometimes, even attacking Allison. As a result, their grades suffered tremendously, almost to the point of flunking out of school altogether. To make matters even worse, when Allison told them that she would get married again, it further strained their relationship.

It wasn't until Brian and Allison allowed their relationship to become a part of their children's lives that they saw a change. They realized that the very thing they feared was exactly what they needed to heal their children. It didn't happen overnight, but with time, determination, and a lot of patience, they began to see a change in their children and their relationships with their children. Brian and Allison were thrilled that everything was falling into place and that there was finally total peace.

27

The wedding is just two weeks away. Brian and Allison have one more thing to do before they say, "I do." It is time to honor the fantasy. Allison schedules a weekend of fun. She rents a suite at the Hampton Inn and Suites, with an open bar, multicolor rose petals, and lingerie so sexy that an impotent man would feel an erection. Allison arranged for Anita to show up earlier than she and Brian and hang out in the room next door, unbeknownst to Brian, who rode with Allison to the room. When they arrive and walk into the room, Brian is impressed by the ambiance. "Babe, this is really nice," he says, admiring what Allison had done with the room.

"You like?" Allison asks with a delighted smile.

"Yes, I do. You've really done a wonderful job in here."

"Thanks, babe. I'm glad you like it," Allison says. She goes into the bathroom to start the shower for Brian.

"Babe, I started your shower for you. Go ahead and freshen up. Then I will take mine when you're finished."

"Okay," Brian says as he undresses. He steps into the shower and enjoys the hot water beating on his flesh. He is excited and anxious about the evening he is getting ready to have with Allison and their plus one. He washes his body, exits the shower, dries off, and slips on a new wife beater and some boxer briefs that Allison bought for him. He seals the deal with a hint of Polo Red.

When he walks out of the bathroom, Allison smells him before she lays eyes on him. "Damn, baby, you smell as good as you look. Shit!" she says, already making love to him with her eyes. "Let me get in this bathroom, so I can get back out here to my man," she says, walking quickly into the bathroom and closing the door.

Brian sits in anticipation. He is excited for her to come out of that bathroom so he can get his hands on her. When Allison opens the door and exits the bathroom, Brian's jaw drops. The sheer lingerie she wore fitted her body like paint and gave the illusion of her wearing nothing. Her skin is glowing, her heels accented her legs, and her perfume has Brian open to eating a human edible arrangement. "Down, boy," Allison says as she watches Brian, almost salivating while watching her. He is like a kid in a bakery, and there is a whole lot of cake to be baked.

"Put some music on, babe," Allison says to Brian as she walks over to the bar and makes him a drink. The sway in her hips and the way her feet glide across the floor overwhelm Brian's senses. He puts Trey Songz in rotation, then sits back down as Allison brings him the drink she made. She leans down and gives him a sensual kiss. Brian is about to lose his cool when Allison stops and moves away from him. "Oh, I see you're gonna be a tease tonight," Brian says, looking at her as if he wanted to dive on her.

"All good things come to those who wait," Allison responds with a devious smile. As Brian enjoys his drink, Allison grabs her phone and texts Anita. It's **showtime!** Brian was mentally mind fucked as he sipped his drink, eagerly awaiting his fantasy surprise. He is just about finished with his drink when he hears the sound of the door opening. Brian sits up straight in his chair when he sees a woman come in wearing a black cloak with a hood hiding her identity. Without saying anything, she walks straight to Brian and stands in front of him. He is trying to figure out who the mystery woman is. The woman lowers her hood.

Brian shouts, "Oh, shit!" His mouth is wide open, thinking he had to be dreaming. *No way,* he thinks as he stares at Anita.

"Babe, you like my surprise?" Allison asks him.

"Ummm, yeah. I mean, wow. Ummm, yeah, babe, I like it," he stutters. Brian considered Anita attractive, but he never imagined she would be the third piece of the puzzle. The moment is sexy. Intense. It feels strange because neither Brian nor Allison had ever had a threesome. Anita is experienced, but it had been years ago. To break the ice, Anita reaches for her bag and pulls out a plastic baggie containing what looks like marijuana.

"Bitch, is that what I think it is?" Allison asks.

"What you think?" Anita responds.

Brian, feeling lost, asks, "What is it?"

"Ganja," Anita replies.

"Ganja?" Brian asks, feeling even more lost and confused.

"Yeah, it's what you Americans call weed," Anita responds.

"Oh no, I can't do that," Brian states.

Allison walks over to Brian, "Relax, babe. I got you," as she lightly strokes his head.

Brian closes his eyes, enjoying Allison's touch, and says, "You got me?"

"Yes, babe. Have I ever let you down?"

"No, babe. You haven't."

"I know you're worried about your job doing a random drug test and this showing up in your urine but you don't have to worry about that because we can clean your system and it won't be detected."

Brian wonders how his soon-to-be-wife had gotten so knowledgeable about weed, ganja, or whatever. "Oh, really?"

"Yes, babe. Trust me and hit this shit," Allison says. As they all take hits of the ganja, Allison sets up a couple of shots of Ciroc. They do the shots and feel friendly and relaxed. Once Allison sees that Brian is loosening up, she kisses him. In no time, Brian's dick was trying to push through his boxers. Anita slides over to Brian, and he massages her breasts. They undress at the same time. They take time to admire each other's bodies. Allison makes the next move when she lays Brian on the bed and begins to suck his dick. She works her magic as she takes his wood in and out of her mouth.

Anita sits on the edge of the bed and watches the action between Brian and Allison. Her pussy is throbbing. She slides over to Brian and positions her pussy on his face, and he goes to town. The taste of her pussy is like Minute Maid watermelon-flavored juice. He is thoroughly enjoying giving and receiving at the same time. Without skipping a beat, Brian slid a finger into Allison. Her pussy juice slides through his fingers like an ongoing hot tub. After a few more minutes of the oral fest, Allison stops.

Anita moves off of Brian's face. It is now time for him to pound some pussy. Brian is hesitant about who to fuck first, but Allison gestures for him to give it to Anita while she watches. Without hesitation, Brian lays Anita down and climbs on top of her. When he slides his dick inside her, it is like putting a log into a fireplace. Her pussy is warm, soft, and wet. As Brian pumps in and out, her pussy begins to talk. The sound of lovemaking is loud and clear in the room as Anita moans in pleasure. Allison sits back and fingers herself until she nuts as she watches her man fuck her best friend.

Allison wants to feel Brian's dick inside her. She nudges Brian, and he knows it's her turn. When Brian pulls out of Anita, Allison gets on her knees on the edge of the bed. Brian stands behind her and pounds her from the back as Allison screams in pure pleasure. Anita moves over and lies in front of Allison. She spreads her legs open, and Allison tongues her pussy.

It is Allison's first time indulging in pussy, but she obviously knows what she is doing because Anita's legs tremble as she nuts in Allison's mouth. Once Brian sees that Allison has taken care of Anita, he pulls out of Allison and lies on the bed on his back. Allison leans down and takes his dick in her mouth again. She moves up and down on it as she sucks and licks it. She climbs on top of Brian, slides down on his dick, and rides it like a porn star in a rodeo.

Anita sits back and watches Brian's wet dick move in and out of Allison's pussy, turning her on even more. Allison comes all over Brian's dick then Anita climbs on him. She slides down slowly on his dick, gets her groove, and rides the hell out of it. He grabs her hips and bounces her up and down on his dick. Anita is not in the least bit embarrassed about how loud she expresses her pleasure. Brian feels so good. As Brian fucks Anita, he thinks that Allison is good, but Anita is different. No pussy or dick is the same, but Anita's pussy is good, to say the least.

He knows the agreement between him and Allison is that this would be a one-time thing, but he almost feels like he could get in this pussy on the regular. As he thinks about how good Anita's love cave is, he fucks her harder. After another two minutes, Brian feels his nut about to explode. He quickly moves Anita off of him and strokes his dick as he releases a load of cum.

"Baby, move your hand and let us have that," Allison says as she and Anita both take turns licking his dick and swallowing his cum. Brian lies back in pure bliss. He is so pleased that his lower extremities tremble. Once his body finally calmed down, Brian sits up, wipes the sweat off his forehead, and shakes his head. What is exciting is that this is only the beginning. He still has the rest of the weekend to enjoy a variety of unlimited pussy. This will be his last time ever having any outside pussy, so that he will enjoy it to the fullest. The night of fun continued, and the sex got better and more enjoyable with a plethora of different positions and multiple nuts that had them all drained by the end of the night. When they finally sleep, Brian closes his eyes with a huge smile as Allison lies on one side of him and Anita on the other. The following day, they are all packing their clothes to leave the hotel when Allison tells Brian she has one last surprise for him.

"You've pulled out all the stops this weekend, babe. What else could you possibly have up your sleeve?" Brian asks curiously and excitedly.

On cue, Anita walks over to him and sits him on the bed. Brian does not know what is about to happen, but he feels he will enjoy it. Anita leans down, unbuttons his pants, and pulls them down along with his underwear. Brian's dick immediately stands at attention. He looks up at Allison as if to ask what is happening. Allison walks over to him and says, "This is your last surprise and parting gift. I'm gonna sit over in this chair and watch as my girl licks your lollipop one last time." She leans down, and tongue kisses Brian while Anita kneels in front of him and begins to stroke his dick with her hand. Back in the day, Anita had always said she could give head like no other, so Allison put her to the test.

Allison planned to take notes so that she would be able to keep Brian happy for years to come. Anita continues to stroke Brian's dick as he watches, anticipating the moment that she will take it in her mouth. She leans up and pushes Brian back on the bed. She kneels down again and spreads his legs. She kisses his inner thighs. Brian closes his eyes and concentrates on holding his nut, as this is a very sensitive part of his body. Anita moves to his balls, takes them in her mouth and loves on them, one at a time, as she strokes Brian's dick with her hand.

She licks his dick, starting from the base. Brian's body begins to jerk lightly as she moves up and finally reaches the tip. She takes just the tip in her mouth and gives it special attention for a few minutes. Brian moans softly, and Allison enjoys watching him squirm with delight. Anita stands up with the tip still in her mouth and slowly goes all the way down and holds Brian's entire dick in her mouth for a few seconds.

"Oh, shit!" Brian yells. And before he could anticipate what would happen next, Anita started bouncing up and down on his dick with her mouth like a bobblehead. As Allison watches Anita slay her man's dick with her mouth, she thinks, *Damn, she is good as hell at this.* As Anita continues to bless Brian, he puts his hand on her head and guides her as he pumps his dick up and down for a few more seconds, then explodes in her mouth. Brian's eyes roll back in his head. "Damn. What a way to end the *fucking* weekend."

The weekend is over, and the threesome is leaving the hotel. When they get to the parking lot, Anita kisses Brian and Allison and wishes them well. Allison and Brian thanked Anita for everything and, most of all, for being a good friend. Anita went on her way, and Brian and Allison went on theirs. When Allison and Brian get into the car, she asks, "Did you like your surprise?"

"Oh, yes babe. I sure did."

"Good. I'm glad you did. But it's just me and you now, and I can't wait to say I do. I'm looking forward to being your wife and having a great life with you."

"I know, babe. Me too," Brian says and reaches over and holds Allison's hand.

28

The weeks pass quickly. Everything is set, and everybody is ready to go. This is going to be a week to remember. Brian and Allison fly to Jamaica together, then separate once they arrive. Brian's room is reserved at the Court Leigh in Kingston, while Allison stays with her parents.

Her family has several questions for her because they had been left in the dark about all her problems with Winston. Allison holds a meeting with her entire family and tells them all at once about the downfall of her marriage with Winston. She lets them know how happy she is to find someone who loves and appreciates her. She also adds that even their kids were happy about her and Brian being together. Once Allison finished filling her family in, her mom still had reservations, but she loved her daughter and just wanted to see her happy, so she was there to support her in any way she could.

RING. RING.

Allison looks down at her phone. It's Brian.

"Hey, babe," she said when she answered.

"Hey. You made it to your room?" Brian asks.

"Yes."

"Have you gotten settled in? Or are you just getting there?"

"I'm settled in and just finished having a talk with my family."

"Oh, okay. How did that go?"

"It actually went good. They were trying to play detective, but I handled it."

"Okay, good," Brian says with relief.

"Now, I'm thinking of what we can eat. Do you have any suggestions?" Allison asks.

"Try the curry chicken. I think you all will like that."

"Sounds good. I think we will have that. How's everyone on your end?"

"Everybody's good. My dude, Tim isn't gonna make it 'til later tonight because he missed his flight," Brian answers.

"Aww, okay. Well, as long as he makes it, we're good."

"He will. He called me as he was getting on the flight."

"Okay, well your mom and sister just arrived. Let me go so I can introduce them to my family," Allison says.

"Okay babe. Tomorrow we will be husband and wife," Brian says proudly.

"I know, babe! I am so excited!"

"Okay, well go ahead and get yourself together, 'cause if I know my mother, she's gonna ask a million questions."

Allison chuckles, "I'll be ready."

"Okay, babe. Enjoy yourself."

"You too. Be careful. Love you."

"Love you too," Brian says and ends the call.

Once he hangs up with Allison, Brian realizes he is hungry too. Jamaican food actually sounds good to him. After all, what better place to eat Jamaican food than in Jamaica? He freshens up and goes downstairs. When he gets to the restaurant, he selects the curry chicken. It is beyond incredible. Brian had hoped that his best man, Tim, would have made it in by now, but his second flight had also been delayed because of bad weather. Brian assures him that he will wait up for him.

Once Brian finishes his dinner, he isn't ready to return to the room. He still had a couple of hours before Tim arrived. To pass the time, Brian heads to the bar for a drink. He meets some local guys who introduce themselves when he gets there and offers him a drink. Brian accepts and introduces himself. There are three of them: Lloyd, who was very friendly, and two others who had little to say.

"So, Brian, what brings you to the Island?" Lloyd asks.

"I'm getting married," Brian replies.

"Oh, congratulations. Are you here alone?"

"No, I have family here."

"So, why are you in here alone?" Lloyd asks curiously.

"Well, part of my family is with my future wife, and the others are in their rooms relaxing."

"Oh, I see," Lloyd says, then offers Brian another drink. Brian accepts the offer and is unaware that Lloyd has slipped a micky ficky into his glass. Brian was already feeling good from the previous drinks he had consumed, so he didn't recognize that he was being set up.

"So, Brian, you wanna party with us for your last night as a single man?" Lloyd asks once he sees Brian consume all of his drink, including the drugs that are in it.

"Sure. What do you have in mind?"

"Ya, mann. I know of a little party in town. Pretty women, ya know."

"Yeah, sounds interesting, but I don't have a car."

"No worries, man. We got you," Lloyd assures Brian.

"Okay then," Brian says, then gets into the car.

They drive for a while when Brian feels they aren't going to a party.

"Hey, where is this party again?" Brian asks.

"No worries, man. We'll be there shortly," Lloyd says, then makes a quick right down a dark, narrow one-way street. The car suddenly stops, and another car pulls up from the rear. A man approaches the car and demands for Brian to get out. Brian's buzz quickly disappears, and he is immediately nervous. He knows this isn't a good situation.

"Out of the car!" the strange man shouts with a deep accent.

"Out of the car, Bombaclot!" he repeats.

"What? What's going on?" Brian asks as he slowly exits the car, wondering what he has gotten into.

"If you want money, take it. Here, you can have it," Brian offers.

"Ras clot! I don't want ya money."

"Then, what do you want?"

"I want your life," the man says, then pulls out a machete.

"Now, wait a minute. Whatever this is, we can work it out," Brian says, pleading with the mysterious man. He looked at Brian with the look of death and then said, "Blood clot! Kill him!"

Brian attempts to run, but he is outnumbered. He is surrounded, and there is no way out.

"Get back here!" the man yells at Brian.

"Ras clot! Kill him!" he repeats.

"Wait! Wait! No, please! Noo!" Brian pleads for his life, but his pleas are ignored as the man takes the machete and slices through his hand. Brian screams as he watches his hand split in half. But, before recovering from the first slice, the machete comes down again and catches him between his neck and shoulder. By this time, Brian is on the ground in a pool of blood, breathing heavily and begging for his life.

"So, ya American boi think you can come over here and steal our women," the man says, standing over Brian and looking down at him with disgust.

"No," Brian tries to scream, but death is all around him, and he feels his life leaving his body. Helpless, his mind goes to Allison. If only he could see her and touch her one more time. She will be torn to pieces tomorrow when he doesn't show up at the altar. He thought about his kids, and the tears began to stream down his face. He cannot believe this is how he is going out. Before he can muster enough strength to plead for his life again, he sees the machete go up in the air, and the next swing kills him. As soon as his life completely leaves his body, the gang wastes no time cutting him into pieces. They scatter half his body parts in the ocean and feed the other half to some hungry dogs nearby.

29

Allison rises early, doing all the things a blushing bride does on her wedding day. She'd gotten her hair, nails, and makeup done and was about to get dressed. Time was moving so fast that she never called Brian to say good morning and to see how his night had gone. However, Brian's mom and Karen went by his room to check on him before the wedding. They knocked on the door but got no answer. His buddy, Tim, who had made it in late, the night before, is in the room across from Brian's. He hears the knocking on Brian's room door and opens his door, and asks if everything is okay.

"Well, we came down to check on Brian before the wedding, but he's not answering," Barbara responds to Tim.

"Hmmm, I spoke to him last night before I boarded my flight but that was the last time I heard from him," Tim responds.

Barbara feels extremely nervous. Deep down, she knows that something is wrong. Karen pulls out her phone and calls Allison to see if she has heard from Brian.

"No, not since yesterday evening. Is everything okay?" Allison asks, now becoming worried.

"We're not sure. Mom and I are here at his room, but he's not answering the door. But I don't want you to get worried, so let us see what we can find out and I'll call you back," Karen says and ends the call.

Tim, Karen, and Barbara then go down to the lobby. They walked to the receptionist's desk and asked the clerk if anyone had seen Brian. They provide a picture and his room number. The clerk looks at the picture but cannot help because he hasn't worked the night shift. Barbara requests to view the surveillance video, but the clerk quickly advises them that it is not allowed. Karen asks the clerk to call the local authorities. However, with very little to go on, they really can't do anything.

They all sit in the lobby with anticipation. A breaking news report comes across the television saying a body part had been discovered in Kingston that morning by a child playing with his dog. The report further stated that an ID bearing the name Brian Fitzgerald was found nearby and that if anyone had any information concerning his whereabouts, to contact the Kingston Police Department. Barbara, Karen, and Tim are stunned as they stare at the television screen.

Meanwhile, Allison hadn't heard anything else from Karen, so she assumed and expected that Brian had been found and everything was okay. She is already fully dressed and is on her way to the waterfront along with Anita to meet her groom. She left her phone in the room, unaware of the calls being made to her. Unable to get in touch with Allison, Karen and Barbara split up. Karen heads to the waterfront, and Barbara goes with the police to the station. The guests are now congregating at the reserved area where the wedding will take place, and Allison is in a private room, waiting on her cue to head to the altar. When Karen finds Allison, she and Anita are in the private room taking selfies before the start of the wedding.

Karen walks into the room, and Allison knows by the look on her face that something is wrong. She stands up and asks, "What is it, Karen?"

"Hey beautiful. I just wanted to let you know that we haven't been able to find Brian."

"What do you mean you haven't found Brian? Where the hell is he?" Allison asks, trying not to get upset.

Karen fills her in on what they just saw on the news report, and Allison immediately panics. Karen tries to encourage her to remain optimistic. Just then, Barbara calls Karen and updates her on what she discovered when arriving at the police station. Allison demands that Karen put the phone on speaker so she can hear what is being said.

Barbara continued talking and said there was a trail of blood in an alley, but they hadn't found a body. All they found was a finger, but she couldn't identify whether it was Brian's or not. Allison had been trying to hold it together, but once she heard this news, she passed out. Anita, standing right next to her, caught her and sat her down in the chair. By this time, the word is starting to get out to the guests that Brian is missing. Although worried, everyone tries to remain hopeful that he will show up.

After hours of waiting and praying, it is clear that what they hoped for was not about to happen. Tragedy had occurred, and no one had any answers. The family and friends who had come for the wedding made arrangements to stay for a week, so they all took that time to look for Brian but came up with nothing. When it was time for everyone to go back to the states, it was clear that Brian was never coming back. Once everyone left, Allison remained. She had family in Jamaica, and she needed to use her resources to try and get answers that she knew she wouldn't be able to get from home.

Allison's brother, Devon, is known throughout Kingston as someone who is not to be fucked with. Allison reached out to him to tell him that she was coming to Jamaica to get married, but because of his background, he didn't want to attend the wedding and be a distraction with his entourage that would have to accompany him. Allison understood and planned to reach out to him after she and Brian were married, so she could set up a meet and greet between her brother and her new husband. But now, she had to reach out to him to let him know about the sudden tragic event that had taken place.

When Devon hangs up the phone with his baby sister, he rushes to see her. He is happy to see Allison, and she is delighted to see her brother, but they are both hurt that she just lost the man she was supposed to marry. Devon vows to his sister that he will get to the bottom of what happened. He quickly began his search to find whoever was responsible. Word went out, and the identities of those responsible were quickly revealed. Because of the street code, Devon could not notify the police. However, Devon did promise Allison that the responsible parties would pay for her pain.

Devon put the word out through his top lieutenant, then, one by one, his crew brought individuals to him. They all confessed that Winston had hired them to have Brian killed. Upon receiving this information, Devon's top priority and sole mission had become to find Winston. He owes his sister an explanation and will give it to her so that she can get closure. Devon reaches out to Allison and lets her know he is on the way with some information he received about what happened. Allison felt like her heart would burst through her chest as she eagerly waited.

Devon pulls up at the house in a black Benz with jet-black tinted windows. At first, Allison is nervous when she sees the car pull up. Devon lowers the window and yells, "Al," his nickname for her. When she approaches the vehicle, the driver gets out armed with a shotgun and opens the back door for her to get in.

"Hey, little Sis," he says.

"Hey," Allison responds, wanting to skip the preliminaries and get straight to the news.

"I know your heart is hurting. I don't even know if I should tell you."

"Boi!"

"Boi, what?"

"If you don't tell me," Allison says with a sharp look on her face.

"Can you handle it?" Devon asks, still hesitant to reveal what he knows.

"I'm here, aren't I?"

"Yeah," Devon says, shaking his head. He pauses, takes a long look at Allison, and says, "It was Winston."

"Winston?!" she shouts. Allison goes into a deep state of confusion. She and Brian had done their best to keep their relationship under wraps, so how did Winston find out?

"Why? How? They didn't even know each other.

"Well, obviously he knew more than you thought he did."

Allison is in disbelief. Winston plotted to have Brian killed. "Okay, I can't wait to get back to the states," she says, going from shocked and hurt to mad as hell.

"To do what?" Devon asks.

"I'm a have his ass locked up!" Allison shouts.

"With what proof? What info? Al, you know that's not how this shit works. You're gonna have to live with this."

"Oh, fuck no! That Ras Clot needs to feel my pain! He is going to pay!"

"Okay, Al. How do you plan to do this?"

"With your help."

"My help?"

"Yes, your help."

"How am I going to do that? You know I'm a deportee from the states. I can't even step my ass on a plane."

"Leave that to me. If I get him here, can you promise me you'll take care of it?"

"You know I will. Just let me know and I will deal with that pussy hole," Devon assures Allison. He kisses her on her forehead, and she exits the car.

Allison thinks about how she will execute her plan. Every move she makes has to be strategically thought out. She sits on the bed in deep thought. She remembers that Winston had a thing for Anita back in the day. She knows that he will if he still thinks he has a chance to be with her. That was it. Anita will be her bait to reel his ass in. Allison calls Anita to see if she would be willing to help her.

"Hey girl," Anita answers.

"Hey, Nita. I need a favor."

"What's up?" Anita asks.

"Do you think you could get Winston to Jamaica in about a month or so?"

"Winston? For what?" Anita asks curiously.

"Just tell him the girls and I are still here and one of them had an accident, but I was too distraught to call him."

"Okay, but why not you?" Anita asks. She then has a thought, and before Allison can respond, she says, "Wait. Did Winston have something to do with Brian's death?"

"Oh, no girl. Unless you know something that I don't," Allison responds, trying to play it down.

"Umm, no, but is there something else you wanna tell me?" Anita asks, not letting it go.

"No, like what?"

"I don't know. Something just doesn't seem right."

"Anita, please."

"Okay, girl. You know I'm willing to help you in whatever way I can. But don't call me to be an alibi!"

Allison feels terrible about lying to Anita, but she is a woman on a mission and is determined to get Winston back at whatever cost. Each week that passes is increasingly hard for her. She is on edge and finds it extremely hard not to act on the information that Devon had shared with her.

Two months. Anita had followed through with her part of the plan and called Winston and told him the story to get him to go to Jamaica. Allison arranges a flight out the day before so that she can perfectly execute her plan. Devon stays out of sight and advises his goons to pick Winston up and bring him to Norwood once his flight lands. To keep Winston from catching on to what was about to happen, Devon had one of Winston's hirelings, who he thought was a friend, pick him up from the airport and offer to take him wherever he needed to go.

Once Winston arrives, he is greeted by his "friend," not knowing that he is now being set up. The 'friend' has to follow through with the plan because Devon is holding his family hostage until he carries it out. Once Winston is in the car and secured, Devon shoots the family members of the "friend" and kills them all.

He goes to the warehouse, where he meets Allison and waits for Winston to arrive. On the ride to the destination, Winston realizes that something isn't right, but it is too late by then. When the car he is riding in makes it to the destination, it is immediately surrounded. When they pull into the warehouse parking lot, the goons open the car door, put a mask over Winston's head, then proceed into the warehouse where Devon and Allison are waiting.

Once the "friend" walks into the warehouse and sees Devon, he demands that his family be released. Without saying a word, Devon walks over to the 'friend,' pulls out his gun, and then shoots him in the head, point blank. "Bumbo-clot pussy-rasclaat!" Devon yells.

He walks towards Winston, who is now sitting in a chair in the middle of the room. He pulls the mask off Winston. When Winston opens his eyes, Allison is the first person he sees. Devon walks behind him and slaps him in the back of the head.

Allison and Winston aggressively stare at each other for a fcw minutes. She takes a few steps toward him and asks, "Why?"

"Because you took my family away," Winston responds dryly.

"So, killing the man who took the time to love me more than you ever did, made you think what? That you would get me back?"

"It didn't matter if I did or not. I just wanted you to feel pain in ya heart," he responds with no emotion. Allison shakes her head as she stands over him. Every memory she had with Winston, good and bad, runs through her mind. Then, every memory she had of Brian ran through her mind. A single tear escaped her eye. She pulled the nine-millimeter from Devon's hip.

CLICK.

Made in the USA
Columbia, SC
04 November 2022

70425817R00126